Drift
River
Romance

Michael O'Gara

This is a fictional work coming from the author's
imagination.
Any similarity to
actual persons, events, places, organizations
and companies, is purely coincidental.

Acknowledgement

Thanks to fellow author and editor, Leslie Thompson,
for her help in editing this book.

ISBN-13: 978-0692600474

ISBN-10: 0692600477

Published by Heartland Indie Publishing LLC

Chapter 1

Nate was heading toward an unexpected and confusing situation that would test his character, abilities, determination, and calling, to say nothing of his sense of humor. He was unaware of all this as he drove with the windows open, enjoying the unseasonably warm early spring day.

About ten miles from his destination, he saw the pickup truck on the side of the road with the hood up. Nate slowed down and pulled over behind the truck. He turned the engine off and got out and walked to the elderly man sitting on the tailgate swinging his legs from the knees. The man didn't seem to have a care in the world.

The man looked up and simply said, "Howdy."

Nate tipped his cap in acknowledgement and sat on the tailgate with the man, who kept on swinging his legs. Nate didn't know why he did it, but he started swinging his legs. He thought it was probably the power of suggestion, but it felt good. He'd driven a long way.

Another pickup truck stopped on the opposite shoulder of the road. A shirtless man in coveralls got out. The laces of his boots were not done up and were flopping as he walked. The man had long hair and a bushy beard. He walked to the front of the pickup Nate was sitting on and looked under the hood before coming to the back of the truck.

The man said, "Ole Beauty threw a rod, Ben."

Ben answered, "Yup."

The man went back to his pickup and drove away.

Nate offered his hand and said, "Nate Christian." The man shook his hand and replied, "Ben Kemp," and kept swinging his legs. Nate did the same.

After a few minutes, Ben spoke, "Sitting here swinging my legs like I did as a wee feller makes me think about gentler times."

Nate just nodded and asked, "Who was the other fellow?"

"That was Jake Harley, a good neighbor. Salt of the earth."

Nate nodded and asked, "How come he didn't offer you help?"

"Why would he? He was going in t'other direction and you is headed to town."

Nate said, "Makes sense."

"I reckon."

Nate patted the truck bed, "You have a classic here."

1

"Yeah. I guess I'll have to replace the motor. At my age that will be a bit too much of a lift though. I'll be needin' hep."

Nate thought for a moment, "I'm not much of a mechanic but I can help with the muscle part when I'm not working."

Ben looked at him curiously, "You don't know me so why the offer?"

"It just seemed the Christian thing to do," and smiled at Ben, who had not missed the play on words.

Ben nodded and said, "I'll take ya up on the offer, Mr. Christian."

Nate said, "I guess we might as well head to town."

"Yup. I live about three miles up the highway and a mile and a half down Kemp Road but I'd best git ta town and git John to bring his wrecker out and tow my pickup home."

"Is Kemp Road named after a member of your family?" Nate asked.

"My grandfather."

Ben shut the hood then got a worn book off the seat of his pickup. He walked to the passenger side of Nate's van and got in. Nate got in behind the wheel. Ben saw Nate's book sitting in the middle of the bench seat, "You have one, too."

Nate nodded and looked at the book Ben had.

Ben said, "I never go nowheres without mine."

"I understand. Me, too."

Ben looked in the back of the van, "Ya on the move?"

"Yes, sir. I'm moving to Bryce Valley."

"It's a beautiful little town, but it has its problems."

Nate asked, "Such as?"

Ben looked at Nate, "You'll find out. My pa, may he rest in peace, taught me if'in you can't say nothin' good, it's best to say nothin' unless someone is in danger."

Nate nodded agreement then asked, "Am I in danger?"

Ben looked at Nate and said, "Jist from the women folk."

Nate thought it was a funny answer, but he couldn't think of anything to say, so said nothing.

Ben asked, "Do you have a place to stay?"

"Yes. I have a little house lined up and a part-time job. I'll have to find other work to make ends meet. What do most people do around here?"

"Some of 'em farm, some works in the businesses here, and some drive the eighty miles to the city to work. Driving that far ain't for me, but it don't matter 'cause I'm of a age where I don't have to work no more. Retired, see."

Nate asked, "Did you farm?"

"I stopped a pair of years back. How old do you think I am?"

"Fiftyish."

"Sixty-three hard but good years on this ole bod. That's what hard work and clean livin' does for ya; it keeps ya young. My sweet wife Emma passed two years ago of the big C and now I live alone. I have a daughter in New York, but she's too busy to spend time here. She does phone every week ta see how I'm gittin' along. She asked me to come live with her, but the big city would be the end of me. I'm happy here. T'is home."

"Please tell me about the county."

"It's a beautiful county. Fishin' is good, huntin' is good, and the soil is good. Lotsa scenic spots here. The Drift River runs through the middle of the county and there's lotsa good swimming holes and a passel of tourists come to tube down the river with the current. There's a fair number of campgrounds and motels around. My friend, Len Cole, has the best one of them campgrounds."

"How come they call the town Bryce River but the river's called Drift River?"

"Nobody no how said it made sense. I reckon you try to make sense out of things around here you'll end up locked away in the funny farm."

Nate chuckles.

"Truth is, the Bryce family started the town after the river was named and as the Bryces weren't much liked, folk kept on a callin' the river by its original name, don't ya see."

"Interesting."

"Ya don't know the half of it."

The drive to the little City of Bryce River, population 2,539, went quickly. Nate enjoyed the drive and the talk with Ben. Ben directed him to Carl's Repair Shop about a mile outside of the town limits on the south side of town. It was a steel sided shop building.

When they arrived, Ben got out saying, "Come on and meet John. He's a good ole feller."

They went into the building through the open bay door and to the workbench where a man was standing over a part muttering to himself, "They make these darn gum thing-a-majigs more complicated than a mind

3

twister puzzle."

Ben chuckled, "Don't whine, John. It keeps ya in work."

The man looked up from his work and smiled broadly, "Well, look what the cat drug in."

Ben said, "John, this young feller here is Nate Christian. Nate, this is John Doyle, our resident mechanical genius. He owns this fine establishment of mechanical mayhem."

Nate stuck his hand out, "Pleased to meet you, sir." He was about to ask how come John owned Cal's Repair but remembered what Ben had said about things here not necessarily making sense. He let it go.

John looked at Ben and said, "Polite, ain't he?" He then shook Nate's hand, "Pleased to meetcha, Nate. And by and by, I ain't no sir. I'm just plain John."

Nate smiled, "Yes, sir."

John smiled and looked at Ben, "Feisty aggravator one, huh?"

"Seems like. Ole Beauty threw a rod about nine miles up the highway. I need a tow back to the homestead. Nate here was good enough to stop and give me a ride."

John looked at Nate, "Why didn't ya jist call on one of those cell phone dealies?"

"Don't have one."

"A man after my own heart," Ben said.

John added, "He can't be all bad if he don't own one of them time wasters."

"It ain't getting any earlier."

John shook his head, "As pushy as always. Well, I'll lock up and we'll mosey on."

Nate said to Ben, "How do I get in touch about helping you?"

"Call me on the phone."

"Number?"

Ben went to a desk in the corner, wrote on a small note pad, tore off the sheet and handed it to Nate, "It's one of them old fashioned landlines. If I don't answer right away, phone back."

Nate said, "See you," then turned and went to his van.

It was a short drive to Jimmie James Hardware where he was to pick up the keys to the little house he was to live in. The main street was somewhat busy and Nate had to bypass the store. He found a parking spot on a side street. He enjoyed the short walk to the shop and went in.

A male clerk asked, "Hep ya, sir?"

Nate said, "Hello. Where is the office?"

The man pointed and then turned his back to Nate. Nate headed in the direction of the office. He went to the back where there was a sign that said "Office." Nate noted a sign by the door over a mail slot that said "Drop rental payments here." Nate went in the door and found a woman at a desk.

"Didn't ur momma teach ya ta knock?" the woman said.

Nate smiled, "Hi. I'm Nate Christian and I believe you have a key for me. The Pine Street house."

"I have keys for ya but they ain't fer the Pine Street house. That uns bin rented."

"I was promised the Pine Street house."

"Ya have that in writing?"

"No but Jimmie James promised me."

The woman scowled, "If'in it's about real estate, it's gotta be in writing."

Nate protested, "But Mr. James promised me. He's a deacon at the church."

The woman said, "Well, that promise was probably made on a Sunday and this is a Monday. What he done said is now just noise on the wind. Look, people pay good money for this place where he's puttin' ya up. Take it or leave it. Makes no matter to me." She handed Nate an envelope.

Nate said, "I'll have a look."

The woman went back to work, ignoring Nate, so he left. He drove to the address on the envelope. When he pulled up, he was shocked. The house, at best, could be called a shack. The weathered clapboards were grey and some were missing. The roof was sagging and the soffits were rotted.

Nate got out and went to take a closer look. He started to climb the steps and noticed one of the steps was rotted. Some of the boards on the porch were in the same condition so he was careful to step over them. He unlocked the door and went in. The inside was filthy. He looked around. The windows were all rotted. Nate could see the ground between some of the floor boards. He went into the kitchen and the smell just about knocked him over. A terrible smell was coming from under the sink. He

5

opened the door and cockroaches scurried everywhere. The sink was leaking and the floor was rotted. Nate closed the door. He opened a kitchen cupboard door and saw mouse droppings.

Looking at the living room and the bedroom, they were in just as bad a condition. The bathroom was filthy and the floor was rotted. Nate turned and left, locking the door behind him.

Returning to his van, he took one of the single-wrapped hand wipes he kept in the van and cleaned his hands. He then headed for the hardware store.

Nate went into the office and the woman looked up, "You didn't knock. Again!" He handed her the envelope, "I think I'll leave it."

The woman shrugged and simply said, "Suit urself."

Nate asked, "Is Jimmie around?"

"That's Mr. James to ya and, no, he ain't here."

Nate said, "So long," and left. He went back to his van. He was hungry and remembered seeing a diner when he drove Ben to the garage. It was just outside of town. He drove there and stopped.

It was way too late for lunch and too early for supper so the place was almost deserted. Nate looked around and the place looked well-kept and clean. He went to the counter and sat. He could see directly into the kitchen, which appeared to be extremely clean and well organized.

A young woman came to him, "Hello, honey. I'm Sue and I'm ya's waitress." She smiled broadly and put a menu in front of him.

"Hello, Sue. I'm Nate." Nate held out his hand and Sue shook it firmly.

Sue asked, "Are ya here on vacation?"

"No, I'm moving here."

"Where ya staying at?"

"I don't know. I just got into town and the house I thought I had arranged was rented to someone else."

"I bet ya made the arrangement with Jimmie James."

Nate nodded agreement.

"He's not known for bein' a man of his word."

An older woman arrived and interjected, "Sue, you shouldn't otta be talkin' outta school like thet."

Sue said, "Sho nuff, ma, but it's true."

Ma added, "Hello, I'm Betsy Conrad."

6

Nate smiled, "I'm Nate Christian," and offered his hand, which Betsy shook. He guessed that Betsy was probably in her early to mid-forties and that Sue was younger than he by several years, probably twenty-one or twenty-two. It was not lost on Nate that both mother and daughter were very good-looking women.

Nate continued, "I guess, after I eat, my priority will be finding a place to hang my hat and take off my boots."

Sue blurted out, "There's room for yar boots under my bed." Sue then went into a deep red blush.

Betsy shook her head, "Don't pay no attention to my daughter. She's all talk and no do. If'in ya tried to take her up on it, she'd run for the hills. She's a terrible little flirt but a good girl. Understand?"

Nate knew Betsy was making a veiled threat and said, "Yes, ma'am, I do."

Sue looked kinda sheepishly at Nate, "Ma is right."

Nate smiled at her, "It's alright. We've all said things we shouldn't have."

Betsy said, "The tourist season is just a startin' so everything respectable is probably counted fer, includin' the seasonal cottages. In town there won't be anything a respectable person would want to live in, though some poor folks have no choice but to rent from one of the slumlords like Jimmie James. You could try the Drift River Outfitters and Campground; it's closest to town. They might still have a cabin but it's kinda late, so maybe not."

Nate replied, "Thank you for the advice. What's your special?"

Sue was still a little red but answered, "Monday special is always finger lickin' good baby-back BBQ ribs. We is famous for 'em."

"Do they come with anything?"

Betsy replied, "Fries and a soda. It's a good deal at seven ninety nine."

"Sold. I'll have a Coke please."

Someone took the seat beside Nate and said, "Hi there, young feller." Nate turned, saw who it was and said, "Hi, Ben."

Betsy asked, "You know this feller, Ben?"

"A little. We met today on the road. Ole Beauty died and he give me a ride ta town."

Sue asked almost shocked, "Ole Beauty died?"

"Yeah, but I plan to revive her."

7

"Good. The county wouldn't be the same without Ole Beauty."

Ben nodded, "I understan'."

Betsy explained to Nate, "Ole Beauty leads all the parades pulling the VFW float."

"You have a VFW branch here?" Nate asked.

Ben confirmed, "Yup," then turned to Sue, "I'll have the ribs with a Mountain Dew."

Sue went to the kitchen counter, "Bubba, two rib specials please."

Nate heard someone say in a deep voice, "Yes, Miss Sue."

Betsy asked Nate, "Do ya have work?"

"I was promised a part-time job. I'll need to find other part-time work."

Ben asked, "What do ya do, Nate?"

Nate explained, "I'm a contractor. I'm state licensed to do electrical and plumbing. I'm also a pretty good carpenter."

Betsy advised, "Well, there's lots of work in the county for a good tradesman but you won't be a workin' in town."

Nate tilted his head, "How come?"

Ben answered, "The mayor's brother-in-law is a contractor and the clerk won't issue no more contractor licenses in the city."

Nate asked, "Is that legal?"

Betsy sighed, "Probably not, but nobody has challenged it in court. Would cost more than it's worth. Most of the new businesses and new houses is started outside of town anyhow."

"I see. Isn't the mayor Carl Johnson?" asked Nate.

Ben agreed, "Yup. He's outta the original Bryce family line. Mother was a Bryce."

Nate found these little revelations interesting. The food came and Ben said the blessing out loud. Sue and Betsy stayed and talked with Ben and Nate. Nate found out a lot more about the county as the little group shared their insider knowledge. He listened intently as he ate.

After he finished his meal, Nate announced, "Well I'd better go down to the campground and see if I can get a place to stay. How do I find it?"

Ben gave him directions and added, "Len owns the place and you can tell him I sent ya. He's a longtime friend and a good ole boy."

"Thanks," Nate said, then paid, said his goodbyes, left a tip and headed out.

Betsy and Sue had a little side conversation in the kitchen when Nate left.

Sue told her mom, "He's good lookin' and he seems nice."

Betsy smiled, "Yes, but he's too ole for ya."

"No he's not, ma. He's too young for ya."

Betsy joked, "We'll flip for him."

"No way, ma. All's fair in love and war, so may the best woman win, or in this case, the youngest."

Betsy laughed, "In your dreams, daughter dear."

Unknown to Betsy and Sue, Ben had overheard every word. He was smiling. He'd warned the young feller about the women here being dangerous. Even Ben had women after him from church and the senior's center. Halfway respectable men were in short supply in the county. In fact, there were few single men of any kind in the county.

Nate found it was a short drive to the campground. He turned off the highway and down a short drive where he found the building that served as the office and camp store. There was a large sign announcing "Drift River Outfitters and Campground." By its appearance, Nate figured the building was probably about fourteen hundred square feet. It had log siding and a covered porch all the way across the front. Nate thought the red steel roof was a nice touch. He also liked that there were several chairs on the porch and there was a railed-in outdoor eating area at the side with a half dozen picnic tables.

Nate got out, locked his van, then went inside. The store was well stocked, as well as clean. Directly across from the door was a snack bar in the left corner with what looked like a pizza oven and a cooktop grill. There were three small old-style sets of chrome kitchen tables and chairs that looked like they were from the fifties. They were near the counter which faced the cook area. There were six stools at the counter.

An older man was sitting behind the store counter to the left of the door and he was reading. He looked up at Nate.

The man said, "Welcome," and rose to greet Nate. He still had the book he was reading in his left hand as he offered his right, "I'm Len. How kin I hep ya?"

Nate shook the man's hand, "I'm Nate Christian. Ben Kemp suggested I come see you. Good book you're reading."

The man smiled, "Yup, the best."

Nate began, "I would like to rent a cabin."

"Sorry. They's all booked. Only have campsites with hookups available."

"How much are they?"

"The serviced sites are a hundred a week or three hundred a month including utilities."

Nate didn't know why he asked but he did, "Do you have longer term rates?"

"I have a few year-round sites for RVs. The annual rental rate is fifteen hundred but electricity is metered and, if you hook up to the sewer and water, it's another forty a month. I sell propane right here."

Nate asked, "You're open year round?"

"Yup. I have a number of campers who come all year. Two couples live here full-time. I have a large number of retired folk who stay here nine or ten months outta the year. My water and sewer lines is buried under the frost line and it don't get real cold here in winter anyways. If you put heat tapes on the water pipes from the service pit, ya don't have freeze ups."

Nate mused, "I didn't realize people lived in campers."

It occurred to Nate that some RVs were probably larger than the efficiency apartment he'd lived in as a student.

"What do you want to do?" Len asked.

"If I rent one for a month and decide to go yearly, would you apply the rent toward my annual?"

"For a friend of Ben's I'd do it. I have only one that's vacant for the whole season and I'll give you a month to decide but no more."

"I'll have to sleep in my van for the time being."

"The rent's the same."

"Understood. Will you show me the lot?"

Len called, "Hildee."

A young woman came out of the office and said, "What ya want, pa?"

"Hildee, this here is Nate. Please show him lot 158." Len turned to Nate, "This here is my daughter, Hildee."

Nate said, "Pleased to meet you."

Hildee held out her hand and Nate shook it. Nate felt a little tingle at the woman's touch. Hildee smiled broadly and gripped his hand like a person used to hard work; her grip was strong.

Nate observed that Hildee was a woman probably just entering her

10

twenties and good to look at but not what most would consider pretty. She had big brown eyes and wore her light brown hair short, but the short hair suited her. Nate guessed she was about five nine; just a few inches shorter than he was. She was very well proportioned, not the very skinny shapeless type of woman that fashion magazines preferred but curvy. She looked fit and healthy and Nate thought there was something extremely appealing and attractive about her. He thought he would describe her as very womanly and striking.

Hildee said, "Foller me, Nate."

Nate followed her outside. He noted she had an attractive backside with womanly hips. Nate had to concentrate to look elsewhere but the temptation continued. Usually he was somewhat immune to such things, but there was something about her that really got under his skin.

Hildee got on a golf cart. Nate followed her lead and got in the passenger seat.

She said, "Lot 158 is a really nice campsite. It's on a little hill overlookin' the river so it don't usually flood in spring. The couple who used to stay there is now gone to meet their maker. Their kids left a picnic table and a portable storage shed when they sold the RV that was there; said we could keep 'em. You can use 'em as long as you're here."

Nate asked, "Is it quiet here?"

Hildee replied, "There are lotsa kids at the beach in the summer as this is really a family camp. Pa don't allow no nonsense and most of the folks thet stay are really nice clean-livin' folks. If ya don't mind the sound of kids playin' until about seven or eight in the evenin', you will like it here."

Nate smiled, "Kids aren't a problem."

The road they travelled was a well-graded gravel surface and, as they neared the river, Hildee turned to the right and drove onto the RV site. "The previous renters poured a concrete pad."

Nate got out and looked around. It was a splendid spot. He looked in the shed, which was about eight by ten with six and a half foot sidewalls. It had one window and was built of two by fours covered with steel siding and had a metal roof but there were no interior walls. Nate made up his mind, "I like it. I'll just have to buy an RV."

Hildee asked, "You don't have one?"

"No, and I think I'll stay here year round."

11

"You'll be number three doin' thet."

They returned to the golf cart. Nate asked, "Would you give me a tour?"

"Sho nuff. I've done my chores."

Hildee started driving and explained the layout of the park, "There are five roads thet runs parallel ta the river and one at each end joining them all ta the road goin' by the store. This is the riverfront road. As you can see, there is campsites on both sides of the road. We have a bathhouse on each road in the middle and toilet buildings on alternating ends of the parallel roads. There's a coin laundry on the middle one."

Hildee stopped at the first bathhouse they encountered and said, "The bathhouses are all the same. Men's and women's shower entrances on either end. Twelve shower stalls in each."

Nate went in the men's and looked. The building was basic but clean and well maintained. There were twelve sinks, one opposite each shower stall. Nate walked out and Hildee was leaning against the cart. Nate said, "It's well kept."

Hildee said, "Yup," and climbed on the cart. Nate followed her lead. She drove him to the laundry building.

Nate got out and went inside. It was a small building with about twenty coin-operated washers and dryers. He was looking at the machines and turned to notice Hildee looking at him. He smiled at her. She smiled back and started walking to the cart. Nate went to the door and watched her. Climbing into the cart, she noticed him looking at her so asked, "Ya lookin' at me?"

"Guilty."

Hildee cocked her head to one side and asked, "Why?"

Nate was, if anything, honest so he answered honestly, "I find you very attractive."

Hildee blushed a deep red. The fact that he had a hard time keeping his eyes off of her didn't help matters. She seemed to realize he was having difficulty controlling his hormones.

As they headed back to the office Nate asked, "Do you work for your father?"

"Yup. I keep the books and keep the place up. I do most of the work until the summer workers git outta school. I do a little bit of everything."

"I have a part-time job lined up but I need to find some contractor work as well."

"If you're any good you'll find lots of work. We don't have a lot of good tradesmen 'round here. You have ur own tools?"

"Yes. The back of my van is full of them."

In fact, it was those tools which had provided the means for Nate to earn his way through his final half year of college. He also realized he would need to store his personal belongings in the shed if he was to sleep in his van in the aisle between the shelves and bins. Then it occurred to him that he could sleep in the shed for a while. The storage shed would be a blessing.

Hildee asked, "When do you start your new part-time job?"

"Sunday."

"So what do ya think?"

Nate smiled at Hildee and looked at her, "I think I'll certainly like it here."

Hildee blushed again, but just a little. She drove Nate back to the office and they went inside. She said to her father, "He's goin' ta take it, pa."

Nate looked at Len, "Yes, please," and offered his hand.

Len shook it and said, "That will be three hundred dollars up front."

Nate took out a debit card and asked, "You take that?"

"Yup," and proceeded to hand Nate a registration card. Nate filled it out and asked, "What's the address here?"

Len told him and added, "Use lot 158. Gayle, our rural carrier, delivers all the mail here to the store." He processed Nate's payment and handed the card back to Nate along with the receipt.

"Well, now I have an address. I'd better get on my laptop and make some address changes. Is there a library in town with computer lines?"

Hildee giggled, "Yup, but be careful!" Nate was not smart enough to ask why. He should have. Hildee told him how to get to the county library.

Nate said, "Thank you, Hildee," with a big smile then added, "See you later, Len."

As Nate was leaving in his van, Len looked at his daughter and said, "He's good lookin'. Ya interested?"

Hildee sighed, "He's gorgeous and he seems nice. I don't think I have a chance with someone like that one, pa. He's probably like most fellers 'round and like's them cutesy, li'l Barbie doll soft, girly types. Besides, I

13

don't know nothin' 'bout his character."

"He certainly seemed to be givin' ya the eye. Be careful, daughter."

Hildee blushed a little, "I done said I don't know 'bout his character, pa."

"We'll find that out soon 'nuff, but Ben has always been a good judge of men and livestock."

Nate drove to what was now his campsite. He unloaded all his personal belongings and some of his larger tools into the shed. He put a wire line up between two rafters and hung his clothes and put a small blanket over the window. He took a padlock off one of his tool boxes in the van and locked the storage shed, then headed into town to the library.

The county library was bigger and nicer than he had expected. He parked and went inside with his laptop. The librarian's counter was at the front and he approached the young woman there.

Nate began, "Good day."

The woman had been concentrating on her computer screen and was slightly bent over showing more cleavage than Nate thought was appropriate. Nate realized with a little effort a fellow could probably see her navel. He avoided looking though it took some effort. The name tag on the desk identified the woman as Chastity. Nate thought that was probably not an appropriate name for the woman and then felt a little guilty for being judgmental.

Chastity was what most men would consider a real looker and Nate thought she dressed way too revealing. She was definitely not his type. Nate thought such sexual temptations were everywhere these days.

The woman looked up, smiled and said, "Hello. How may I help you?"

Nate said, "I'm new. I'm Nate Christian."

The woman smiled broadly, "Hello. I'm Chastity Bell," and offered her hand. Nate shook it and noticed Chastity did not immediately let go.

"Do you have Wi-Fi?"

"Yes, we do. We also have lines for more secure connections at the computer table. Would you like a library card? For residents they are five dollars and twenty for non-residents."

Nate said, "Please."

Chastity handed him a form and he filled it out and handed her five dollars. "You didn't put down no phone number."

"I don't have one."

"That's unusual these days."

"I guess it is."

Chastity asked, "Will your wife want a card as well? You can git one for her while you're here. No extra cost." She was smiling broadly.

He wondered about the motivation to that question but answered anyway, "I'm single."

"Well, that is interestin', honey."

Nate was not a complete moron when it came to women, but he thought this would be a good time to act like one. He didn't let on he recognized the flirtation signals she was giving off. She started playing with her necklace which was obviously a way she had of drawing attention to her ample and exposed cleavage. He asked, "Do I need a code to get access to the system?"

Chastity said, "Just a minute," and started working on the computer. Nate turned away so he would not be tempted to look at Chastity's inviting cleavage. He stood half facing away from Chastity and examined the library.

Nate heard the printer. Chastity said, "There it is." He turned to face her. She was now standing bending over the printer to retrieve his card and her dress was way too short. Nate turned away. Chastity came and sat back down, "Here's your card, hun."

He turned around and she handed him a library card and said, "Your card number is your access code." In the process, their hands touched and Nate thought it might be intentional on Chastity's part. Her hand lingered a moment on his. It was obviously intentional.

Nate nodded and took his hand away with the card saying, "Thank you, Chastity."

Chastity offered, "The best place to access a signal is at the center table where there's wired hook-ups." She pointed.

Nate nodded and set out for the table. He sat down at the table, opened his laptop case, and took it out along with the power cord. There was no use in running down the battery. He used another type of cord to connect to the library system so he could check his bank accounts more securely. Glancing at Chastity, he noticed she was watching him like a hungry cat watches a mouse. She smiled and was still playing with her necklace.

It took Nate forty minutes to get online and send the notices he needed to. He checked and reconciled his bank accounts, cleared his emails, then signed off. After packing up his gear, he headed for the door. As he passed Chastity, he said, "Thank you for the help, Chastity."

Chastity gushed, "If you need anything else, anything at all, I'd be pleased to help." Nate noticed the emphasis on anything and said, "Thanks. Bye."

He left as families were arriving at the library. Nate looked at the sky and figured it was probably after dinner time and he was hungry. He drove to the diner and found people were coming out as he went in. It was obvious as he entered that the evening rush was ending. He sat in a booth and Betsy came over.

"Hi, Nate."

"Hi, Betsy. Looks like you had a busy dinner service."

Betsy nodded, "It's always busy but more so durin' tourist time. I have to hire a lot of student workers full-time durin' the summer. What can I git ya?"

Nate said, "How about a grilled cheese and soup? What's the soup of the day?"

"Homemade chicken noodle."

"Sounds good and a glass of water, no lemon."

Betsy smiled, "Comin' right up."

Sue came over, smiled, and said, "Hi, hun. Has mom served ya?"

Nate smiled, "You know she has."

"Yup. Mind if I sit with ya?"

"Please," and Sue took the seat opposite Nate.

"Well, did you get a place to stay?"

"Yes. I'll be staying at Len's campground."

"Good."

"Do you go to church regularly?"

"Yeah. Me and ma go over to Chesterville every Sunday."

"Isn't that a long drive when you have a church right here in town?"

Sue replied, "We like it better over there. Would ya like to go with on Sunday?"

Nate answered innocently, "I'd accept but I have another commitment."

"Too bad."

Betsy came with Nate's water, soup and sandwich, "Here ya go, Nate."

Nate said, "Thank you, Betsy." Instead of being wise enough to leave it there, Nate added, "Would you care to sit down and join us?"

Betsy smiled and looked at her daughter, "Sure thing."

She slid in beside Nate and Nate slid over, noticing the look Sue gave her mother. Nate now regretted his careless but innocent offer. He was a little uncomfortable because Betsy was sitting very close and their thighs touched. Nate moved over but just a little because he was now against the wall.

They seemed not to notice when Nate bowed his head and silently gave thanks and started eating. Betsy stopped the glaring contest with her daughter and asked, "So did ya git a place ta stay?"

Sue answered, "He's stayin' at Len's campground."

Betsy asked, "Would ya go to church with me on Sunday?"

"I already asked. He has another commitment."

"Some other time then?" asked Betsy.

"Sorry but I can't go on a Sunday morning."

Betsy smiled, "Too bad. I'd better git back to work."

Sue agreed, "Me too."

The two women went to the kitchen and Sue said, "Well, that tears it. I reckoned fer sure Mr. Christian was a Christian."

"Seems not. It looks like he's out fer the both of us."

Sue sighed, "Too bad. Did ya see how he looks in that tee? He has a six pack, ma."

"Don't I know it. He is certainly a temptation."

As she cleaned a table, Sue was thinking this was an opportunity to witness and she was sure God wouldn't mind that she had ulterior motives. She went back to see Nate who was finishing his meal. She asked, "Would ya like coffee, Nate?"

"Yes, please."

Sue went and got two cups of coffee and went back. She asked, "Mind if I join ya?"

Nate said, "Please."

Sue sat down and asked, "Nate, have you ever told a lie?"

"Yes."

Sue asked, "Have ya ever taken anything that didn't belong to ya?

17

Even a pen or some food that wasn't offered or even a cookie or candy as a kid?"

"Yes."

Nate knew where Sue was going with this and he smiled. He was not put off but appreciated what she was trying to do. It spoke well of her character.

"Nate, have you ever used the name of God as a curse word?"

"Guilty."

Sue smiled, "Well, what do they call a person who tells a lie?"

"Sue, I'll save you time by admitting I'm a liar, a thief, a blasphemer and much more. I have broken all the Ten Commandments either in thought or deed. I deserve to go to hell for my offenses against God but, because I have accepted Jesus as my personal Lord and Savior, He has taken on the penalty for my sins, taken my punishment for me."

Nate smiled at Sue. Sue had her mouth open in disbelief. She paused then said, "I thought ya was a heathen. You turned down my invitation to go to Sunday church."

Nate smiled, "That's because I'm a preacher and I'll be busy."

"Oh." Then Sue blurted, "That means ya are an available and acceptable bachelor."

Nate smiled, "Is there such a shortage of single men here?"

"In case ya haven't noticed, there is a shortage big time. Ya might as well be a ten-point buck during deer huntin' season. Every unhitched woman 'round will be after ya. There are only a few unmarried men here and there's reasons no respectable woman will have anythin' to do with most of 'em 'cause they're lay about womanizers, drunks, and such."

"I see. Is that why you were witnessing to me."

Sue sighed and looked down, "Only partially. I thought about it and figured there was no harm in both God and me having an interest in ya."

Nate laughed and then said, "Good point."

Sue said, "I've probably said too much."

Nate smiled, "I don't think so. I like your directness and honesty. I never imagined though that I'd be compared to a ten pointer."

Betsy came out of the kitchen and said to Sue, "Don't ya have work ta do?"

"No, ma. The tables are all cleared and my shift was over a half hour ago."

18

Betsy looked around and shrugged.

Nate said, "Well, I'd better get going. Thank you ladies." Nate left a tip and got up. Betsy followed him to the cash register and checked him out.

Sue sat smiling at the table. She decided what her ma didn't know just might work against her in the hunt. Sue was not going to tell her ma what she had discovered about the "ten-pointer" Nate.

Chapter 2

Nate slept well considering he had made his bed on the floor of his van. He went to the shower building and shaved and showered then headed back to his site. On the way, he ran into Hildee emptying waste barrels. She seemed to have no trouble hefting the fifty-five gallon barrels to empty them. He stopped and watched her just because he found her so attractive. She seemed to realize someone was there and turned to look at him.

Nate smiled and said, "Like some help?"

Hildee smiled, "Well, aren't ya a gentleman. No thanks, though, 'cause this is my job and my responsibility."

"Alright," then had a brainstorm. "I haven't had breakfast. If you can get away, how about letting me buy you a meal at the diner?"

"Well, I ain't eaten out in a while. I reckon I'd like thet. Give me ten and I'll meet up with ya at the store."

Nate simply said, "Ok."

For a smart man, Nate could sometimes be more than a little dense. He did not notice that Hildee had blushed ever so slightly at his invitation. What Nate took as a neighborly gesture, well, probably more than neighborly when he'd look back on it, Hildee was interpreting correctly as romantic interest. Of course, it could just be that Nate's initial attraction to Hildee was growing and he was not yet willing to admit it. It was, in fact, the reality.

Nate was at the store a little ahead of schedule. He went inside. Len was sitting behind the counter and said, "Mornin'," just a little gruffly.

Nate asked, "Something wrong, Len?"

"I hear ya is takin' Hildee to breakfast."

"Yes, sir."

"My Hildee is a good girl. Don't go toying with her feelin's or you will answer ta me."

"I understand."

"Well, what is your intent? I thought ya was a nice young feller."

"I try, sir. I really do. I have no intention of taking advantage of Hildee."

"See ya don't. She's quite capable of knocking yar block off and if she don't, I will if'in ya hurt her. There's too many fornicating fast-talking,

20

liquored-up men in this county already."

"So I've been told."

"Who told you that?"

"I think it was Sue at the diner."

Len gave Nate a stern look. Nate was saved as Hildee came into the store and announced, "I'm ready."

He noticed she had changed from her plaid work shirt and was wearing a nice blouse which accentuated her highly feminine qualities ever so modestly. It occurred to Nate that there was no way of hiding that God had endowed Hildee greatly with apparent good character and personality, handsome face and a killer body.

Nate said, "See ya later, Len."

"Ya."

Nate held the door for Hildee as they left. He walked beside her to the van and opened the door for her.

Hildee said, "Thank ya."

"You're welcome."

Nate got in and started the van.

Hildee asked, "Why did ya ask me to breakfast?"

Nate was surprised, "What do you mean?"

"Well, ya could have just about any single woman, and some not, in the county. Ya are very good lookin' and have a good personality. Unless ya is a drunken lay-about, which I doubt, ya would be considered quite a catch."

Nate smiled and said with a touch of humor, "Well, shucks ma'am, you are just too kind."

Hildee said seriously, "Ya didn't answer my question."

Nate knew then that Hildee was no one's fool, so he said, "Well, I wanted to get to know you. The women I have met so far, you being the exception, seem almost like hunters and they make me feel like the hunted."

"So I'm safe?"

Nate didn't know why but he decided to be candid, "Not likely. I think you are for me a great temptation. You seem to be of good character and have a nice personality. To boot, I find you very, and I mean very, attractive."

"You didn't say pretty."

"No. That word would not be truthful or do you justice. You are what I would call a handsome woman."

Hildee cocked her head to one side looking at Nate. Nate continued, "Now before you take offense, in my defense, I would point out handsome means you have striking and imposing good looks. To me, that is much more attractive than regular old pretty."

Nate looked at Hildee, who was looking at him with an intensity Nate did not find uncomfortable.

Hildee simply said, "Ya definitely has possibilities."

"I was hoping you'd think so."

Hildee laughed lightly. She then said, "Ya don't talk like any construction worker I ever met. What do ya really do?"

"Oh, I'm really a contractor and licensed. I do electrician and plumber work as well as general contracting. I will probably do that until I'm old and grey. It is how I paid my way through school. I'm also a preacher."

"Really?"

"Yes. Bi-vocational. You know, preach part-time and work at another job full-time."

Hildee asked, "Couldn't you get a full-time church?"

"I was offered several but that's not what I'm called to do."

Hildee simply replied, "Hmmm."

"That a problem for you?"

Hildee smiled, "God didn't ask my permission."

It was Nate's turn to chuckle, then he said, "Good point."

They arrived at the diner and Hildee got out before Nate could go around and open her door. She met him at the front of the truck and took his arm and they went into the diner. The only thing that could have caused more shock than their entrance was if the president had shown up for breakfast.

Time seemed frozen. Betsy and Sue stopped dead in their tracks with their mouths open. Chastity was sitting at a table and spilled some of the coffee she was putting to her lips. She started wiping at it while still staring at Nate and Hildee, who were arm-in-arm. The rest of the customers had stopped to see what was causing the reaction.

Nate said, "Good morning, everyone." The sound of his voice seemed to set time back in motion. Everyone went back to what they had been doing. Nate led Hildee to a table. He pulled a chair out for her and she sat down. This time neither Betsy nor Sue rushed to Nate's table.

Hildee remarked as Nate sat, "Well, that was interestin'."

"Yes, it was. You'd think we had two heads."

Hildee smiled, "Well, we does, between us that is."

Nate chuckled, "Good one."

Betsy came to serve them, "Good mornin'."

"Yes it is, Betsy. Betsy, do you know Hildee?"

"Yes, I do. Hi, Hildee."

"Betsy."

Nate said looking at Hildee, "Betsy and Sue were kind enough to invite me to church. Sue even tried to evangelize me so I told her about my part-time job?"

Betsy asked, "Part-time job?"

Hildee said, "Nate is a preacher."

"What?" Betsy turned and looked at Sue, who was standing nearby serving another table. She looked at her mother somewhat timidly. She looked like the child caught with her hand in the cookie jar.

Nate looked at Sue and knew she had not shared the information with her mother. Nate thought Advantage Sue. Sue's mother would probably get even, if only good naturedly.

Betsy regained her composure and asked, "What can I get y'all?"

Nate looked at Hildee, "Ladies first."

Hildee ordered the country breakfast platter and Nate ordered the country pancake platter with sausage. When Betsy left, Hildee smiled broadly at Nate, "They were both on the hunt fer ya, Nate."

Nate nodded agreement, "The fact did not escape me completely, even though I can sometimes be dense where women are concerned."

"Well, in ya's line of work ya is askin' for trouble if ya are too dense 'bout it."

Nate sat back, "It never occurred to me but you are right." Nate paused and looked at Hildee, "I can see that added to the many advantages of a pastor being married."

Hildee blushed ever so slightly, "Tease."

Nate smiled broadly and Hildee threw her napkin at him and he laughed. The people around them glanced in their direction. Hildee smiled broadly. She could not remember when she had enjoyed small talk so much.

Betsy brought their food and said, "You two make a good couple." She looked at Hildee, "If I is havin' to lose in the hunt, I can't think of a better person to lose to."

Hildee replied, "I haven't bagged him yet."

"Yeah, ya have. He just hasn't realized it yet. Watch out for the claws though."

Hildee smiled, "Thanks, Betsy."

Betsy looked at Nate, "Good choice."

As Betsy walked away, Nate thought she wasn't talking about the food. He realized there was something profound happening between him and Hildee and it was too fast, way too fast. Or was it?

Nate said, "It seems my future is decided for me on my first full day here."

Hildee smiled, "It's in the Lord's hands. Now hurry up like and say the blessin' afore the food gits cold."

Nate smiled, bowed his head and prayed. When he finished, he noticed people were looking at him. He looked at Hildee and they started eating. The syrup Betsy provided was the real deal; maple syrup.

"Would you come to service with me on Sunday? I'd like you to be there the first day I preach."

"Where ya preachin'?" Hildee was afraid of the answer.

"First Community Church of Bryce River."

"I don't usually go ta church there, but fer ya I'll go."

"Thank you, Hildee. You will be my cheerleading section."

Nate did not see Ben coming until he sat down, "Hi, Nate."

"Hi, Ben."

Ben turned to Hildee, "I see you have met my new friend."

Hildee smiled, "Yes, Ben. We bin havin' a good time."

Ben told her, "Your pa called me all in a uproar about this young feller takin' ya to breakfast. I told him about the most honorable date a man could take a young woman on was breakfast at the local diner. Your pa is a real worrywart since your ma passed."

Hildee nodded agreement as she chewed.

Betsy came to the table and asked, "You want breakfast, Ben?"

Nate offered, "I'm buying."

Ben told Betsy, "In that case, I'm eating." Ben ordered the breakfast special.

Nate asked, "When do you want to start work on Ole Beauty?"

"I ordered me a rebuilt engine. It won't be in until next week at the very earliest. Probably it'll take a lot longer."

"Let me know when you're ready."

"You livin' in a tent?" Ben asked.

"Nah. I slept in my van last night but I'm going to buy a camper RV. I'll stay in that until I eventually build a home, God willing."

"So you plan to stay in these parts."

Nate looked at Hildee, "I find this place suits me."

Hildee blushed slightly and Ben laughed, "Oh, this is goin' to drive yar pa crazy, Hildee."

Hildee looked at Ben, "Well, he's a little crazy anyhow. A little more can't hurt."

Ben started laughing and very loudly. It was contagious and Nate and Hildee started in. Everyone was looking in their direction. Betsy came over with a cup of coffee and sat down.

"If'in you're gonna party in my diner, I'm invitin' myself."

Ben said through the laughter, "The more the merrier."

Nate asked, "Can I buy you breakfast as a peace offering?"

Ben looked at Nate and started laughing again. Now all four of them were laughing. It was a contagious thing, the laughter. Those nearby were smiling.

Betsy looked at Ben, smiled and said, "Ya know all of a sudden ya aren't looking all that bad, Ben."

There was a second round of laughter.

Ben finally caught his breath, "Well, Betsy, you're young enough to be my daughter but, oh boy, what fun we'd have."

Betsy jumped in, "Alright then, you can take me to the dance Friday."

The group stopped their laughter and Nate looked at Ben. The look on his face was priceless and the three of them saw it at the same time and started laughing.

"Alright then, it's a foursome for Friday. We otta chaperone these here kids."

Nate said, "You sure it isn't the other way around?"

They started laughing again. Several people at the surrounding tables had been listening to the merriment and now they were chuckling. The diner had become breakfast party headquarters.

More customers arrived and Betsy left to help Sue serve.

By the time Nate finished eating, his breakfast was cold. The pancakes were good so he finished them anyway.

"So you're looking for a camper, huh?" Ben asked.

"Yeah, I am."

"I have a neighbor who has un he's a lookin' to sell. It needs work inside but he'd probably sell it at a good price. Wanna go see it?"

"I have to take Hildee home, but I'd like to go afterward."

"I'd like to tag along," Hildee put in.

"Oh, this will be fun. Let me call your pa," and left to use Betsy's phone. When Ben came back, he was smiling from ear to ear. "Your pa is fit to be tied. He was muttering something about taking this gallivantin' time out of your pay."

Hildee laughed and Ben smiled. Nate looked at them and said, "What?"

Ben chuckled, "Len is tighter than a cross-threaded nut on a rusty bolt. He don't pay Hildee. He 'spects he don't have to seeing as she is kin."

Nate shook his head, "No wonder she's desperate for a husband."

Hildee poked him none too gently on the arm and all Nate did was smile. Hildee smiled back.

"It's disgusting that's what it is!"

Nate and Hildee looked at Ben.

He complained, "Ya two is actin' like a long-time couple. One know's what the other means and when it's good kiddin'."

"Stop complaining," Hildee said. "Ya got a date with a young woman 'cause of us. Ya think that would a happened if we'd left ya to tendin' yar own business. Ya needed us to be matchmakers."

Ben smiled, "There is that. She's way better lookin' than them old heifers down at the seniors' center."

Nate asked, "By the way, where is the dance?"

Hildee answered, "The county fairgrounds center. It's a regular dance and social thing. No liquor and the parking lot is patrolled by county mounties. It's a family affair."

Nate just nodded. They all got up, Nate paid the bill, said so long to Betsy, and the trio left. Nate's van only had two seats so they went in Ben's old Buick. It was a short drive to Ben's neighbor's place. As they drove up the lane, Ben said, "Let me do the talking and stay inside until I motion to you." Ben got out of the car.

The man reached for a shotgun beside him. He yelled out, "That you, Ben?"

"Yeah, Billie. I got two friends with me. Hildee and a new friend Nate."

"Come on in then."

Ben motioned to Nate and Hildee and they got out of the car and followed Ben toward the porch. Billie put his shotgun back against the wall. Nate noted a large dog was sitting beside Billie. Nate had seen dogs like that before. They were very sociable but could get very aggressive if their owner was threatened or if they were given a command.

As they went up the porch steps Billie said, "Take a load off."

The three of them took chairs.

Hildee said, "Hi, Billie. How ya bin?"

"Good, Hildee. Who is thet with ya?"

"His name is Nate."

Nate asked, "Can I put my hand out to shake, Billie?"

Billie noted, "You ain't no slouch are ya." He made a signal to the dog and Nate reached out his hand and said, "A little left of your breastbone."

Their hands engaged and they shook.

Billie said, "You been around blind guys before."

"Yes."

"Vet?"

"Yes."

Billie asked, "Where and how long?"

"Two tours in Afghanistan. Six years in."

Nodding, Billie remarked, "I take it this ain't purely a social call."

Ben began, "Nope. Nate here is needin' a camper to live in and ya needs to sell one. I reckoned ya should meet."

Billie offered, "It's in the field to my left. The tires are shot, dry rot, and the thing needs work inside. You want it and I'll sell it to you at a good price."

Nate asked, "What do you figure?"

"I reckon five hundred 'cause it needs a lot of work."

"Can I have a look?"

"Go ahead. The key's on top of the front tire on the door side. Ben, why don't ya keep me company?"

Ben said, "Sure thing."

Nate and Hildee got up slowly, left the porch and walked to the camper. Nate examined the outside and, though the grass was tall, looked underneath.

When he crawled out, Hildee asked, "What do you think?"

"It looks solid. Just a couple of very small dings and the windows look tight."

Nate took the key and went inside. It appeared there were no leaks but the thing would need upgrading and chances were the appliances and air unit would probably need work or replacing. The mattress was kaput and the carpets would have to come out and the seats would need recovering. Nate figured with his skill and a little money he'd have a sweetheart of a trailer for about two grand.

Nate looked at Hildee, "I can fix this up really nice."

They went outside and locked the trailer then looked at the trailer tires and noted the sizes. He looked at Hildee and said, "Let's go back." It just sort of happened that they were holding hands on the walk. Neither said anything. When they arrived back at the porch, they sat down and Nate said, "Four hundred cash."

Billie nodded, "Sold."

Billie put out his right hand and they shook. "You got cash on you?"

"Yes."

Billie got up, "I'll go get the ownership." He made his way into the house. When he came outside he said, "Ok, pay up and she's yours."

Nate took four one hundred dollar bills out of his wallet and handed them to Billie. Billie took out a pen and Ben held his finger where Billie needed to sign. He did and handed the title to Nate.

"Ya kin come and get it anytime. Call out before gettin' out of yar car and, if'in I'm not outside, just honk but don't git out until I tell dog here it's alright."

"Understood. You get out much?"

"Where would I go?"

"The Friday night dance."

Billie tilted his head, "And how do you propose I git there?"

Ben offered, "I'll drive ya. I might even try to fix you up with a dance partner."

28

"And I suppose you have a date like Nate here?"

Nate knew Billie was blind but he wasn't stupid. He figured there was something going on between him and Hildee. Nate was now hoping there really was something.

Ben told him, "As a matter of fact, I'm going with Betsy."

"The good lookin' one from the diner?"

"Yeah."

Billie exclaimed, "Man, she's almost young enough to be your daughter."

"Eat your heart out. I'll try to fix ya up but you need to get cleaned up. Go to the barber and get trimmed and buy some new jeans and stuff. Maybe some cool sunglasses like the blind guys on TV wear. I'll even take ya."

Billie smiled at his friend's half teasing, "Yeah, but what about the dancin' part?"

"I'll just let everyone know ya's as clumsy as a bull in a china shop and ta give ya room."

"Really?"

"Yup."

"You're on."

"Alright then, when we get ya spiffed up, I'll take you to lunch at the diner so I can try to fix you up with a blind date who isn't really blind."

Billie chuckled, "No, but I is, so I guess that's good enough to call it a blind date."

Hildee smiled, "That's a good one, Billie."

Billie grinned, "It ain't half bad, is it?"

Ben advised them, "Well, we have to get Hildee back before her pa has a conniption fit. He ain't used to her gallavantin'. I'll come by tomorra."

"See ya, Ben. Good meeting ya, Nate."

"Back at you, Billie."

The trio got in the car and Ben said, "God sure does work in mysterious ways. I've been trying to get him out social like fer the longest time. I'm sure between Betsy and me we can git him a date. Billie don't look bad at all when he's cleaned up all nice. He's spry, too. He gets around better than he lets on. He can make out dark and light but not so's to tell faces. Everything's sort of shadowy blurry is how he told me."

Ben took them to the diner. They said goodbye and Hildee got in the van with Nate. Nate pulled out and went to the service center to gas up. As they pulled up to the pumps, he turned to Hildee.

"You're quiet. I'm going to get a soda. Do you want something?"

"Yes. I'll use the ladies room and I'll meet you inside."

They left a few minutes later. Hildee was sipping an orange soda and looked at Nate.

Nate commented, "You're quiet all of a sudden."

"It just sunk in that you are serious about stayin' here."

"Yes. I'm staying."

"What if the church job doesn't pan out?"

"I have other reasons to stay. Besides, this is where I was called to go. It'll work out."

Nate looked at Hildee and she was looking at him with her head tilted. She said, "This is happenin' very fast."

"It happens at the speed of God, whether slow or fast."

Hildee nodded, "Makes sense, maybe 'cause I want it to."

Nate nodded agreement, "Yes, there is that."

They arrived back at the campground and Hildee got out saying, "I'd better change and git back to work."

Len was sitting on the bench in front of the store. Nate got out and went and sat beside him. Len asked, "How'd it go?"

"We all had a good time. I also bought a camper. It needs repair. Do you have a problem with me doing work on it at the campsite?"

"What's it like?"

"It's boxy and basic; no slide outs but it's a good size. It's almost too big to pull with my van. It's all white and the structure is good. The outside is pristine and just needs a cleaning. The inside needs an overhaul. I plan to work on it pretty much full-time for a couple of weeks."

"I don't have no problem with you workin' on it here as long as you don't do it when folks kids is normally layin' back for the night."

"Understood. I'll knock off early. I'd also like to put up one of those aluminum carports to park it under. It will help keep the trailer cool in the summer sun and provide a shady sitting area. I see the two other year round folks put them up."

"No problem."

"Thanks."

Len asked, "Ben said ya and Hildee are hittin' it off."

Nate nodded, "Oh yeah."

"Ya an honorable feller? Ben says he reckons ya is."

"My intentions are right. We are going to the Friday night dance. Ben and some friends are going too."

"Me, too."

"Good. Maybe we can all sit together."

Len seemed surprised by Nate's answer and after a slight pause said, "I reckon."

Nate got up, "I have to go to town. I'll see you later."

After Nate left, Hildee came out in her work shirt. She sat down beside her father.

Len asked, "What do ya think 'bout him?"

"I think ya is 'ventually goin' to lose a daughter and gain a son."

"It's too soon."

"It is now, but it won't be."

"I see. He worries me."

"Cause you might lose your free hep or because of him."

"Maybe some of both."

Hildee smiled, "Well at least ya's gettin' honest in yar old age."

"I ain't that old, daughter."

"Then why don't you git out more?"

"I'm going to the dance Friday."

Hildee surprised him by saying, "Good thing. I'm going to work now."

She had no sooner left then Len phoned Ben. They had a long talk. Len felt better afterwards.

It didn't take long for Nate to get into town. He went to the church and went inside. The building was a nice single story brick building and was about twenty years old. It sat on a large corner lot. Nate walked to the office. A woman was busy on the computer. Nate looked at her and wondered why so many women here were so ready to expose the major portion of their breasts to public view.

The woman didn't look up but asked, "What do ya want?"

Nate stood there stunned by the rude response but gathered his thoughts and asked, "Where is the office?"

"Jimmie ain't here."

"No, I mean the Pastor's office."

The woman still hadn't looked up and said, "There ain't one. The only office we got is for the chairman of the deacons."

"I thought he promised it to the new pastor."

"He's slept since then. Jimmie don't have a good memory 'cept when it suits him; usually when money for him is involved."

The woman looked up, "Well, ain't you the cutie hunk. Sweetie, you can park in my bed anytime."

Nate asked, "Who are you?"

"Cindy Crawford and yes, that's my real name and no, we are not sisters, though we look alike."

Nate said, "I see," though he didn't mean he saw the similarity with the famous Cindy Crawford because there wasn't one. He asked, "How long have you worked here?"

"Since Jimmie hired me 'bout a month back. I needed a job."

"I see."

"What's that supposed to mean?"

"I don't understand."

"Don't believe them rumors 'bout Jimmie and me bein' a thing."

"Isn't Jimmie married?"

"Yeah, but he has a reputation, but that don't mean I'm his kept woman."

Nate was stunned. He asked, "Do ya go to church here?"

"Do I look like I'm a church biddy, honey?"

Nate said, "No."

Cindy stood and bent over revealing more than Nate cared to see so he said, "I have to go. See you later."

"I sure hope so, honey."

Nate left the building his mind boggled. He walked across the street and sat on a sidewalk bench facing the church. An old man came and sat beside him.

The man said, "It's a nice looking building but it's rotten on the inside."

Nate looked at the man, "What do you mean?"

"It's nuff to say that around here some folks call it Satan's Little Church. The deacons are all slumlords, sleazy businessmen, or corrupt politician types. Ya won't find many real Christians there. Churches is supposed to be hospitals for sinners but that place is a hotel for Satan's disciples."

"Where do you go to church?"

"I don't. A long time ago I used to go there. I don't have transportation and the city passed a law keepin' other churches from sending their vans here to pick people up. Now I have a Bible study group at the Bryce Seniors Home down the block. The mayor is trying to get the study group shut down. He says it's subversive to the church. I'm probably going to get kicked out for teaching the Bible study. Can you believe that?"

Nate shook his head, "Hardly."

"Still it's true. Ask anybody."

"I see. What's your name?"

"Willie Washington."

Nate offered his hand saying, "I'm Nate Christian."

Willie smiled, "Of the Christian Christians?"

"Yup."

The two men shook hands.

Willie said, "My advice is if you are thinking about going to church there, don't. I'd better head back. I don't move as fast as I used to but I need the exercise."

Nate sat there watching Willie walk away. It was probably more than a chance encounter; Nate was thinking divine intervention. Nate got in his van and drove out to Ben's place. He found Ben mowing his front yard with gang mowers pulled by a farm tractor. Ben saw him coming and drove up near the porch. They both arrived at the same time. Ben climbed off his tractor and met Nate at the porch.

Ben asked, "What's up?"

Nate sighed deeply, "I need to know about Satan's Little Church."

"Ya sure do work fast."

"Why didn't you tell me?"

Ben asked, "Would ya have taken me seriously?"

"Maybe but maybe not."

"It was better ya find out fer urself."

Nate sighed again, "So it's true about the deacons?"

"Yeah, and you can't make a silk purse out of a sow's ear."

Nate added, "Yeah, but God can."

"True, but he can also start a new work." Ben looked at Nate seriously.

Nate asked, "Do you think that would work?"

"Well, there's no real church within thirty-five miles and the church in town is just a social club and a milk money producer for a few corrupt men who run the place and play at church. Some say it's just to give them respectability don't ya see. I reckon they have their reasons, but it ain't got nothin' to do with God. Some folks go there 'cause there's no expectations about how theys's livin'. There's also a reason half the county drives thirty-five miles up the road to go worship on Sundays. It ain't gossip me tellin' ya this 'cause it's for the right reasons and it's true as the fact you don't get chocolate milk from a brown cow."

Nate just nodded, "I need to think about this and pray over it."

Ben got up and went to his tractor and Nate left. On the drive it occurred to him Hildee had agreed to go with him on Sunday. She was going to stand in the line of fire with him. He drove to the diner and went in. He sat down and Sue came to his table.

"Hi, Nate."

"Hello, Sue. Just coffee please."

Sue went and got a cup and brought it to the table and poured fresh coffee out of the pot she brought.

"You seem troubled."

Nate asked, "Would you sit down and tell me about Satan's Little Church?"

Sue sighed, "Not much ta tell. Most respectable folks stay away from the place." Sue sat down and that drew Betsy's attention and she came over.

"What's up?" Betsy asked.

"Nate found out about Satan's Little Church."

"Well it didn't take him long. You look troubled, Nate."

"That's an understatement."

Just then Jimmie James came in and looked in Nate's direction. Betsy saw Jimmie, looked at Nate, and then turned to her daughter and the two women left.

Jimmie came over and sat down. He asked, "How's the new boy doing?"

Nate said, "I'm getting by."

"I expected you'd drop by and wait to see me. Where you been?"

"Getting settled in."

"I was offended you didn't take my generous offer of a place to stay."

Nate sighed, "You broke your word."

"Don't be a crybaby. Business is business. I had a better offer."

Nate said, "Me, too."

Jimmie ignored the answer, "Ah well, I'm a forgiving man. I need to see your sermon for Sunday by Friday morning."

"I may not have it ready by then. It depends where and when the Spirit leads me."

"Well, if you want to work for me, you'd better have it done by Friday morning. By the way, I'll expect you to start at the store Monday."

"Pardon?"

"Well, you didn't expect us to pay you just to preach. You have to work at my store."

"That wasn't part of the deal."

"Well, it is now." Jimmie smiled evilly and added, "I don't think you have many options."

"Sure I do. I quit. Find yourself someone else."

Jimmie looked stunned. He responded, "You'll not work in Bryce River. I'll see to that."

Nate smiled, "Bryce River is not the center of God's creation."

Jimmie got up angrily and said, "It's your funeral, boy," before stomping out.

Betsy came to the table and sat down, "We couldn't help but hear with no one else in the place."

Nate shrugged, "It's not going to be a secret long."

"And his story will be something along the lines that he fired you, for this reason or that, which he'll make up. It's how he works. There will be some lies, half-truths or innuendos. Some will believe him but most won't."

"I have broad shoulders."

Sue came and sat down beside her mother and added "Yeah, but does Hildee? He's likely to drag her into this when it's all said and done. It won't take long for the news to spread that you and Hildee are an item."

Betsy said, "Could be."

Nate decided, "I'd better tell Len and Hildee."

Sue smiled, "That'd be a good thing, Nate. By the way, we release ya

35

from your promise to go to church with us if you weren't working."

Nate got up with a smile and left two dollars for the coffee, "Thank you, ladies. You are nice people."

It took Nate no time to drive out to the campground. Len was sitting on the bench in front of the store. Nate got out and went to him asking, "Is Hildee close by?"

"Yeah. Why?"

"I need to talk to you both."

Len went to the door, "Hildee, come out here please."

Hildee came out and saw her pa and Nate sitting and came and sat down beside them. Nate told them about his afternoon. He mentioned how it might affect Hildee. When he finished, he added a personal note, "Hildee, I really appreciate that you were willing to go into the lion's den with me on Sunday."

Hildee smiled, "Uh huh."

Nate assumed that was local for you're welcome.

Len asked, "What's ya goin' to do, Nate?"

"Fix up the camper, get some work and wait for God's leading. Ben suggested I start a new church."

Hildee jumped in, "That's a great idea. I'll help. I play the keyboard and pa plays the guitar."

Nate looked at Len, who nodded agreement.

Len said, "Let's pray," and they did.

When they finished, Len asked, "Why don't we sit right here and eat sandwiches?"

"I'll go make 'em. Pa. You get us some sodas outta the cooler."

Ten minutes later they were sitting eating sandwiches and drinking soda in the mild late spring air.

Nate offered, "It's quiet here."

"Wait until after Memorial Day. This place will be a hoppin' and filled with families. Between Memorial and Labor Day, we are full weekends and about ninety-five percent or better full during the week. Those are our make or break months."

Nate said innocently, "Too bad there isn't a place close by for them to go to church."

Len looked at Hildee, "There's the pavilion."

"Great idea, pa." She turned to Nate and said, "We could have

Sunday morning service there for the campers and any other folks who wants to come."

Len grinned, "That would drive ole Jimmie crazy. Let's do it."

Nate cautioned them, "We can't be doing it for revenge against Jimmie."

Len answered, "I reckon." He bowed his head and said, "Lord, forgive me."

Hildee said with a mischievous grin, "But if God uses it to chasten Jimmie, it wouldn't be a bad thing."

Nate just shook his head in disbelief but had a big smile on his face. He was trying to keep from laughing.

Len said, "I'll play the guitar and, Hildee, you can play that electronic piana ya got. We'll sing and Nate can preach."

Hildee asked Nate, "You game?"

Nate smiled, "Sure why not. We have everything we need."

Len said, "But to get the word out."

Hildee asked as they ate, "What are your plans, Nate?"

"Tomorrow I'm going to take the wheels off the camper and drop them off to get new tires put on. Then I'm going to go to the county courthouse, get a contractor's license and find out about local building codes then transfer the title for the camper. I also have to open a local account for my banking. After that, I'll put the wheels back on the camper and bring it back here."

Len told him, "If Hildee will look after the store, I'll come with ya and hep ya with the wheels and stuff. I could use a little time away before it gits busy."

"Sho nuff, pa, I'll look after the store. Maybe tonight we could practice some hymns at the pavilion."

Nate approved, "Then it's settled."

Len asked, "Ya got jack stands to hold the trailer up?"

"No I don't. I'd planned just to use some cement blocks and the van jack."

"I got some jacks and stands at the maintenance shop we can use."

So it was that, after an evening of talking on the porch, Nate retired.

On Wednesday morning, Nate rose early and went to the closest shower building and got cleaned up. It was more than a little cool in the unheated building, but the water was hot. When he finished, Nate took his morning kit back to the campsite. He spent some time reading his Bible and praying, both of which were part of his morning routine. When he finished, he locked up then went up to the store. Len was already waiting outside sipping a cup of coffee.

As Nate was getting out of his van, Len said, "I got fresh coffee. Hep yarself."

"Don't mind if I do."

Nate went inside and found Hildee pouring coffee behind the counter. She saw him coming and grabbed another cup saying, "Mornin'."

"Good morning, gorgeous."

Hildee smiled, "I like compliments. Keep 'em coming, ya silver-tongued preacher."

Nate smiled and took the coffee cup she offered. They went outside and sat near Len.

"This evenin' we should go over to the pavilion to practice fer Sunday," Len said, "sort of git a feel for what's what, ya know."

Nate agreed, "Alright by me."

Hildee said, "Uh huh," to agree with the suggestion.

After finishing their coffee, Nate and Len picked up the jacks and stands then went to fetch the wheels off the camper. While they were at Billie's, Billie went with them to the trailer and sat on the van's bumper sipping coffee and talking to them as they worked. They were on their way to the tire shop by eight-thirty.

They went inside where Len introduced Nate to the owner. Nate told the man what he needed and the man sold Nate four tires and promised to have them mounted and ready to pick up after lunch. Nate and Len, helped by the owner, took the wheels out of the van then left to run the other errands. As they were driving to the county courthouse, Len made a comment out of left field.

"Hildee's been tryin' to git me out socializin' like. I reckon it's jist the time I needed to heal my heart, after losing my wife, was longer than Hildee 'spected."

Nate didn't say anything but just nodded in acknowledgement.

Len continued, "She died in a car accident on her way home from shoppin' on a Saturday afternoon. Drunk driver ran a stop sign, t-boned her pickup and crushed her. Imagine, drunk as a skunk in the afternoon. They said she died hurry up quick. I guess it was a blessin' she didn't suffer. Hildee got over it quicker than me. Girl's is stronger in the feelin's department it seems ta me. She cried for days and then got over it. I kep it in and I bin sufferin' for years. Maybe it's time to let go. You think?"

Nate said, "I reckon."

Len nodded and nothing else was said about it as they were at the courthouse building. Nate grabbed his envelope that he'd left on the dash, they got out, and went inside. Len knew where they should go and led Nate to the right office.

When they walked in, a woman who appeared to be in her late forties or early fifties greeted Len with, "Well, look what the cat drug home."

Len said, "Hi, Marilee. This is my friend, Nate Christian."

"I'll bet you're that new preacher fella that Jimmie has been badmouthing; Hildee's beau."

Nate smiled and offered his hand, "Well, I'm new and I'm a preacher fellow, but I can't speak to the badmouthing part. As for Hildee, I can't say anything in front of Len because you know how pa is about his little girl."

Marilee laughed and shook Nate's hand, "Well, ya must be alright if Jimmie is spouting off bad 'bout ya and Hildee likes ya. What can I do for ya?"

Nate took his papers out, "I'd like a local contractor's license. I've got my papers here." He took his papers out of the large brown envelope.

Marilee looked at everything, "You've obviously done this before 'cause you have all the right paperwork. I need to make copies of these for yar file. You fill out this form while I do it."

Marilee slid a form to him and went and made copies of Nate's documents. When she came back, Nate had finished the form. Marilee handed Nate the originals and looked at the application form. "Well, all you need to do now is pay me the fees and I'll give ya the contractor and business licenses."

Nate pulled out his checkbook and wrote a check. As he was writing Marilee said, "The county has only issued three contractor licenses so I'd suggest ya git a phone. There's more work here fer good men than the two others kin handle."

"I guess I'll do that."

"Git some business cards, too."

"Yes, ma'am."

Marilee looked at Len, "It's good to see you out and about. You goin' to the dance Friday?"

Len nodded, "Yep. Nate and Hildee is goin' and I said I'd go to make sure they is behavin'."

Marilee declared, "I don't have a date."

Len was a little taken aback but said, "I'd be honored to take ya, Marilee."

Marilee smiled, "Pick me up about seven then."

Len smiled back, "Will do, Marilee."

Nate thought romance was sure in the air and said, "Nice meeting you, Marilee."

Len and Nate walked back to the van in silence. When they got in Len asked, "What just happened?"

"You made a date with a woman who it seems, for reasons that escape me, finds you attractive."

Len punched Nate playfully on the shoulder.

Nate continued, "There is no accounting for taste. I guess you'd better get some new jeans to wear and get spiffed up for Friday. You could use a trim."

Len looked at Nate and muttered something Nate couldn't make out, so Nate asked, "What was that you said?" Len shook his head but smiled.

They drove to the license bureau agency where Nate got the camper title transfer processed and paid the required fee. He could not get plates until he had the trailer insured. Nate also opened accounts at the local credit union and transferred some funds in. He and Len then returned to the campground. It was just a little past eleven when they got back. They went into the store and Hildee was behind the store counter working on the computer.

Hildee looked up, "How did it go?"

"We have to pick the wheels up after lunch and then we can bring the camper here."

Nate added, "And your pa has a date for the dance on Friday."

Hildee's mouth dropped open, "What?"

Len blushed and Nate replied, "He's taking Marilee; you know, she works at the courthouse."

Hildee recovered and smiled broadly and said, "It's about time, pa." She turned to Nate, "It seems ya is a good influence on pa."

"Whatever it takes to win you over."

Now both father and daughter were blushing.

Nate asked, "May I use your phone to arrange insurance on the camper? It's an 1-800 call."

Hildee offered, "Hep yarself."

Nate finished the arrangements using his card to pay the premium. The insurer would confirm by email with a liability card and gave Nate a confirmation number.

He finished the call and turned to Hildee. She said without being asked, "Yes, you can print off your insurance card."

She moved away from the computer and Nate sat down to get his card printed off, then signed out. While he had been working, Len and Hildee had gone outside. Nate went out and found Hildee was the only one sitting on the porch.

Nate asked, "Where's your pa?"

"Went for a walk. He said ya is good at hepin' people with their problems."

"I didn't do anything."

"Well, pa sure reckons you did. It is a miracle what happened today. He went direct from hermit to social butterfly."

Nate smiled at the thought.

"I'm reckonin' next he'll be buyin' new duds."

Nate put his head back against the high back of the rocking chair he was sitting in and said, "I suggested that and that he get a trim and new jeans. I think he will."

"I woulda lost money on thet bet."

"Which bet?"

"That pa would come out of his doldrums all of a sudden like after all this time."

Nate just nodded. He changed the subject. "I feel right at home here."

Hildee offered, "I'm hungry and I'm goin' to make a burger. Want one?"

Nate smiled, "Please. You'd better make an extra for your pa."

After lunch, Nate got tags for the trailer then he and Len got the new tires on the camper in the afternoon. They took it to the campground and Nate parked it off the concrete pad so when the carport was put up the camper would not be in the way.

At seven that evening, Nate went to meet Len and Hildee at the pavilion. Len was tuning his guitar to Hildee's keyboard when Nate pulled up. Nate brought his guitar out and went to where they were.

Len looked up, "I didn't know ya picked."

"It never came up."

"We got electric here. We also got us a small sound system we'll bring on Sunday. Didn't think we'd need it this evenin'."

Nate just nodded and smiled at Hildee.

Len asked, "I got an ole buddy who plays the banjo comin' to join in if'in that's alright."

"Another musician is always welcome."

Just then a pickup pulled up. The truck was obviously a four-wheel drive with large tires and was jacked up to give maximum clearance. A big fellow got out and pulled a banjo case out of from behind the seat. He looked the part of a bluegrass player. He had a long beard and long hair. His hair was in a ponytail trailing out of an old worn baseball cap imprinted with a tractor logo . He wore a T-shirt under jean overalls and wore work boots.

The man walked over and said, "Hi, Len. Where's this preacher feller?"

Nate began, "I'm Nate," and held out his hand.

The big man shook it and said, "You don't look like no preacher I ever met."

Nate smiled, "Yeah, well, we don't look like no church choir I ever seen either."

The big man's laugh boomed. He turned to Len and said, "I like this preacher feller."

Len just nodded.

Smiling, the big man said, "I'm Kyle Dixon but they call me Tiny 'cause I'm not."

Nate smiled broadly and Tiny returned it. They were soon "tuned up" and they started playing some of the old hymns. It was just one of those things that sometimes a group of musical types are just naturally suited together. It happened with this group. Their instruments and voices were very complimentary. They had been playing and singing for just a few minutes when people started coming over and sitting at the picnic tables in the pavilion. Soon there were about thirty people stomping and clapping to the music and joining in. It went on for almost two hours before the music just petered out.

Len announced, "Folks, we'll be having Sunday mornin' service at ten here. Same place. Same kinda music. Nate here will be doin' some preachin'."

Several people came to talk to the members of the group and they spent another half hour talking before the group packed up their instruments.

Len noted, "We had jist 'bout everybody who's stayin' here come."

Tiny added, "If'in church was like this all the time I'd go every Sunday."

Nate said, "You're on."

Tiny was taken aback but after a pause said, "You snookered me, preacher, but I'll be here." He offered his hand to Nate and they shook.

Nate spent the rest of the weekdays working on his camper. He took the carpet up and it, with the mattress, went to the campground dumpster. Nate would go to the campground store a couple of times a day to buy a sandwich or have a beverage with Hildee. Mainly it was to see Hildee.

By late Friday afternoon, Nate had ordered the carport which would be put up the next week. He was also ready to put the new floor down in the camper and start on repairing the cabinets. He still had not taken the built-in furniture for reupholstering. He stopped early so he could shower and get ready for the dance.

Chapter 3

Friday evening Nate headed to pick Hildee up then realized he didn't know where she lived. He was at a loss as to what to do. He decided he definitely had to get a cell phone. He was standing there at his lot thinking about what to do when Len pulled up with Hildee.

She got out and said, "Pa suggested you'd be like a lost sheep 'cause you didn't know where we lived."

Nate shrugged, "I reckon. It seems my lady friend likes to keep me guessing."

Hildee smiled, "I like that - lady friend."

Nate couldn't help teasing, "Well, girlfriend seems too much like high school."

Hildee shook her head and sighed, "What am I goin' ta do with ya?"

"You'll think of something."

Len yelled out the window, "I'll see you two at the center," and drove off.

Nate opened the door of his van for Hildee and she climbed in. Nate closed her door and then got in and drove to the highway. He looked at Hildee, "Which way?"

Hildee smiled, "Right."

"You are going to have to tell me where to go."

Hildee teased, "I imagine before you're done some other folks will tell ya where ta go."

"You're making a mountain out of a molehill."

"We'll see."

When they arrived at the fairgrounds, the parking lot was filling up quickly. With Hildee's help, Nate found a place relatively close to the building. They went in to find a large number of people had arrived and were standing around talking.

A young man came up to Hildee, "Hi, Hildee. Who's this guy."

Hildee replied, "This is my date, Nate Christian. Nate, this is Cal Cartwell."

Nate offered his hand, "Pleased to meet you."

The young man looked Nate up and down and grunted, "I ain't so pleased," and walked away.

Nate asked Hildee, "What's that all about?"

"Cal's not so nice and he's been trying to get me to date him fer years, but no way I would. He's nothin' but trouble with a capital T and he thinks he's all that because he played football in high school. Typical jock."

"Ouch."

Hildee giggled, "Don't tell me ya was one."

"Ok, I won't."

"But ya was."

"Guilty."

The band started playing so Hildee grabbed Nate's arm, "Let's dance." Nate didn't object. Hildee was a good dancer and she immediately recognized Nate was a good dancer as well. When the number ended, Hildee spotted her father.

She pulled on Nate's arm, "Let's go say hi to pa's date."

Hildee went with Nate in tow and as they got to Len and Marilee, Hildee said, "Hi, Marilee."

Marilee smiled, "Hey, Hildee. I haven't seen you since last Sunday. I heard some rumors you'd found yarself a beau."

Nate chimed in, "No ma'am, I was lucky enough to find her. A handsome woman like her doesn't need to find a man."

Hildee laughed and Marilee said, "A true gentlemen."

The band started in again and Hildee took Nate's hand and said to her father, "Come on, pa, they's line dancing."

Len shrugged and offered his arm to Marilee and soon they were all dancing. About ten minutes later, Ben and Betsy joined the line with Billie and a woman Nate did not know. Billie did pretty well. Most of the folks knew Billie, and his date and Betsy sort of kept him hemmed in and his date led him around. Nate eventually got introduced to Billie's date, Jessica. They were all having a good time so it was inevitable someone would try to ruin the night.

The little group had left the dance floor to get a beverage when it happened. A man grabbed Nate's shoulder. Nate turned around and a man he did not know tried to coldcock him. Nate easily sidestepped the punch and moved out of the way. The man's swing took him off balance and he fell into a support pole holding up the roof. He screamed and fell down. Blood was pouring out of his nose and mouth.

He screamed, "Ya hit me."

The folks standing nearby knew that wasn't the case.

45

Ben said, "Joe, you are considerable drunk. Trying to take Nate on in your condition is about as smart as puttin' new paint on a demolition derby car."

Joe sat there bleeding and crying. He blurted out, "Ya scumbag. You leave my sweet Chastity alone. Ya got another gal. I only got Chastity."

Hildee looked at Nate and Nate shrugged and held up his hands, palms up in front of his chest. He signaled he had no idea what the man was talking about.

Two deputies showed up, "What's going on?"

Joe screamed and pointed at Nate, "He hit me for no reason. He tried to steal my gal."

The older deputy looked at Ben, who shook his head no. The deputy looked around and everyone close by was shaking their head no. The deputy said to Nate, "You ok?"

"His punch missed me. He can hardly stand up."

The deputy looked at Ben and Len explained, "Joe tried to coldcock Nate and he moved aside and Joe is so drunk he fell into that pole there. See, it's got blood all over."

The deputy looked around and several people were nodding in agreement. The deputy asked Nate, "Do you want to press charges?"

Nate shook his head, "Nah. No harm was done."

The deputy nodded again and his partner tried to help Joe up, for which he was repaid by Joe biting his forearm. Now they had no choice. Joe was cuffed and arrested all the while protesting all the men were trying to steal his sweet Chastity.

When the deputies led Joe away, Nate asked, "What was that all about?"

"You bin to the library?" Ben asked.

Nate answered, "Yeah, to get my library card and use the internet."

"And Chastity tried to get ya interested."

"She was flirting and flaunting her cleavage."

Hildee snorted and Nate looked at her, "It's not funny."

Hildee started laughing, "It is, too."

There was snickering and light laughter from his little group.

Ben explained, "Chastity flaunts it to every feller that goes in there and then tells Joe they were hot after her. She's been trying to get Joe to propose for five or six years but Joe ain't havin' it. Chastity is driving him 'round the bend with all her crazy talk 'bout the men hot after her. Married or single don't matter. She's driving Joe mad. It's pitiful is what it is."

Billie said, "She even flirts with old Ben."

"Well, Joe ain't never tried to deck me," Ben said.

Billie said, "Well, look at ya agin the young feller." It struck the group as funny that Billie had made the sight comparison and they started chuckling.

Ben grumbled, "I don't like where this is a goin'."

Nate said grinning, "Better it's on you now."

Hildee did the snort laugh thing again and Nate asked, "You always laugh like that?"

"Only when I try to hold it in."

Nate said with a smile, "Then don't." That remark sent Hildee into fits of laughter and the others followed her. Nate was smiling broadly. He was having fun.

Soon the little group was back on the dance floor having a grand old time. The rest of the night passed quickly and it was almost midnight. The last dance was announced and Nate and Hildee took to the floor. It was a slow dance.

Nate started out with a little space between them but Hildee moved in and they were cheek to cheek as she was almost as tall as he. Nate then realized Hildee's body was pressed against him. Nate had a male reaction and Hildee whispered, "Well, Nate, I guess even preachers is men."

Nate moved away slightly, "Sorry. You have an effect on me."

Hildee moved in close again and said, "Good."

Nate whispered, "Please, Hildee, have mercy."

"Not a chance," and wiggled just a little against him.

Nate sighed and they finished the dance. Nate hoped his state wasn't too noticeable; after all his jeans weren't skin tight. He and Hildee left with their group.

Outside, Ben said, "Why don't we all go to the diner for coffee and pie?"

It was agreed and they all parted to head for the diner. Nate opened the door of the van and closed it after Hildee got in. He saw them coming as he walked around the front of the van. It was Cal and one of his friends. Nate jumped in the van and drove away before they could get there.

Hildee asked, "You afraid of Cal?"

"I'm afraid of what I might do to him if he provoked me into defending one of us. He's just a kid and he only thinks he's tough. It's going to get him in trouble, but I don't want the trouble to be me." Nate glanced at Hildee and she had her head tilted looking at him in that way she had when she was carefully considering something. She just nodded. He went back to watching the road.

Hildee told him, "I'm not usually a tease."

Nate's reply was typical of a redneck who didn't have a clue, "Huh?"

Hildee said, "You know." She paused, "The gettin' ya hot and bothered."

Nate blushed deeply and Hildee could see it even in the dark and started laughing. He said, "It's not funny!"

Hildee proclaimed with a snicker, "Oh ya, it is!"

"Well just because I'm a preacher doesn't mean I'm not a man subject to a man's temptations and, woman, you are a gigantic temptation."

"And just because I'm a virgin don't mean I don't know what it's all about. I think betwixt us we can keep it under control."

Nate didn't say anything, but he wasn't so certain. He would certainly need help from his Maker.

Hildee looked at him, "I take it ya aren't so sure."

"I'm a good swimmer but these waters are deeper and faster than anything I've encountered before."

"I see," Hildee said then went silent.

It seemed to Nate the seriousness of the situation had dawned on her. He realized it now as well. This was way beyond playfulness. They drove the rest of the way in silence and Nate was considering what was happening. It was hitting him like a ton of bricks and he was supposed to be a temperate man. Well, at least that was expected.

When they arrived at the diner, Hildee proclaimed, "Oh, am I glad we're finally here. I need to use the ladies' room in the worst way." They got out and Hildee hurried ahead of him into the diner. Nate followed Hildee inside and saw Len sitting alone. He went and sat opposite Len and asked, "Where's Marilee?"

"Ladies' room."

"Hildee, too."

"Ya seem to be hittin' it off with my Hildee."

"Yeah. We need to talk when we're alone."

48

Len sat back, "Serious huh?"

"So hard and fast it scares me. Don't say anything to Hildee. She is going to be my greatest temptation." Nate looked Len directly in the eye, "and I'm telling her father because I'm going to need help in that department."

Len chuckled, "Well, seein' as you know it you're likely to deal with it better."

"Well, you're a big help."

"In case ya didn't reckon it, I has my own temptation."

"You're no help at all!"

The ladies were coming back and Hildee asked, "Hep with what?"

Nate said, "It's guy talk."

Hildee slid in beside Nate and purposefully got close enough that her hips were against Nate. His reaction was immediate and Nate was glad the table hid it. Hildee seemed to know what was happening and moved her thigh against his. Nate sighed.

Len started laughing.

Hildee looked at her father and asked innocently, "What?"

Len answered, "Your ma used to do that to me. Drove me crazy. Ya's jist like her."

Hildee started blushing and Marilee laughed. Len followed and it was contagious so Nate started as well. Hildee was just sitting there beet red.

Len commented, "Daughter, I weren't born yesterday. You done already chose him and he knows it and now the tormenting has started. It's the female way."

Marilee said, "You are just better at it than Chastity."

Hildee put her head in her hands. "I'm so embarrassed."

Len said, "Ain't no need. It's kinda cute."

Hildee finally looked up and Marilee not to be outdone snuggled against Len and he started to blush. Hildee broke out in fits of laughter and now it was Len's turn to be the focus of the laughter.

Ben came in with Betsy and they pulled a small table over to the end of the booth and sat down.

Betsy asked, "What's all the laughing about?"

Marilee recounted the events and it was even funny during the telling. Nate noticed Sue was standing there taking it all in.

Sue shook her head and said with a grin, "I give ma the night off and y'all just corrupt her with all this romance stuff. What can I git y'all?"

The group put in their orders. Nate got to know the others as they talked. All of them but Nate knew the backgrounds of the others. The talk was for Nate's sake. Marilee was a widow and had worked for the county since she got out of high school. She and Len had been dating in high school and Len had even taken her to the senior prom. Then Hildee's mom moved to town and that was the end of that.

Nate learned Betsy had never been married and Sue's father had run off when she was born. He died several years later. Betsy shared that had all been before she had gotten right with God. Nate found it all very enjoyable.

Around one o'clock, Sue came to the table with a broad smile. "I got to run y'all off. Closing time is one o'clock and the boss will have my hide if'in I stay open later. Besides, it's been a long day." She gave them all their checks and went to the cash register. The gang paid and piled out of the diner and Betsy locked the door after them. Sue waved from inside.

"Will Sue be alright?" Nate asked.

Betsy said, "Yeah, Bubba will make sure she gits to her car. He makes sure we both git away safely when we work late."

Nate nodded. He took Hildee's hand and they walked to the van. He opened Hildee's door and she climbed in. When Nate started the van, Hildee said, "I reckon' this has been an entirely fun evenin'."

"Yes, it has been."

"I never thought I'd see pa carryin' on like thet again. It seemed the world has been lifted off'in his shoulders."

"Seems so."

"Pa has been in a funk for years. Tonight was like he used to be when ma was alive, at least best I kin remember. It's good fer him."

"I think so."

Hildee sat in quiet until they were near the campground when she said, "That road on the right is the lane to the house."

Len's house was on a road behind the campground. Nate could see the security light of the campground store through the opening in the trees. He pulled up beside the house and Hildee said, "Pa ain't home yet." Nate got out and walked Hildee to the porch. She tried to open the door but then went and sat down on a swinging love seat on the porch.

Nate asked, "Aren't you going inside?"

50

"I don't have no key. Never needed one before 'cause pa was either with me, here, or at the store."

Nate sat down beside Hildee and they swung gently. It was a nice evening and warm for this time of year. Still Hildee snuggled up against Nate. He put his arm around her.

She said, "The sky is clear tonight and the stars are bright."

"It is beautiful here."

"You think a city boy like you could be happy here."

"Yup. What was it like growing up here?"

"Good. I always was content with my life. In school I had a lot of friends and I know most folks hereabouts. There's a lot to do round here. Ma and pa were so happy and so was I. It just about was the death of pa when ma died. Even so, he loved me so much he kept on and I think it was for my sake. I always felt loved and so my life was good."

Len's truck came up the lane and he got out of his truck and came up on the porch. Hildee looked at her watch and said smiling, "I was worried about you. It's past curfew ya know. You coulda called."

Len laughed, "I guess I'd better git ya a key."

"That would be good."

"Well, this ole boy is going to bed. I've had enough excitement for one weekend. Well, at least to last until Sunday."

"What does that mean?" Hildee asked.

"Marilee is coming for our service on Sunday then I'm takin' her fer lunch at the diner."

Hildee looked at Nate, "Give 'em an inch 'n they take a mile."

Len laughed out loud, shook his head, unlocked the door, and went inside.

Hildee said, "We don't open the store on Sunday until after Memorial Day. Then we open in the afternoon."

Nate smiled and Hildee turned to him, put her hand on his cheek, and kissed him and not a closed lips kiss. Nate felt his pulse start to race and his temperature, among other things, start to rise. Hildee held the kiss just long enough to fire him up and then got up and said, "I always wondered what that would be like. I think I like it. Well, I'd better get some sleep. I've got to work in the morning. Thanks for a wonderful evening."

Nate watched her walk away. He thought, oh Lord, what am I to do? He then figured he knew, but what he didn't know was how long he should wait. It occurred to him that God would not allow him to be tempted beyond what he could deal with.

It was difficult getting to sleep that night. Thoughts of Hildee kept sliding through his mind. As a result, he got up and wrote a sermon in the middle of the night using his work light. He slept late. It was almost ten o'clock by the time he got to the campground store. Len was there, sitting behind the counter. As usual, he was reading and drinking coffee.

Len held up his cup and said, "Hep urself."

Nate got a cup. When he returned, Len had put down his book and motioned to the chair beside him behind the counter. Nate took the invitation.

Len smiled, "Good times last night. That Marilee is a real pistol. We always did git along. I could a talked her ear right off."

Nate smiled back, "Yeah, but you had curfew."

Len laughed, "Ya there was thet. Beside Marilee is a decent Christian woman. The neighbors might a got to talkin' if we'd stayed on the porch any longer."

Nate just nodded and sipped his coffee.

"She said I cleaned up nice. You were right about the trim and new duds. She noticed. I told her she looked like a sweet Georgia peach glisten'n in the sun. I don't know where it come from, but she seemed to like it."

"Women like compliments that come from the heart."

"And they seem to know, don't they? I mean when it's a true thing, even if it is corny."

"Yup."

Len paused, "You think maybe my Hildee will become yar Hildee?"

"Seems likely."

"I reckon' you'd make her a good husband and I wouldn't have no objections to it."

"I'd sure work at it when the time comes."

It had not escaped Len's notice that Nate had said when, not if.

Len just nodded, "Her mom and I didn't know each other very long when I popped the question. It was but a few weeks. I think I knew thet first week."

Nate shrugged, "I suppose sometimes it's like that."

"I was sort a like ya, but ya seem to have a few dollars. I didn't hardly have two pennies to rub together, but we built a life."

"That's what is supposed to happen."

Len changed the subject by asking, "What ya got planned today?"

"I guess I'll putter at putting a bamboo floor in the camper. It'll wear better and clean better than carpet. The stuff I'm using is light weight."

Len nodded, "So you're not going for the 'from the factory' look?"

"Nah, I'm going for practicality and glitz."

They watched through the front window as Hildee pulled up in front of the store in the pickup.

She came inside and said with a big smile as she took off her work gloves, "Did you two lay-abouts drink all the coffee?"

Nate replied, "Not yet. You got back too soon."

Hildee surprised Nate and came around the counter and kissed him square on the lips then went to the coffeepot.

Len smiled, "She sure knows how ta shut ya up."

"There is that."

Hildee came back and grabbed the chair from the desk near the counter and rolled it over to where the two men were sitting. She asked, "What have you two been up to while I was out workin'?"

Len said, "Reckonin'."

"What about?"

Len looked at his daughter, "If'in I could convince Nate to take you off'in my hands."

Hildee blushed deeply. Len looked at Nate, "She might be interested."

Nate was in a mischievous mood, "So what's her dowry?"

"A horse and two sheep but you'd have to take an I.O.U. note."

"I'll think on it."

Hildee was sitting beside Nate and punched him in the shoulder. He said, "Ouch. Girl, watch it; you can hit."

Hildee smiled, "And don't you forget it!"

Nate smiled, even though he knew he'd have a bruise. Hildee was no slouch.

Hildee asked, "What you got planned for today, Nate?"

Len said, "He's a gonna put a floor in his camper."

Hildee looked at Nate, "Want some help? I finished my work."

Nate nodded, "Sure thing, soon as we finish the coffee."

That was how Nate found Hildee knew her way around tools. Nate

53

assumed her pa had taught her well. They had cut and laid the new flooring in just under three hours. Nate had literally stripped the trailer out beforehand and laid a new subfloor.

Hildee was looking at the finished job, "That's gonna look real nice when you put everything back in."

"Yeah. Thankfully the walls just needed a little touch up. Next, I've just got to find someone to do the upholstery."

"I know someone. Let's throw the stuff in the pickup and go over."

"Shouldn't we phone first?"

"Nah, Herman don't have no phone at his shop."

They walked up to the campground store and went in. Len was just finished checking out a customer. When the customer left, Hildee said, "Pa, we're goin' to take Nate's stuff up to Herman's in the pickup."

Len asked, "Ya finished already?"

Nate remarked, "Hildee is good with tools. We did it in no time; like we'd been working together for years." Nate looked at Hildee and they both smiled.

"You two is disgustin' is what."

They took the truck to the camper and took all the seats and backs of the built-ins out of the shed and loaded them into the pickup. Hildee noticed the folded camp cot in the shed.

"That what you've been sleepin' on?"

"Yeah."

They got in the truck and Hildee drove them out into the county. Herman's shop was off a gravel road out in the middle of nowhere. The upholstery shop was a converted machine shed with a homemade painted sign over the door. When they walked in Herman was working on upholstering a sofa.

Hildee called out, "Hi, Herman."

Herman looked up, "Hi, Hildee. Who's this with ya?"

Nate offered, "Hi, I'm Nate Christian," and held out his hand.

Herman put down his tool and shook hands with Nate saying, "I heard of ya. The new preacher feller that's hot after our Hildee here."

Nate looked at Hildee and shrugged, "Guilty on both counts."

Herman shook his head, "An honest preacher. What's the world coming to? What can I do fer ya?"

"I'm redoing a camper to live in."

"I suppose ur keepin' it down at Len's."

Hildee said with a big smile, "Where else?"

Herman chuckled, "Well, at least there yar pa can keep a watchful eye on this city slicker."

Nate smiled broadly. He really enjoyed the people here.

Herman commented, "Well, I ain't got all day so let's see what ya need?"

They led Herman to the pickup and Nate explained what needed to be done.

"I don't know if in I kin git thet exact fabric," Herman said.

"I don't need it to be the same. Just something that will wear well and clean easily."

Hildee added, "And looks good."

Herman pretended to ignore Hildee's comment, though he looked at her and smiled, then said, "Man after my own heart. Let me show you some fabric."

With Hildee's help, Nate picked out a fabric and Herman quoted a price to cover and put new padding in the pieces. Nate agreed and the three of them unloaded the truck.

Herman asked, "What ya do for a livin', Nate? Preachin' don't pay."

"I have a master contractor's license. I do carpentry and am state licensed to do electrical and plumbing."

"Thet so. I needs a new electric service in the shop. Could ya do thet?"

"Sure could. I can have a look while I'm here and give you a price."

Herman showed him what needed to be done. Nate did an inspection and showed Herman some things that were hazardous and needed to be repaired and told Herman why. Nate got a pad out of the truck and did up an estimate on the spot. He gave the sheet to Herman, "That price is good for thirty days."

Herman looked it over and said, "When ya finishes yar camper, come on up here and do the fixin'. That's a fair price. How's about we swap out? I'll do your upholstery and pay ya the difference cash money."

"Alright but don't advertise this because I'm going to need to start doing strictly cash jobs."

"I understand. A feller can't get hitched without havin' money comin' in."

Hildee set to blushing again and Herman said, "Girl, ya's more redder than a new stop sign on a county highway." Nate chuckled and Hildee, who was next to him, elbowed him but very gently. It was a playful thing.

Herman grinned, "When they start that elbowing stuff, it means they done laid claim to a man."

Hildee shook her head, turned around and walked back to the truck, waving over her head.

Herman said, "Ya got a good un there, preacher."

"Don't I know it. By the way, have you got a church home?"

"Nah. We go sometimes but it's too far a drive to Chesterville every week. Can't afford to go all the way over there. Besides my ole truck don't have the legs left to go a long ways regular like."

"We're having service at the campground pavilion on Sunday at ten. Consider you've been invited."

Herman announced, "I just might show up outta pure curiosity."

"Whatever it takes, Herman."

The two men shook hands and Nate headed to the truck. Nate got in and Hildee said, "This is gettin' embarrassin'."

"Who are you kidding? You're loving seeing me squirm."

"You don't look to be doin' no squirmin' as far as I kin see."

"You're right. I'm coming to see the possibilities for the city slicker preacher and the country bumpkin gal."

Hildee smiled and shook her fist at Nate, "Watch it, city boy."

Nate looked Hildee up and down, "Oh, I am." Hildee went to blushing and Nate laughed.

When he stopped laughing, Hildee said, "You seem to be fittin' in here well."

"It won't always be this easy. Satan will surely try to throw a monkey wrench into things. He's pretty much got Bryce River sewn up to hear people talk."

"Yeah, but we know the ending," Hildee said.

Nate smiled, "That we do, my love, that we do."

He had said it without thinking but it had been from the heart. Hildee seemed to sense it and she got that tilted head and seriously thinking thing going again. Nate just smiled at her and she stuck her tongue out at him.

"Don't do that woman. It sets my hormones to raging."

Hildee blushed again and Nate started laughing so hard he was

56

doubled over. Hildee couldn't help herself and started laughing so hard she had to pull the pickup over. They were both laughing so hard their eyes started to water. When they finally stopped, Hildee pulled back onto the road and started out again.

Nate asked, "Do you like doing the kind of work we did on the camper?"

"Yeah, I do. I know it ain't girly like, but I really like working with my hands. I guess it's why, when I graduated from the community and technical college, I went to workin' with pa."

Nate asked, "What did you study?"

"I did the one-year building trades program. I also took a course in welding. Pa says I'm better than any son he could have had. I can do most minor electrical, the plumbing, the carpentry, and all that needs doin' round the campground. I'm not good at the mechanical though. You know the pumps and stuff, though I can do the HVAC basic work."

Nate nodded.

Hildee said, "Are yar wheels turnin' for a reason?"

Nate simply said, "We make a good team," and glanced at her. He knew she was thinking about what he had said.

"I guess there is possibilities for us."

On the way back, Hildee had to stop to gas up the pickup. Nate insisted on paying and she let him. They arrived back at the campground store around four. It didn't seem like they'd been gone that long. When they pulled up, they found Len was sitting on the store's front porch and had dozed off. He woke when they closed the doors of the truck.

Len looked up, "How did it go?"

Hildee spoke, "Herman's going to re-up Nate's built-ins. Nate also got his first job."

"What's thet?"

"He's going to put a new service in for Herman. I'm goin' to tag along and see what I kin learn and maybe hep out."

Len looked at Nate, who just shrugged. It was, after all, news to him, but it made sense so he was agreeable.

Len said, "It can't hurt learnin' new things. Jist remember the canoes need to come out of storage and there's work to be done around here, too."

Hildee looked at Nate, "Maybe ya could hep me with movin' canoes

Monday mornin' and I'll help you with your work in the afternoon."

"Ok," and he took the seat next to Len.

"Not much gits to ya does it?" Len observed.

"Not usually."

Hildee came and sat down, "Herman says Nate and I are an item. Everyone jist about has us hitched."

Len asked, "That so?"

Hildee answered, "Yup. Wonder where thet got started?"

"There's no tellin' how these things start. I reckon' the way you two go about makin' goo-goo eyes at each other has somethin' to do with it."

"Pa, we do no such thing."

Nate disagreed, "Yes, we do."

Hildee shrugged, "I reckon it's so. I'm goin' to have an orange soda. Anybody want somethin'?"

Nate and Len both shook their heads no. Hildee went into the store. Len gave Nate a knowing look and Nate just shrugged. She came out and handed her pa a root beer and Nate bottled water. They accepted the drinks.

Nate said, "Thanks."

Len said, "Uh huh," which meant me, too.

The three of them sat quietly for a few minutes enjoying the spring breeze. A few children could be heard in the distance.

Nate broke the silence, "What's this about canoes?"

Len explained, "They don't call this drift river fer nothin'. In season, we rent canoes and float tubes. People leave their wheels parked here and rent float stuff. The staff go downriver later and pick the tubers or canoers up and bring them and the gear back here in the two busses. The truck goes along to get the canoes and tubes. It takes all day to drift the fifteen miles down to the bridge."

Nate asked, "There good money in that?"

"It's a livin', but I ain't getting rich. Hildee don't know it, but I been puttin' what I'd normally pay her in wages aside fer her. She has quite a little nest egg."

"You didn't tell me, pa."

"You didn't need a dowry 'til now. Besides, if you'd known, you'd have spent it on woman things." Len put his head back and wore a huge grin.

58

"If'in I wasn't enjoyin' this soda so much I'd heave it at ya," Hildee giggled.

"Sure ya would, daughter."

Nate shook his head. He enjoyed these people.

Len asked, "What do your kin do, Nate? You never told us about 'em."

"My father and two older brothers are in the construction trades; family business. My mom is still alive and my parents are still happily married. Both sets of grandparents live in Florida. Both sets of grandparents had just one child so no aunts or uncles."

Len asked, "So construction is in the blood?"

"Yeah. I was licensed before I went in the service."

"When do we get to meet your family?"

"I don't know. I suppose during vacation."

Hildee asked tongue in cheek, "What's vacation?"

Len piped up, "It's when you set time aside to do things you've been puttin' off. You know, like gettin' hitched."

Hildee exclaimed, "Enough already, pa!"

Len chuckled and Nate couldn't help himself and smiled.

Hildee groaned, "Don't ya encourage him, Nate."

Nate said meekly, "Yes, dear," and that sent Len into fits of laughter and he slapped his thigh. Nate and Hildee followed him into laughter country.

When they finished Hildee said, "Ya know we're all off'in our rockers."

Len agreed, "Destined for the funny farm."

"I'm sure glad they're all full up." Nate added.

Hildee added, "Ain't that the truth."

Len said, "Well, it's four-thirty so let's close up and I'll grill us some burgers up at the house."

They locked up and the trio walked the path through the trees to the house. Nate and Hildee walked hand-in-hand.

There was a deck behind the house and they sat there and talked as Len cooked burgers on a gas grill. Len told Nate all about his business and Nate explained his plans for his business. It was an enjoyable evening.

Nate went back to his site about nine and turned in, slept like a log, and was up at the crack of dawn. He was sitting in a lawn chair reviewing his sermon notes when Hildee showed up in the pickup about eight. She called out, "Get in. Pa's cookin' breakfast."

Nate gathered up his things, put them in the van and got in the pickup. He looked at Hildee and said, "Good morning, good looking."

Hildee smiled at him, "Hey. Ya don't look so bad yarself, gorgeous."

Nate leaned across and kissed her. When Nate moved away, he could see she was blushing. He sighed before saying, "Oh, what a delightful way to start the day."

Hildee didn't say anything and just drove up to the house. They went inside and Len called out, "It's just about ready. Better wash up."

Hildee pointed and she and Nate went to the main floor half-bath and started washing their hands. The bathroom was small and they couldn't help but make contact. She jumped back when the sparks flew. "What was that?"

Nate said, "Static electricity."

Hildee grimaced, "I ain't no dope. That ain't like no static I ever seen."

Nate smiled, "Then it's just that together we create sparks." He went out, leaving Hildee open-mouthed. Nate went into the kitchen alone.

Len asked, "Where's Hildee?"

"You know women."

There was a knock at the front door and Len said, "Will ya git it, Nate?" Nate went to the front door and opened it.

Marilee said, "Good mornin', Nate."

"Good morning, Marilee. It's good to see you. Len is in the kitchen." Nate held out his arms and hugged Marilee appropriately and when he let go, she was beaming from ear to ear.

He turned to find Hildee standing there and Hildee said, "Good morning, Marilee. Welcome." She embraced Marilee and then the two women headed for the kitchen. Nate closed the door and followed them.

"You're timing is perfect, Marilee," Len said. "Everyone grab a chair." He took biscuits from the oven and put them in a basket, which he placed on the table. He took pancakes and sausage from a warmer and put them on a platter on the table. A pot on the stove held syrup and he poured hot syrup into two small glass containers which he also put on the table then sat down. "Let's pray and eat. I'm hungry." He said the blessing and then they all started to put food on their plates.

"Quite a spread, Len. I didn't know you could cook," began Marilee.

Hildee told them, "His biscuits and gravy are to die for. His pancakes and syrup ain't bad neither."

Marilee asked, "How many do ya think will come this mornin', Nate?"

Nate finished his mouthful, "There's no telling. We had about three dozen at the sing along Wednesday so I'm hoping for the same."

Nate had miscalculated the curiosity factor of the people of the area and the fact that Betsy and Sue had been telling everyone who came into the diner about it. Then there was the curiosity about the fellow who had gotten Hildee's attention. It was well known Hildee had turned away not a few potential suitors, which was unheard of in these parts.

The group left the house about nine fifteen. They loaded the small public address system, Hildee's keyboard and amp, microphones, and Len's guitar into Len's truck. Hildee drove Nate to get his guitar and Bible. When they arrived at the pavilion, people were already gathering. It took about fifteen minutes to get tuned up and set up. They were ready to go with more than twenty minutes left before the scheduled start.

The picnic tables were already full so Len, Tiny and Nate went to gather up chairs from storage. They brought a truckload back and, with the help of some men, unloaded them. There still weren't enough places to sit. Some of the campers went hurrying off and came back with folding chairs leaving the other seating for the visitors.

They barely started on time. Len welcomed everybody to the first open-air service of the Drift River Church. It was ad lib and meant to be humorous but it would stick. He introduced the music team and Nate then said an opening prayer. Len then said "We think most of you will know these songs so please join in."

The group started playing and singing and there must have been angels about. The people sat mesmerized. The little group sounded like nothing the people had ever heard. They were meant to be together. It wasn't until the second chorus of the first song that somebody started clapping, then there was foot stomping and a few started singing. Soon almost everyone was into the praise music. The group sang five hymns then Len introduced Nate.

Nate was a pretty good preacher under most circumstances but the Spirit was with him here. This was where God wanted Nate. By the time he finished his very short fifteen minute sermon, some were crying and

61

others were praying. Nate made an altar call and three people came forward, including Tiny. Hildee hurried and got paper and gathered their names and contact information. They would be baptized in the river on the Memorial Day weekend.

The group started playing again and Ben went about with a friend actually passing the hat. After three more songs, the service ended. Len invited everyone back next Sunday, same time, same place, same music, same preacher and, as always, the same Jesus. There was clapping and Len said a short prayer.

People lingered around talking to their neighbors and waiting to meet Nate.

Betsy came to Nate with Ben in tow. She said, "Ya sure can preach, Nate."

Nate acknowleged, "If it's good, it's from God, and if it's bad, it's me."

Betsy smiled, "That's a good one, Nate. Good job."

"Thanks for the encouragement."

The others standing around were listening to what Nate was saying. Others came and introduced themselves and that day Nate met a lot of people. He did not see the person with the camera.

It was almost noon when the crowd began to break up. While Nate was talking with people, Tiny and Len packed up the public address gear and put it in the pavilion storage and locked it up. It was after twelve when Nate got in the pickup with Hildee.

"Let's drop your stuff at your place. The gang's goin' to meet for a late lunch at the diner. Pa's going to take care of the store."

When Nate and Hildee got to the diner, the place was packed. A lot of the people had been at the campground. Hildee saw Ben waving to them and pointed it out to Nate. They started making their way in that direction. Many of the folks greeted Nate as he passed and he exchanged a word or two and a handshake with most of them.

They finally got to Ben's table and he said, "We saved ya'll seats. Take a load off." Nate pulled a chair out for Hildee and then took the seat beside her. Tiny was at the table with Ben.

Nate asked, "Where's Betsy?"

"It was so busy she had to grab an apron and go to work. Seems they ain't usually this busy Sunday afternoons. The part-timers were swamped."

A teenager came and took Nate and Hildee's order. Everyone else at the table was waiting on their food.

Ben began, "The collection was good this mornin' and we locked it up?"

Nate said, "I hadn't planned to take up a collection."

Ben grinned, "First rule ah church runnin' is always take up a collection."

Tiny added, "Even I knows that."

Nate asked, "Where did Drift River Church come from?"

Ben answered, "Len said it was a God thing. We got to make it formal as we got checks made out to Drift River Church. You know how to do that, Nate?"

"Yeah, but I can't handle the money. Lesson one of being a pastor is that the preacher and the money are always separate."

Ben affirmed, "Well, ya is certainly the preacher."

Nate agreed, "Then that makes you the church treasurer and Len the worship leader. Tiny you are officially part of the worship team."

"Well, don't that beat all. Do I have to shave and dress up?" Tiny said.

"No way. Don't change a thing. Our motto is God's more concerned about what's in your heart than what's on your back."

Tiny asked, "What about Hildee?"

Ben said, "She'll be the pastor's wife, ya know, and play the piana."

Hildee couldn't help it and blushed and Tiny smiled stating the obvious, "She sure do turn a pretty shade ah red."

Ben commented, "I guess this means we're going to do church."

Nate concurred, "I reckon. At least until it gets too cold to be outside."

The young waitress brought the ordered food. The team ate and planned how they were going to go about doing church. Nate and Hildee returned to the campground about two in the afternoon to find Len and Marilee sitting on the store porch drinking coffee and talking.

Hildee was out of the vehicle before Nate and got to the porch first and sat on the love seat rocker. She patted the seat next to her and Nate went and sat down. Hildee put her arm through his.

Marilee said, "Interesting day, Nate."

"It was indeed and it's not over."

Hildee told her father about the lunchtime conversation with Ben and

Tiny. He just nodded.

Marilee quite innocently asked, "And what role did you get Hildee?"

Hildee smiled, "Ben suggested pastor's wife."

Len was in the middle of swallowing coffee and it choked him. Marilee started laughing and Len kept choking. The coffee had obviously gone down the wrong way.

Marilee asked, "Has he proposed?"

Hildee laughed, "Not yet, but he's giving every indication he will."

Marilee looked at Nate, who just shrugged. He didn't mind at all how he was being pushed into this. He was totally open to the possibility.

Marilee asked, "Will it be a long engagement?"

Hildee replied, "I doubt it. He's kinda passionate for a preacher."

Len said in fake shock, "Hildee!"

Hildee responded, "Don't lecture me. I see how you look at Marilee."

It was Marilee's turn to blush, but she didn't. Instead she smiled and looked at Len and said, "That's so sweet."

Len surprised everyone and blushed.

Nate commented, "I'm glad I'm not the only one on the hot seat."

Len suggested, "It's gotta be somethin' in the water."

Nate agreed, "I reckon."

The two women exchanged looks which was not lost on the men.

Hildee offered, "Marilee, what say you we go inside and I'll make us some grilled cheese sandwiches? I'm still hungry."

Marilee said, "We haven't eaten," and the two women went inside.

Len said, "Things are movin' as fast as a rabbit bein' chased by a fox."

"Don't I know it. Thing is, I'm not against it going so fast."

Len nodded, "Me neither."

"Then so much for that."

"Yup."

Marilee and Hildee came out a few minutes later with a pile of sandwiches and some soda.

Hildee stated, "Thing about a commercial grill is ya kin make a bunch of sandwiches at one time."

Len said, "Uh huh," and proceeded to say the blessing and they set to eating.

Marilee confessed, "This is nice."

Chapter 4

On Monday morning, Nate finished his daily start-the-day routine early and then walked up to the store. There was a bit of a chill in the early morning air and he wore a sweatshirt over his T-shirt. As he walked, he thought about Hildee and all that happened in the short time he'd been here. It was as if this was the place he was meant to be and he seemed to fit in naturally.

Nate got to the store a little before seven and found Len and Hildee were already there. Nate went inside and Hildee said, "Coffee's ready." Len was sitting at the snack bar counter so Nate went and sat down, saying, "Good morning. Looks like it's going to be a nice day to work outside."

Hildee put a cup of coffee in front of Nate and said, "I'm makin' eggs and hash browns. Want some?"

"Please. I expect to have a busy mornin' moving canoes."

Hildee said with a big smile, "Ya got that right, city boy."

After they ate, Hildee took Nate to the pole building under which the canoes were stored. They lifted an aluminum canoe rack into the back of the flatbed truck, fastened down the rack, and then loaded it with canoes.

Nate remarked, "I haven't ever seen racks like those."

Hildee confessed, "Made them myself and, yes, I can weld. Even all-you-mini-um."

"In the city we call it aluminum."

Hildee smiled, "Well, you ain't in the city now, are ya?"

"Good point."

They got in the truck and drove down near the river. There was another pole building there and they unloaded the canoes onto the racks there.

Nate asked, "Why don't you just leave the canoes here?"

"This is in the spring flood plain. We don't want the canoes floating away so we store them in the winter on high ground and bring them down here after the spring run-off."

"I see."

Nate found that Hildee was a hard worker and very strong for a woman; probably stronger than a lot of men. She was obviously used to physical labor. By ten o'clock they had the canoes all moved. They went to the store to get a beverage. Len was stocking shelves when they went in.

He asked, "Taking a break?"

Hildee said, "Nah, we finished."

Len looked up, "Really? That's got to be some kind of record."

"Nate here is no slouch and we work good together, pa."

Len got up off his knees, "Seems so."

Hildee asked, "We're going to have a drink. Want one pa?"

Len nodded yes and said, "Uh huh."

The three of them went outside to sit and take a break. Len asked, "What's next?"

Nate said, "I have to make some calls on church business. That shouldn't take but a few minutes. Then I'll call Ben. Hildee offered to help me work on the camper so I'm going to ask her about some ideas I have for new cupboards for the trailer. Depending on how that goes, we may have to go pick up some materials."

Len looked at Hildee and said, "Uh huh."

They finished their soda and Nate made his phone calls resulting in the necessary arrangements. He also used the office computer to do a little work online. He and Hildee then took the pickup down to the camper.

As they got out of the pickup, Hildee asked, "What have you got in mind?"

"Let me show you," and they went inside, "Well, I could make the new cabinets out of wood to replace the plastic covered particle board ones I took out, but that would still be heavier than I'd like. That concerns me because this is, after all, a camper and it may need to be moved at some point."

"Like if'in the spring flooding is bad?"

"Yes. So I was thinking, seeing as you know how to work with aluminum, if we could make aluminum frames with aluminum shelves then fasten a lightweight plywood covering to the aluminum we'd have lighter cabinets."

Hildee thought for a moment, "It's doable if the frame matches. We can't be fastenin' all-you-mini-um to steel."

"The frame is wood. I checked."

"I can do the welding, but I'll need some special rods and they're not cheap. I do know where we might be able to buy aluminum for the job at a decent price."

"I notice you didn't say all-you-mini-um."

Hildee smiled, "I can talk city."

Nate asked, "How far do we have to go to get the material?"

"Just a few miles; well, about thirty. You'd better let me do the talkin' though. I done business there before."

"Well then, let's do it."

They took measurements of the cabinets that had been removed and Hildee figured how much material she'd need. They talked about how they'd make cabinet door frames. Hildee had ideas on how to overcome the issues Nate raised. He was impressed.

It was almost noon when they started out on their thirty mile trip to the scrap yard that Hildee had dealt with in the past. In their search for framing aluminum, they came across some small panels of brushed aluminum. They all were of different sizes. Hildee was examining them intently.

Nate asked, "What are you thinking?"

"Well, folks is hyped up about stainless steel kitchens. Why not cover the cabinets and counter top with this brushed aluminum if I can haggle a good price?"

"That's genius and it'll be better than that stuff they used in the old cabinets."

Hildee smiled and started measuring. They piled up everything they were interested in and Hildee got the owner. They set to haggling. The owner argued the sheets would make good tool boxes and should fetch a higher price. Hildee pointed out the sheets were too flimsy for such but didn't volunteer what they would be using it for. It took almost twenty minutes for them to agree on a price. When they finished, Hildee turned to Nate. "Pay the man, Nate."

"Yes, dear."

Hildee didn't blush this time but just smiled.

Nate paid and they loaded the material into the pickup and went off in search of the right kind of welding rods. They drove another forty miles to the city and, after a late lunch, were able to get what Hildee needed at a welding specialty supply.

As they were leaving the supply shop, Nate said, "I think I'd better stop while I'm here and get a cell phone. I'll need it for business."

"Good idea. Also, that way you can call your dear one."

"Sounds good. Ma will be happy to hear from me."

Hildee popped Nate lightly on the shoulder, "Tease."

"Takes one to know one."

The rest of the week Nate and Hildee fell into a routine. In the morning, Nate helped Hildee with her work. They'd have lunch with Len. In the afternoons, they'd work on the camper. By Friday, the cabinets had been made and installed. The result was even better than they had anticipated. They went and got Len to show him their handiwork.

Len went into the camper and looked at the cabinets and said, "Well, that's sho nuff some fine work. Them floors ya'll done look good."

Hildee grinned, "Ain't it fine? Jist wait until the built-ins are back."

"Then I'll just need to put in a new refrigerator and stove and wire them up."

"No fillin' propane bottles huh?" Len asked.

"Except for the outdoor gas grill I plan on buying."

Len went and looked at the toilet and shower room. He came out, "It's small but it'll work. It's good that didn't need work."

"Yeah, and the bedroom, aside from the flooring, was in good shape. As soon as I get a mattress, I can start sleeping on the bed."

Len asked, "Wanna move this here camper under the carport while I'm here?"

"Might as well."

Thirty-five minutes later the task was done and they had the trailer leveled. The jacks were manual, but with two people it was an easy job and they had three people to get it done.

Len asked, "Ya got any plumbing leaks?"

Nate shook his head, "Nah. I hooked her up and tried everything before I put in the new sub-floor."

"It's gonna be nice when ya finish. Real comfy-like but a little close for two."

Hildee said, "Enough, pa!"

Len just smiled and shrugged, "Didn't say nothin' bout ya, Hildee."

"Pa, stop it."

Nate was smiling, "Better stop, Len. She hits like a mule kicks."

Len said with a broad smile, "So I've been told, but she's always been kind to her ole pa." He looked at Nate, "I've seen she's not so gentle with other men folk."

Hildee looked at Nate, "See what I have to put up with!"

68

"He sure is a trial, but he is your pa, so I guess we're stuck with him."
Nate put his right arm around Hildee's shoulders. She smiled and said,
"Well, what now?"

Len remarked, "Seein' how you finished braggin' on your work, ya
should get back to it."

Hildee turned and looked at Nate, "It's Friday night so why don't you
come up to the house and we'll watch a movie and I'll make popcorn with
lotsa butter."

"Sounds good to me."

Len told them, "I can't. I got a date."

Before Hildee could say anything Len walked off. Nate and Hildee
stood speechless watching him get in his truck and leave.

"It's good pa is back to the land of the living."

"I reckon. You do know we have to change our plans?"

"Why so?"

Nate sighed, "Well, I have a responsibility to protect your reputation.
It would not be proper for us to be alone at your pa's without a chaperone.
It also might be more temptation than I could handle."

"What if we weren't alone? Give me your cell."

Nate handed it over and Hildee dialed a number. Nate listened to
Hildee's side of the call.

"Hi, Jean. Yeah, it's me. No, it's my boyfriend's phone. Yeah, that's
him. You still goin' with Shocky? How would you like to bring him out to
pa's to watch a movie and gobble popcorn? Good. How about seven?
Nate don't know it yet but he's treatin' me to dinner at the diner. That
would be great. See ya then."

Hildee handed her phone to Nate, "Jean and Shocky are meetin' us at
the diner at five-thirty."

Nate simply said, "Alright then. I'll walk you home then I'll get
cleaned up a bit."

Hildee smiled, "I should hope so. You smell all manly and stuff."

Nate shook his head, took Hildee's hand and started walking. He
muttered, "You're just too much, Hildee."

Hildee answered, "Ya just have to try and keep up with me."

They arrived at the diner at twenty after five and took a seat. Sue came
to greet them.

"Hi. I'm not happy with you two."

Nate asked, "Why?"

Sue put her hand on her hip, "I'll have you know your little match makin' is causin' me to have to work on a Friday night. Len and Ben are on a double date with ma and Marilee. It's all your fault." Sue smiled, "Ain't it great?"

Hildee agreed, "It is."

Sue looked at Hildee, "You owe me."

Hildee asked, "How you reckon' that Sue?"

"Well, you bagged the hunk there, fixed my ma up, but for me, yar friend, nothin'. What are you gonna do 'bout it?"

"We'll think on it."

"In that case, I reckon' I'll serve you."

Just then Jean and Shocky came to the table. Sue greeted them. Hildee got up and hugged Jean and Jean then hugged Sue.

Nate looked at the fellow with Jean and said across the table, "I'm Nate."

"I'm Jack but everybody calls me Shocky."

Nate asked, "How come?"

"You'll find out," and put his hand out to shake. Nate took his hand and there was a snap of static.

Nate started laughing and so did Shocky. The girls stopped and looked at the two men. Jean said, "I ain't never seen anybody react like that to Shocky before."

Hildee put in, "Nate does electric work among other things."

Jean said, "Explains it."

Sue nodded agreement and said, "I'll never understand men, but I sure would like one of my own. Good Christian one, mind ya."

Hildee looked at Jean, "We gotta find her one."

Jean agreed, "Ok by me. May take a while. Ya know homely women folk is hard to fix up."

Sue said with a smile, "Careful or ya won't get no grub no how."

The four of them sat down and Sue took their drink orders.

Nate started the conversation, "Shocky, do you have static all the time?"

"Nah, but enough that the shock thing happens pretty regular. You should have seen Jean jump the first time I kissed her."

Jean smiled, "It was electrifying and 'bout scared me to death. I thought God was goin' to strike me dead for kissin' a boy."

Hildee added, "Jean moved here in her junior year in high school. Her and Shocky been socializin' since then."

Jean showed Hildee her finger, "It's official. We's gittin' married. He asked me last night. Wanna be a bridesmaid?"

Hildee smiled, "Do fish swim? Do birds fly? Do dogs bark?"

"It's settled then. We haven't told Shocky's dad because there is no way we are going to be married at the church here."

"Nate's an ordained preacher. He can hitch ya," Hildee told her.

Jean asked, "Really?"

Nate inquired, "How old are you?"

Shocky said, "Twenty-two, preacher."

"Twenty-one," Jean said.

Hildee added, "And I can vouch they's both good Christian folk."

Nate concluded, "Yes, I can definitely marry you."

Hildee added, "No charge. That'll be our wedding present."

Shocky grinned, "Cool. Where's the church?"

Hildee proceeded to tell her friends about Drift River Church and how it happened. When she finished, Shocky said, "So you're the feller who was supposed to preach at the church in town that Jimmie James says he fired, though everyone knows it was you what quit him 'cause you wouldn't knuckle under."

"That 'bout sums it up," Hildee noted.

Shocky said, "If'in you marry us, my dad will be really upset, but that's a burden for his mule to carry. He's goin' to be agin us marryin' on any account."

Nate asked, "Why's that?"

Jean sighed, "My family is poor farmers and Shocky's pa don't think I'm good 'nuff for him."

Nate murmured, "Hmmm."

Shocky asserted, "I don't think bein' rich or poor has to do with character."

Nate just said, "True."

Jean changed the subject, "I was surprised you and Hildee were datin'."

"How come?"

Shocky jumped in, "Hildee ain't never really dated."

71

Nate asked, "What's that all about?"

Jean looked at Hildee, "You ain't told him?"

"Never came up."

Jean said, "I love my girl Hildee, but she's dense 'bout some stuff. She ain't done much datin'. There's a story behind it."

Nate looked at Hildee, "Tell me."

Hildee sighed and started the telling, "When I was thirteen, my best friend Molly got in the family way. Her pa sent her to kin folk outta state. The baby was adopted and Molly came back bent."

Nate asked, "What do you mean bent?"

"She kilt herself a couple weeks after gittin' back."

"That's sad."

"Tain't all. The boy who done her was charged with rape 'cause of her age and him bein' older. He was kin to the Bryce clan and he got away with it. Folks knew it weren't right. After Molly's funeral, her pa got to him. Beat him to death with his bare hands, then kilt himself."

Nate looked at Hildee. Hildee looked into his eyes, "I didn't date 'cause I didn't want ta risk that kinda misery for me or my pa. Molly and me was close and I took her passin' hard. Only bin on two dates and they was doubles. I reckon I had a real hard time with trustin' 'til ya came along."

Nate just nodded.

Jean added, "Cause she didn't date, Hildee was teased. Boys called her the ice queen."

"Sure didn't make me more sociable with the men folk hereabout."

Sue came and took their meal order. They all had a pleasant meal and Nate enjoyed listening to the conversation. It occurred to Nate that Hildee, in some ways, seemed older than her friends Jean and Shocky, but she wasn't.

After dinner, the four of them retreated to Len's to watch movies, eat popcorn, and talk. Jean and Shocky decided they'd come to service at the campground Sunday. Nate learned Shocky played bass in the country and western band that had played at the fairgrounds dance. Nate invited him to join in on Sunday.

They were watching the second movie when Len and Marilee came in. The little group greeted them and Nate learned everyone knew each other. Len and Marilee sat on a love seat and joined the young people. After a few minutes, Nate felt Hildee elbow him gently and she nodded toward her pa. He had his arm around Marilee and she had kicked off her shoes, had her feet under her and was snuggled against Len. Nate smiled and looked at Hildee, who gazed into his eyes. It was a magic moment.

The little group finished watching the movie then Shocky announced he had to get Jean home or her pa would beat him to a pulp.

Jean laughed, "Ya, but we can tell pa we were at the preacher's arranging to get hitched. That'll take the wind out of his sails."

Shocky laughed and Len looked at Nate.

"They are engaged."

Marilee clapped her hands and got up and hugged Jean. It would be another ten minutes before the couple left.

Shocky said to Nate as he went out the door, "We'll talk to ya later, Nate, as preacher, ok?"

"Certainly. I look forward to it."

Len closed the door and looked at Nate, "I never thought 'bout you marryin' people."

"It's part of what a preacher does, Len."

"Yeah, but with ya datin' my daughter, I guess it jist didn' sink in. I guess if I ever git hitched again I'll get a freebie."

Hildee piped up, "It's gonna be our weddin' gift to Jean and Shocky; Nate's marryin' them, I mean."

"Let's have coffee, then we'll all take Marilee home."

Saturday morning Nate was sitting on a lawn chair under the carport listening to the rain drum lightly on the metal and reading his Bible. The sheriff's car pulled up and two deputies got out. They came toward Nate.

Nate stood, "Hello there. Come in out of the rain and have a seat." Nate offered his hand, "I'm Nate Christian."

The two deputies shook his hand and Nate sat down, "Please have a seat. How can I help you gentlemen?"

One of the deputies said, "We have a report that you are scammin' folks out of their hard earned money?"

Nate asked, "How so, Deputy?"

"The report is you're playin' at being a preacher and collectin' money for a church when there ain't none."

"I think I can clear this up quickly. Who filed the complaint?"

The deputy said, "I shouldn't say."

Nate said, "It's a matter of public record, isn't it?"

The other deputy said, "He's right, Cob. Best tell him."

"Jimmie James."

Nate remarked, "If you'll allow, I'll get some things out of my camper. I think I can clear this up."

The older deputy nodded agreement. Nate went inside and retrieved what he needed. He brought it back to show the deputies.

"This is my degree from Bible College. This is my ordination certificate. This is the state registration as a non-profit for Drift River Church. I don't handle the money. The church treasurer is Ben Kemp. Do you know him?"

The older deputy said, "Everyone knows Ben. He's as straight an arrow as there is."

The deputy examined all the papers and handed them to his partner who made notes.

Nate said, "Ben can tell you all about the banking details."

The older deputy handed Nate back his papers, "Sorry to bother you, preacher."

"Drop by anytime. We are having service in the pavilion here at ten tomorrow. You are invited. It's humble but you might enjoy it. It's very informal dress; jeans and shorts seem to be common."

The older deputy asked, "Why do you think there was a complaint?"

Nate shrugged, "I think you can guess the answer, but I can't say because I'd only be speculating."

The younger deputy looked at his partner, "Sounds right."

The deputies got up as did Nate and he shook their hands and sat back down to watch them drive away. They had no sooner left than Len pulled up in his pickup and came and sat down by Nate.

"What's that all about? They came askin' fer ya at the store."

"Jimmie James filed a complaint that I was pretending to be a preacher and ripping people off collecting money for a church that doesn't exist."

Len spat, "Sounds like some underhanded ornery thing Jimmie James would do. Is it going to be trouble?"

"Not with the law. I had all the paperwork to show I'm who and what I say. They'll check it all out and it'll go away. It's still going to be spiritual warfare. Satan isn't done with us yet."

"He ain't never tired of attackin' the true followers of Jesus."

"That's so."

"Come on up to the store and I'll make us some breakfast."

"I'll be there as soon as I call Ben and warn him."

Len left and Nate called Ben. Their talk was short. Ben knew the sheriff well and would call him at home. Ben also told Nate the delivery date for the new engine for Ole Beauty had been delayed.

The rain stopped and the sun came out so Nate walked up to the store. Len was already cooking eggs and bacon on the grill and said, "It'll be done directly."

Nate sat at the counter, "Where's Hildee?"

"She went off early with Jean. They went shoppin' fer wedding and bridesmaids' dresses. Women stuff. Jean called early this mornin' and Hildee didn't have yar new number. Better fix that quick."

"Yup. She should have one, too."

"She do."

"What is it?"

Len told him and Nate saved the number on his cell. He called it and Hildee's voice answered, "Hello?"

"Good morning, dear one. You should capture this number so you can track me down."

Hildee laughed, "Ok, it's done."

"Have a good time. Bye." He ended the call.

Len asked, "What's with the dear one?"

"Inside joke."

"Chow's done."

Len scooped the food onto plates and got the coffee pot and put it on the counter. They prayed over the food and started to eat. The bell on the door rang and Len yelled out, "We don't open 'til eight."

A young man walked toward them and drew a pistol, "Give me your money."

Nate stood up slowly and faced the young man, who was obviously nervous. Nate said, "If you needed help, you could have just asked."

The young man was within arm's length, "I want the money."

Len said, "There ain't no cash in the register."

The man turned the pistol toward Len and Nate acted. He disarmed the man, stepping in just the right way and grabbing the man's wrist,

75

grabbing the gun barrel and bending the man's hand back and took the gun right out of his hand. The young man found himself staring down the barrel of his own gun.

Nate remarked, "Didn't your mother ever teach you not to point a gun at people?"

The young man was shaking and urinated in his pants.

Nate tossed his phone to Len, "Call 911. He may not be alone."

Turning back to the young man, Nate ordered, "Turn around and get on your knees. Cross your ankles and interlace your hands behind your head."

The young man did as he was told and asked, "You a cop?"

"I'm the one asking the questions. You got friends outside?"

"Two."

Nate handed the gun to Len, "If he moves, cap him."

"I ain't that good a shot. I'll just unload the pistol into him."

Nate reckoned, "That'll work."

Len winked, "I got half a mind to do it anyhow."

The young man sobbed, "Don't shoot, mister. Please don't shoot!"

Len said, "There's a nine in the desk drawer," then called the emergency operator.

Nate went and got the weapon and the spare clip. He peeked outside and said, "They aren't getting out of the car."

Nate decided to wait and see what happened. A couple of minutes later, Nate watched the two in the car drive away. Nate knew they met deputies at the highway because Nate heard the siren then gunshots. A couple of minutes later two sheriff's cars pulled up. Nate put the nine back in the desk and went and sat beside Len.

The deputies came in guns drawn. Len said, "We got this un."

Len lowered the pistol and handed to the deputy and said, "He used this five shooter to try and rob us."

The deputy asked, "How'd you end up with it?"

"He got too close to Nate here and Nate did some stuff like in them movies and took it right outta his hand."

The young man whined, "I think he broke my wrist."

He was formally arrested and taken away. By the time Len and Nate had given statements and the sheriff's deputies left, two hours had passed.

Len dumped the cold food in the waste and said, "Well seein' as we didn't' get breakfast, how about burgers for lunch? 'Citement gits me hungerin' for meat."

"Sounds fine."

"Finer than frog's hair split three ways."

They had just finished eating when the local newspaper reporter showed up. Len introduced Nate and the reporter asked if he could get a picture of them and they agreed. He asked them a few questions about the attempted robbery and Len answered for them. Nate didn't pay too much attention to it all, but he should have.

Hildee and Jean got back around five to find her pa and Nate sitting on the porch of the store staying out of the rain that was now coming down quite hard. Jean parked as close as she could to the porch and she and Hildee made a run to get out of the rain. Once under the roof, Hildee took her jacket off and sat down beside Nate.

"What have you two bin up to?"

"Arrestin' robbers," Len informed her.

Hildee ignored the remark thinking her pa was joking. She turned to Nate, "What have you been doing really?"

"Like your pa said. We spent most of the day speaking to folks who came by. A few this morning but just one this afternoon."

Jean jumped in, "Well, we found me a wedding dress. It's beautiful but I'm so tiny waisted compared to my boobs, I had to buy one size bigger and they have to take it in around the middle."

"TMI," Nate announced.

Jean asked, "What's that mean?"

"Too much information; TMI."

Jean said, "Meanin' I shouldn't have ought to said boobs in front of a preacher?"

Nate went to say something and realized Jean was having him on so said, "Women!"

Len said, "Yup."

Hildee giggled, "You behave pa or I'll tell Marilee on ya."

Len said, "This ain't high school, dearie, and Marilee's my squeeze, not my mommy."

Hildee giggled again and Jean laughed lightly and finally took a seat saying, "This is fun, so I think I'll stay for a while."

"You ain't' foolin' me, girly," Len said. "You're just waitin' until we put the feed bag on, thinkin' we'll take mercy on ya."

Jean smiled, "I reckon. Besides it's a rainin' and I don't want to melt."

"Well, I reckon I can fire up the pizza oven and we can try them new uns we got to feed the campers." Len went to do it.

Jean recounted, "Shocky told his daddy we are gittin' married and he had a spaz fit. It isn't like Shocky is livin' at home and moochin'. His daddy forbid it and Shocky told him he had no say and was sorry he felt that away. Shocky's daddy said there ain't no way he's gittin' married at the church and Shocky told him they didn't have a pastor anyhow. I guess it was ugly. It was right in the diner and his daddy tried to hit him. Shocky didn't hit his daddy and his daddy is lucky 'cause Shocky would've creamed him."

Hildee agreed, "Shocky's in good shape and his daddy is a creampuff."

"I love Shocky and we are gittin' hitched and that's that. At least my parents will be at the wedding."

Nate asked, "What does Shocky's father do?"

"He's the mayor of Bryce River and a businessman. Some say he's a slumlord and it seems that's so. I don't think he's a nice man and Shocky's not anything like him. My parents were worried until they got to know Shocky."

Nate asked, "What does Shocky do?"

"He's a lineman for the rural electric co-op. We waited for him to git his journeyman's before gittin engaged. Now he makes a good livin' and he don't hurt no one in the process. He's even helped pa out on the farm on some of his days off. He's a real hard worker, my Shocky."

Nate sighed, "If you and Shocky want to talk to me, give me a call."

Len came over and said, "The oven's heatin' up, it won't be long," then sat down.

Hildee said, "I wonder if we'll have a big crowd tomorrow."

Nate sighed, "It's all in God's hands."

The four of them sat and talked about nothing special and everything in general that had to do with what was happening in the county. Nate and Len didn't think to mention the visit by the deputies after Hildee had ignored the remark about the robbery. That was a mistake.

After they ate, Nate excused himself because he had yet to write a sermon. The rain had stopped so he walked back to his site. The topic of the sermon came to him right away so he was able to retire early. He also woke early. He had water hooked up in the camper but he had not changed out the propane water heater so he had to go to the shower building to clean up. He was sitting outside in a lawn chair reading his Bible at seven when Len pulled up.

"Better come with me."

They drove over to the pavilion. The pavilion had been spray painted with obscenities and satanic symbols. The storage room had been broken into and the public address system was in pieces all over the pavilion. The picnic tables were gone. Deputies had put crime scene tape up and were searching the site for clues.

A camp guest came up to Len as he got out of his truck and said, "You'd better come see this, Len. I know where the tables are."

Len went to the closest deputy and they all followed the man down to the river. They could see one of the tables had been swept onto a sandbar. "Recoverin' twenty tables from the river is going to be about as much fun as falling into a outhouse pit." He turned to Nate, "What are we going to do about the service?"

Nate shrugged, "It's going to be a fine morning; the weather is good. We'll have folks sit on the grass or on lawn chairs in the playground, or on the gates of pickups and have service under the big blue dome."

"I guess that works. I have some heavy extension cords."

That was how it was arranged. Tiny and Shocky came early and a few campers did as well. They started arranging things. They rounded up every lawn chair, picnic table and bench they could find and put them out. They ran an extension cord for Hildee's keyboard and Shocky's bass guitar amp. They brought Len's flatbed truck out to use the bed for a stage. Things were pretty much arranged when folks started showing up. All of them went to see the vandalism.

At the appointed time, people were sitting on pickup tailgates, on lawn chairs, and on blankets laid out on the grass. By now everyone knew what was happening. Len got up on the bed of the truck and got everyone's attention then asked them to join in an opening prayer.

They prayed for a heart of forgiveness toward the person or persons who had committed the vandalism and that they would repent of their sins. They also prayed for strength during these times of trial.

Len, Nate, Shocky, Hildee, and Tiny played their best yet. An added surprise was that Shocky's voice fit right in. The little group sounded like they had been together all their lives. It was another hand-clapping, boisterous praising of the Lord in song. Some of the small children got up and started dancing and swaying to the music. After five songs, Nate got up to preach.

Nate started out with, "I had planned a sermon on gossip for today. This morning though God leads me to a different message. A message about forgiveness and spiritual warfare."

The sermon lasted about twenty minutes as Nate told about the requirement for Christians to have forgiving hearts. The crowd sat listening intently because the Spirit was there and leading Nate. Nate next talked about spiritual warfare and that there should always be rejoicing in the worship of God because Christians know who had already determined the outcome of the spiritual war. He talked about putting on the full armor of God and not being discouraged by temporary setbacks and that was what they were. When Nate finished, the assembled sat quietly thinking about the message until the group started singing and playing.

Everyone joined in and Ben and three trusted and chosen men went about passing hats to take up the collection. Len ended the service with a prayer and people went about talking to their friends and neighbors.

A small slim man came up to Nate. He was wearing a tweed sports coat and a cowboy hat. He said, "You are the real deal, preacher." He held out his hand and Nate shook it and said, "I'm Nate Christian, sir. I am pleased to meet you."

"I'm Cory Pilcher, Sheriff of Pearce County."

Nate smiled, "Welcome, Sheriff."

"We checked ya out pretty good."

"I'd have done the same if I were in your shoes, Sheriff."

"Jist Cory please, preacher."

"Please call me Nate."

"Alright, Nate. Sorry about yar troubles."

Nate shrugged, "Thank you, Cory. As you can see, it may have worked to God's glory. It provided good material for a message. Thanks for coming, Sheriff. You're welcome anytime. Please come back."

Cory tipped his hat and said, "I'll do that," then left and others, who had stayed at a distance in respect for the sheriff, came to talk to Nate. Nate noticed quite a few of the families had brought sandwiches or picnic lunches. A social had spontaneously developed. Campers and locals were mingling.

Len came over, "We had a bigger crowd today than last Sunday."

"I think so."

Hildee finished talking to some people and came over and took Nate's arm, "I have some folks you should otta meet."

It was after two o'clock before Nate got to eat some lunch that Hildee prepared for him at the snack bar. He was sitting with Hildee at a table sipping coffee when Len came in and sat down.

Hildee asked, "You want something to eat, pa? I can make ya a small sub sandwich."

"Yes, please."

Hildee got up to make it.

"I'm goin' to miss her when ya two is hitched."

"If she accepts me, we won't be goin' anywhere." Nate noticed he'd dropped the "g" and that he was starting to talk like the locals. He didn't care and took another sip of coffee.

Len changed the subject, "The sheriff says it was probably teenagers. If'in it were after Memorial Day, the place would a been packed and they would a been seen or heard."

"Probably so."

"Some of the men offered to come over tomorrow evenin' and hep me paint the pavilion."

"Uh huh. We could go fish out those picnic tables during the day."

"We'll do it in the mornin' and start early. I'll put a sign in the store window sayin' gone fishin' for picnic tables. Open at noon."

Hildee brought her father's sandwich and sat down. Ben came into the store, "Well, that was quite a service. Lotsa folks."

Len asked, "Where ya been?"

Ben smiled, "I made a drop deposit at the bank. There was too much cash for me to want to keep it on me. One of the young men run shotgun with me."

Nate couldn't help it and laughed lightly.

Ben said defensively, "It were a sizeable amount."

"I just had a picture in my mind of you driving a stage coach with a young fellow with a shotgun beside you."

Ben smiled and Len said, "Uh huh. I can see how that would be hoom-er-us."

81

While the men had been carrying on, Hildee had gotten a cup of coffee for Ben. She put it down and asked, "You want a sandwich, Ben?"

"Not with the prices Len charges the tourists."

"Tightwad," Len responded.

Ben retorted, "The pot's callin' the kettle black. Besides, I'm jist a poor ole retired farmer. The prices you charge would give a poor ole feller like me a heart attack."

Len smiled, "I don't wanna see you have no heart attack so it's on the house."

Ben allowed, "Well that proves it's a day of miracles."

Hildee went and made another sandwich and brought it to the table.

Ben said, "Thank you, Hildee."

Hildee said, "Uh huh," and sat down.

Ben started, "In case anybody's interested, we had sixty-six come last Sunday and eighty-seven this mornin' with collections of three hundred eleven dollars and change and five hundred seventy-two dollars and change."

Nate commented, "I guess we should replace Len's public address system and fix up the pavilion with it."

"I'll arrange it and give an accounting next Sunday."

Nate nodded.

Hildee said, "The Lord provides."

Ben said, "Amen," paused and said, "You even startin' to talk like a preacher's wife."

Hildee sighed deeply and said, "You fellers keep it up and ya's gonna scare poor Nate away on me."

Nate was looking at the coffee in his cup and said, "Not likely." The three of them looked at him then each other. The talk changed.

Len reflected, "Ain't no need to replace the speaker stuff. I got insurance."

Nate replied, "Ok, but the church pays the deductible."

"Fair enough. The sheriff said they'll take the crime scene tape down in the mornin'."

Ben offered, "Maybe I kin organize and sidewalk supervise a few fellers to hep paint the pavilion in the evenin'. If a few fellers work on it, it shouldn't take long."

Len said, "Appreciate that."

After they ate, they went to sit on the porch. A camper came up and asked Len if he'd mind selling some ice as he'd run out. Len obliged and they went back to sitting and talking. After a half hour, Ben headed home and Len locked the store door and did the same. He left Nate and Hildee sitting there. They talked for a while then Nate walked her home and they went hand-in-hand. They didn't say anything on the walk.

At the door Hildee said, "You are something, preacher man."

Nate blurted out, "And I love you, woman," then kissed her tenderly and he could tell it took her breath away. He turned and walked away, leaving Hildee standing there with her mouth gaping. It had been so unexpected. She stood there watching him until he was out of sight then went into the house.

The next morning Nate was up and about early. He was waiting, sitting in a lawn chair under the carport, when Len pulled up in the old flatbed truck pulling a trailer with a large Jon boat on it.

Len hollered, "Come on. We gotta go fishin' and I hear the picnic tables is biting."

Nate smiled broadly, locked up, and jumped in the truck with Len who said, "Hildee is already at the launch. She's puttin' in another boat she hauled behind the pickup. Can ya swim?"

Nate smiled, "Yes."

"Good. It'll be easier haulin' in them tables without a life jacket on ya. I see ya was smart enough to wear shorts and sandals."

"I reckoned I'd need to get in the water. I didn't reckon an old fellow like you would be jumping in."

Len hit Nate playfully on the arm, "Seniority, son. Seniority has privileges."

Nate handed Len his cell, "You'd better keep this for me so it doesn't get wet."

When they arrived at the boat launch, Hildee was already there. She had launched the other boat and had it tied to a tree. She was also in shorts and Nate thought she looked fabulous in them. Nate realized the love of his life had long shapely legs and that brought up lustful thoughts he had to pray to suppress. It was going to be a long day. She walked toward him and he greeted her.

"Hi, love."

Hildee stopped in mid-stride and started crying. Len looked at Nate.

"Don't ask me."

Len went to his daughter, "Did he do somethin' to hurt ya?"

"No, pa. He told me last night he loved me."

"Girl that ain't nothin' to cry about."

"Ya it is, pa. I'm so happy."

Len handled the situation in the redneck way and said, "Ok, nuff of this foolishness. Let's git to work. Outta the way so's I can launch this boat." Hildee moved and Nate went and stood beside her. He put his arm around her waist and she put her head on his shoulder and they watched Len back the boat trailer into the water.

He got out and said, "Don't ya'll just stand there moonin'. Come hep me git this thing in the water." Hildee laughed and ran to help her pa. Nate followed along. Once the boat was launched, Len pulled the flatbed into the parking area and unhooked the trailer. He knew they would need full access to the bed to load the tables.

They took the boats out to look for tables. The first eight tables were along the shoreline, close to the campground and easy to get onshore and onto the flatbed. They were tables made of heavier wood and not apt to float well. The next seven they found relatively easily and Nate and Hildee had to get wet to get them onto boats laying them upside down across the gunnels.

There were still five missing so the hunt began. They went slowly downstream on opposite banks. The problem was that these tables were made of aluminum so they would be easy to move and, as a result, floated well. It had never occurred to Len when Hildee made them that he would have to worry about the tables floating away. Eventually they found and brought back the five remaining tables.

After two trips with the flatbed, they had the tables stacked on the lawn beside the pavilion. They went back to fetch the boats. When they got out of the flatbed, Len said, "Let's get the little one out and then we'll take a trip down in the big one while we got it out and see how the river's lookin' between here and the bridge."

They cruised down the river at a leisurely pace though they could have gone fast with the large motor that was on the large aluminum boat. Nate and Hildee were sitting together on the middle seat enjoying the view while looking for hazards.

Hildee called out, "Slow down, pa." She pointed and Len slowly approached what looked like a sunken boat.

Nate said, "Hand me the cell, Len."

Len did and Nate called the 911 operator to make a non-emergency report. The operator asked him to stay on the line. They were asked to stay on the scene until a sheriff's boat could get there.

Nate told Len and Hildee, "They want us to stay until deputies can get here."

Len nodded agreement and Nate told the operator they'd stay. Len threw and anchor overboard and Nate said, "I'm going to have a look."

Nate took off his sandals and T-shirt. He slipped over the side into the water and went diving. The water was clear and he could see well. On his third dive, he came up and climbed into the boat. He motioned for the phone and called the 911 operator and identified himself.

"I went into the water. There's a body pinned underneath. It's been there for some time. We'll continue to wait but you'll need to send resources for recovery."

Nate sat down and said, "Let's pray," and they did.

When they finished, Len said, "How long do you reckon it's been there, Nate?"

"I have no idea."

They sat quietly for a bit and Hildee asked, "I wonder how come someone didn't report a missin' person in a boat?"

Len answered, "Good question. Can't be nobody from here. Folks here woulda missed 'em."

It was forty minutes before the first deputies arrived. Len told them about retrieving the tables then deciding to survey the river before the tourist season and how they'd come across the boat stern sticking out of the water.

They left ten minutes after the deputies arrived. Len brought them back at full speed and no one said anything on the trip. When Len beached the boat, Nate tied the bow line to a tree and they went to hitch the trailer to the truck. They loaded the boat onto the trailer and brought it to the storage area where they unhitched the trailer and "dropped" it. Not a word had been said since they left the scene.

Nate broke the silence, "Well, as a wise man once said, enough of this nonsense. Let's go to the diner and eat. My treat."

"Another time, Nate. I need to git the store open 'cause a delivery truck is bringing a load of stock this afternoon. I need Hildee to help me unload and price."

"Understood. I have other business I can take care of anyway so I'll get to it." Before Hildee realized what was happening Nate kissed her and said, "See you later, love."

Hildee broke into a smile a mile wide. Len said as they watched Nate walk away, "Daughter, ya both got it bad."

"Sho nuff, pa. Sho nuff."

Nate had made a decision and he was, after all, a man of action. His mission resulted in his not getting back to the campground until almost six in the evening. There was a note on his trailer door. "Come to the house, please. Hildee."

Nate walked up to the house and found a number of cars parked in the drive including a sheriff's car. He went to the front door and knocked. It was Marilee who opened the door, saying, "Good. It's about time."

"What's up?"

"We're just startin' so come listen."

Nate walked in and found all the living room seating full of people including the sheriff. He said, "Hi, everybody. Sheriff."

"You forgot this," Len said, and handed Nate his cellphone.

"Thanks. Good thing I didn't need it."

Hildee countered, "I tried to call ya but it jist rang in pa's pocket." Hildee looked accusingly at her pa, who just shrugged.

Nate went and sat on the arm of the sofa next to Hildee. The sheriff said, "This is a real mess. The body we found was Tye Bradson, the young un of Terry, who owns the funeral parlor. I got no doubt and neither do the state crime fellers that Tye's death was accidental like. It appears he was speedin' down the river when his boat hit a submerged log. It went through the bottom of his boat and a branch went plumb through him. His boat was a movin' on and hit so hard it overturned right off. Tye drowned but he would've probably died of bleedin' anyhow. We didn't think he was by his self at the time. Thing is, the time of death was 'bout the time your campground was vandalized.

"My deputies put two and two together and questioned some of Tye's friends. One, Tommy Crenshaw, has fessed up they did the vandalism and he was in the boat when they had the accident. Tommy was throw'd from the boat and swam to shore. In the dark, he didn't know what happened to

Tye and couldn't find him. He walked home thinkin' Tye swam to the opposite shore and hoofed it home. Tye's dad didn't report him missing so that raised questions. I 'spect his father put him up to the shenanigans."

The sheriff paused and then continued, "I sent deputies lookin' to talk with Tye's dad and to tell him about Tye but they couldn't find him. He'd already heard about his son's death. His wife was boo-hooing and told my deputies Terry was heavy into the bottle. Terry'd left with a mess of guns. He'd been ranting about how it was all the fault of the Drift River Church folks. We considered y'all may be in danger so I came to tell ya all to be careful 'til we find him. Thing is, I don't have enough deputies to protect y'all and look for him."

Ben said, "We understan', Sheriff."

Nate asked, "What's Terry driving?"

"Dark blue Yukon."

Len declared, "Thanks for the heads-up, Sheriff. We'll think on a way to circle the wagons 'til he turns up."

Nate agreed, "That's good work, Sheriff. Tell the deputies thanks from all of us as well." Ben said, "I second that." Everyone expressed agreement.

The sheriff got up, "Be careful, hear." They all shook hands with the sheriff, who then left.

Ben asked, "How do we handle this?" They were all looking at each other.

Len noted, "There is safety in numbers so we should stay together at night and always have our guns close. We only go out in pairs during the day and armed at that. Who's got concealed carry permits?"

Everyone raised their hands.

Len looked at Nate, "It don't upset ya we all go about armed?"

Nate shook his head no and said, "Maybe I should preach on what the Bible teaches about self-defense."

Ben asked Nate, "You got a concealed carry permit?"

"Yes."

"I'll be," Len said.

Nate quipped, "Be what?"

Everyone chuckled and Len answered, "Surprised." He smiled broadly and continued, "Here's what I think. Ben, you can stay here in the small upstairs. It's got a double. Marilee and Hildee can stay in the guest room that has two twins. Nate, you sleep down here on the sofa and guard the main floor.

"Ben, you and I will drive Betsy and Sue to work, pick them up, and bring them back here. Marilee, you will be pretty safe at work with all 'em metal detectors at the court house. Nate and Hildee will take you to work and fetch ya after work. Ya stay inside 'til they come. Hildee, you and Nate are attached at the hip during the day anyway. Ben, if yar agreeable, ya can tag along with me and watch my back. What y'all think?"

Marilee jumped in, "It's a good plan, but how many bathrooms ya got here?"

"Two and a half. Two upstairs and a half down. Fellas get showered at night and women folk in the morning."

Sue spoke for the first time, "We ain't got clothes and necessaries here."

Nate told her, "Hildee and I will take you and your ma to get your stuff. When we come back, Len can go with Ben and Marilee to get what they need."

"Everybody agree?" Len asked.

Marilee spoke up, "Yeah, and make sure to bring all yar guns back with ya."

Len agreed, "Sure and bring towels. I ain't got enough big uns."

By eight o'clock, Len's house was a merry but armed camp. The group had stored their stuff and they all sat in the kitchen drinking coffee or soda while Marilee and Hildee prepared something to eat.

After supper, Nate and Len went down to the campsite so Nate could get his stuff. Later Len, Ben, and Nate showered before retiring. Nate took a cold shower and that wasn't enough. Thoughts of Hildee were tormenting him. Nate prayed and hard.

Nate was the first to get up in the morning. He stuffed his Glock in his waistband, grabbed his rifle and went outside locking the door behind him. He went to have a look around. Everything was quiet and he found nothing out of the usual. When he returned, he found Ben was sitting on the porch with a shotgun in his lap drinking coffee.

Ben said, "I take it you didn't find anything."

"So far all clear."

"You must ah done sneakin' 'round afore 'cause I didn't see or hear ya until you came out of them woods and ya didn't even have camo on."

Nate shrugged and sat down beside Ben.

Len came outside, "The ladies are about ready to go. Everything clear, Nate?"

"Seems so," and went to Len and said quietly, "If I was going to ambush us, it would be when we got back and had let our guard down."

Len asked, "What ya suggestin', Nate?"

"When we get back, we all meet up at the campground parking lot and come up here on foot on the chance we have a visitor."

Len nodded and went to lock up the house. When the ladies had been safely escorted to their work places, Nate, Hildee, Len and Ben gathered as planned. The little group went quietly through the woods. They were getting close to the house when they heard a door slam. Nate was leading and signaled the group to stop and to stay. He disappeared to come back a minute later.

Nate told them, "There's someone in the house," then took out his cell phone and called 911.

The group waited and listened. It wasn't long until they heard the sheriff's cars going up the drive. They heard a door slam again. They eased forward to see what was going on. Terry came racing around the side of the house at a dead run, carrying a rifle in one hand and holding up his pants with the other.

Terry ran into a deputy, who tackled him. The other deputy arrived and held Terry down while he was handcuffed. The group watched and could tell he was being read his rights.

The foursome came out of the woods and the deputies saw them coming and recognized them. The little group was armed to the teeth. A deputy came to meet them, "It was good you didn't take matters into your own hands."

Nate smiled, "Less chance of anyone being hurt if the professionals did it. Of course, if you'd needed help, we would've obliged."

The deputy laughed and said, "You is the most unusual preacher I ever met."

Nate smiled and shrugged.

The deputy turned to Len, "We got him dead to rights on burglary. He was apparently using your toilet when we arrived and he smells of booze. Given his threats against ya'll, I think the prosecutin' attorney will speak against bail, but there ain't no promises."

Len stated, "If he makes bail, we'll circle the wagons again. I guess I'm goin' to have ta keep on lockin' up the house durin' the day."

The deputy smiled, "Good plan."

Len drawled, "All right," and pointed in the direction of the store, "Let's saddle up and meet there."

They went back to the vehicles and drove them up to the store. Len got out and unlocked the store then he and Ben went inside. Nate and Hildee took seats on the porch.

Hildee remarked, "Interestin' twenty-four hours."

"Wasn't it."

"I don't think there'll be much more a happenin' fer a while."

"Don't count on it."

Hildee looked at him, "Well, I'm hopin' so."

Nate slid out of his chair and went down on one knee and asked, as he pulled the ring out of his pocket, "Hildee, will you marry me?"

Hildee jumped up and then did something unexpected. She started to wobble and Nate jumped up and caught her as she fainted. Nate held her in his arms and yelled, "Hildee. Hildee!"

Len came runnin' out and said, "What's the matter?"

"She fainted. Let's get her to the clinic."

Nate carried her to the pickup. He and Len drove her to the clinic without regard to the speed limit. When they arrived, Nate picked Hildee up and carried her inside the clinic and a nurse directed them to a treatment room.

A nurse came running in, "What happened?"

"She fainted."

The nurse asked, "How long ago?"

"About five minutes."

"Did anything unusual happen just before she fainted?"

Nate said sheepishly, "I proposed."

Another nurse brought smelling salts and waved them under Hildee's nose and she came awake. She blinked once, looked at Nate, smiled and said, "Ya."

Nate sighed and took the ring back out and Hildee let him put it on her finger.

Len said, "All that over a ring!" and stomped out of the room.

Nate bent over and kissed Hildee then the nurse started taking

Hildee's vital signs.

She asked, "Has this happened before?"

Hildee was smiling and replied, "No, but the man I love never proposed before."

The nurse finished taking Hildee's vitals and looked at Nate, "Git her out of here. It's on me; an engagement present."

Nate smiled and said, "Thanks," and helped Hildee up. They walked hand-in-hand out of the clinic.

Len was waiting in the pickup when they got in and asked, "And how much is thet gonna cost me?"

Nate proclaimed, "It's taken care of, but I'm putting you on notice that I'm not taking an I.O.U. for the horse and three sheep."

Len smiled, "It were two sheep, city slicker."

"That was before I knew she was prone to fainting."

Hildee smiled and took Nate's arm and put it around her shoulders and snuggled up. They met Ben coming in the opposite direction so pulled over onto the shoulder. Ben did the same and backed up on the opposite shoulder and shouted, "She ok?"

Len yelled back, "Yeah, she just had a fainting spell 'cause Nate finally popped the question."

"He ain't too romantic, is he?"

"Yeah, but preacher's sometimes don't use the good sense God gave 'em. He didn't give her no warnin', like takin' her fer a fancy dinner so she'd be spectin' it. Boy's as dumb as a box ah rocks."

"Appears so. We should go tell the lady folk. I left a note sayin' the store will be closed for a couple hours due to a family emergency."

"Ok." Len pulled a U-turn and followed Ben back toward town. It was mid-morning so the diner was almost empty when they went in. Sue came rushing over, "We heard they caught Terry. Ma called Marilee and told her."

Ben announced, "We come to tell ya. Nate and Hildee's engaged."

Betsy came over and gave Ben a peck on the cheek, "Well, news travels fast around here. Deputies already bin in for coffee. Why didn't ya 'all tell us about the 'tempted robbery?"

Hildee asked, "What robbery?"

Sue said, "It's in the bi-weekly River Crier how Nate disarmed the robber and how the deputies captured the two other fleeing desperados.

There was a shootout and everything. The three robbers is in the jail."

Hildee confessed, "I thought you were a pullin' my leg, pa."

"Nope."

Betsy put in, "And there's pictures about the open-air church and a big write-up, too. There's also a piece about a malicious report maligning the new church and its pastor."

Sue added, "That's you, Nate."

"Sit down," Betsy said, "and I'll git coffee and I'll show ya the paper."

Hildee scolded Nate, "You told me you only talked to people that day."

Nate replied, "Yeah, several deputies and such in the morning and a reporter in the afternoon. You didn't seem to believe us about the robbery, so I didn't see any sense in going into detail."

Hildee shook her head but she was in too good of a mood to let this bother her. She said, "You'll pay for that, my love."

Sue jumped in, "Pretty familiar with the preacher ain't ya, Hildee." Hildee displayed her ring, smiled and said, "Eat your heart out." Sue started jumping up and down like a little kid repeating, "Hildee's gettin' hitched. Hildee's gettin' hitched."

Betsy came and looked at the ring then looked at Nate and asked, "That real?"

Nate beamed, "Of course."

Betsy asked, "You rob a bank or somethin', Nate?"

Nate smiled, "Or somethin', Betsy."

Hildee looked down at her ring. It was breathtaking and it hit her this was a very, very, expensive ring. Hildee bent over and whispered to Nate, "I don't need a ring this fancy."

Nate smiled and whispered back, "It was on sale so I'm not taking it back. You are stuck with it."

Hildee said to tease Nate, "Preachers ain't supposed to tell fibs about fancy rings being on sale."

Nate shrugged.

Hildee said in a whisper, "The rock's giinormous."

"Well, you got a ring so stop complaining."

Hildee giggled and then kissed him. The talking at the table didn't stop and no one was paying attention to Nate and Hildee's interaction.

That evening, Nate and Hildee called Nate's family to tell them the good news. Len was in on the conference call. Nate's parents wanted to meet Hildee and Len and were not willing to wait until after Labor Day, so they said they would all have to arrange to visit.

Chapter 5

The time leading up to the Memorial Day weekend was a very busy time for Len, Hildee, and Nate. Nate finished his camper and put in Herman's new service and helped Len and Hildee out as well. He also met with a few people as pastor. Ben's engine came in and Nate helped Ben put it in. In the process, he learned quite a bit and bonded further with Ben. Ole Beauty would be available to tow the VFW float for the Memorial Day weekend parade.

After the report in the River Crier, Nate was approached on the following Monday about being involved in the local VFW and he agreed, providing a copy of his DD-214 document and filling out an application card. At Tuesday's meeting, he was fast-tracked. His membership was approved by a quick afternoon meeting of the Post Review Committee as a result of a Monday phone call by one of the more prominent members to Washington. That evening, Nate was elected to membership at the general meeting, and even though he wasn't there, he was appointed chaplain. Nate received a phone call congratulating him and he just went with the flow.

What happened next was what some people would call good fortune but Nate would call it a God thing. He went out to give an estimate on some electrical and plumbing work on a farm near the campground. As he started up the lane, he saw the stone barn with the collapsing roof. Nate had seen such places made into upscale homes up east. It sat on a hill overlooking the river.

Nate drove past and up the road about an eighth of a mile. He stopped his van and got out and went to the door of a very large home. It needed work but it was grand old place. A new Cadillac Escalade was parked out front.

Nate went to the front door and used the door knocker. A middle aged gentleman answered the door.

Nate said, "Hello, I'm Nate Christian. I came to give you a quote on work."

The man smiled, "I'm Dorcas Smith." The man held out his hand and Nate shook it. The man said, "Come in, please."

Nate went in and found the house was in the process of being gutted to be redone. There was a sofa and chair in the middle of the living room and not much else. Nate said, "You have taken on quite a project."

"It's what we expected."

An attractive, middle-aged woman came into the room. Like her husband she was well dressed. Dorcas said, "This is my wife, Bethany. Dear, this is Mr. Nate Christian."

The woman offered her hand and Nate shook it gently. Nate knew by the way she offered her hand it was to be a genteel shake. She said, "Please have a seat, Mr. Christian."

Nate said, "Thank you, ma'am. Please call me Nate."

The woman nodded.

Dorcas said, "You came highly recommended. We bought this home for our retirement. It seems, due to unforeseen circumstances, I will be retiring earlier than anticipated. I was told the electrical and plumbing is in terrible shape and I should do the work before closing the rest in."

Nate asked, "And what exactly would you like from me?"

"A price to do all the electrical and plumbing upgrades. We'd like to keep all the old fixtures which I'm told are in good shape. I'd like your advice."

"Have you had an assessment done of the septic system?"

"What is that?" Dorcas asked.

Nate explained it to him. After he finished his short explanation, Dorcas said, "We always lived in the city and I just took it that you hooked a pipe up somewhere and the government took care of it."

Nate nodded, "Yes, that's how it works in cities."

"But not in the country," Mrs. Smith put in.

"No, ma'am."

Dorcas said, "Well, I suppose I should show you around."

Nate spent almost three hours looking at plumbing and electrical issues. The fact that the walls were open made the job easier. Nate had to put on overalls to inspect the dirt-floored basement which was accessed from outside. Nate took a digital camera and flashlight with him. When Nate finished, he took his coveralls off outside and went back to the living room.

Mrs. Smith had tea on a serving table and asked, "Would you like some tea, Mr. Christian?"

Nate said, "Yes, ma'am."

"Sugar or cream, Nate?"

"No thank you, ma'am."

The woman poured and gave Nate a cup and saucer. Nate took a sip and said, "This is a fine quality Oolong. Thank you for sharing it with me."

"You know your tea."

"My mother loves her tea and she taught her boys to appreciate the finer teas. Her tea is perhaps her only vice."

Dorcas took a sip from his cup and asked, "What do you think?"

Nate replied, "All your wiring is outdated and worn as you were told. It doesn't meet code. It's also antiquated and too small for a house this size with modern demands. There is no electric in the basement. All the wiring should be pulled and replaced and you need a new larger service. You'll want a laundry room so you need to decide where you want the plumbing and electrical for that. In summary, everything electrical needs to be taken out and new put in. The plumbing isn't as bad but it's not good news either. About half of it has been updated at some point, but it was poorly joined to the old pipes which are now failing."

Nate took out his camera and showed Mr. Smith what he'd discovered, "The bad news is that the pipes are leaking in the basement. Before I can make a recommendation, I'll need to do camera work."

Dorcas sighed, "In short, it's going to be expensive."

"Yes, sir. This is a large house and, if it is structurally sound, you could end up with a very fine home."

"Will you give us a free estimate?" Dorcas asked.

"No, sir. I will have to spend considerable time putting a camera down the pipes to find out what we're dealing with."

Mrs. Smith said, "Oh dear."

"How much will that cost?" Dorcas asked.

Nate told him what he would charge for the camera inspection.

Mrs. Smith advised, "That's a lot less than we've been told by others."

Nate assured them, "What I quoted you is a fair price."

Dorcas got up, left the room and came back with some papers and handed them to Nate. Nate looked at them. They were bids on the work and Nate knew the prices were high. He knew why; the contractors were from the city and they would have to pay to have their union employees put up and fed in local hotels. They also didn't want the job unless they could make a profit equivalent to what they'd get working in the city.

"What do you think, Nate?"

Nate answered, "I can do it for a lot less."

"How much less?"

"Probably twenty percent less for the interior work. There is no provision in the quotes you have for septic or buried pipe work if it's needed."

Mrs. Smith asked, "How long would it take you to do the work?"

Nate told them.

Dorcas looked at his wife and she nodded. He said, "Then do the camera inspection and we'll pay you for it, then give us a bid. When can you do the camera work?"

"Day after tomorrow."

Dorcas agreed, "We'll be here. If we agree on a contract, we'll provide you a key."

"That's agreeable."

Nate prepared a work authorization and gave it to Dorcas to sign, which he did.

Mrs. Smith said, "You're not from around here are you?"

"No, ma'am."

Dorcas asked, "This your family business?"

Nate answered, "Well, I'm a third generation contractor. My father and brothers run a family business in the big city. My business is here and I work with just one helper."

Mrs. Smith commented, "I can understand why you want to live here. It is beautiful. We bought almost two hundred acres we didn't want to get this house with its view and some of the land it sits on."

Nate asked, "Would you consider selling some of it?"

"Are you interested?" Dorcas asked.

"Yes, sir."

"Which part?"

Nate told him, "The old stone barn area. Looks like there's about three or four acres down to the river."

"How much would you be willing to pay to take it as is and the old barn becomes your problem?"

Nate, thinking it was a ridiculous offer said, "Fifteen hundred an acre for five acres down to the river."

"It's a deal if you pay for the survey."

"Agreed," and the two men shook on it.

Mrs. Smith said, "I'll write up a sales agreement."

Dorcas added, "My wife is a real estate broker."

They signed papers and Nate gave Mrs. Smith a hundred dollar bill for a deposit to make the agreement binding. Mrs. Smith gave him a copy.

Their business and the tea being finished, Nate said, "It's a pleasure doing business with you. Thank you for the tea. I had better get going. I have a lot to do."

Nate got up and Dorcas shook his hand. Nate stopped on the way out and looked at the old stone barn. It was small for a barn but the right size for what Nate had in mind. It definitely had possibilities.

On the way back to the campground, Nate made a call and booked the rental of the equipment he needed for the camera work. Nate got back to the campsite to find Hildee sitting on a lawn chair under the carport. Nate got out, leaned over her, and kissed her. It was a passionate kiss and, when it ended, Hildee said in a hoarse voice, "Love, we've got ta set a date soon."

Nate affirmed, "I know."

Hildee asked, "How did your day go?"

"I have a job I'll need your help with."

"What're ya going' ta pay me?"

"Fifteen an hour. Cash. It'll be a day's work."

"Deal. It will go into my dowry fund."

Nate laughed.

"Some of the summer students have started so pa will have lotsa hep here. What will we be doin'?"

"A camera inspection of pipes. I have to give a bid on rewiring and re-plumbing a very big house."

"So we're building the family business."

Nate said with a broad smile, "I can see the sign now, Nate and Sons."

Hildee grinned, "Nah, it'll be Ma and Daughters."

Nate laughed and sat down saying, "Life is good."

"Seriously. I do pa's books and taxes and I can do our business. I can also hep with the regular work."

"That's what my mother and father do, only mom sticks to managing the office."

The next morning, Nate and Hildee worked at the campground. In the afternoon, they went and got the rental equipment, picking it up just before closing. The next day, they went to do the camera inspection. They arrived at the house early and Mr. Smith answered the door. He took one look at Hildee and smiled.

"Nate, is this your assistant?"

"Yes, sir. This is Hildee Cole, my fiancée and assistant. Hildee studied building trades. Hildee, this is Mr. Smith."

Mr. Smith said, "I'm pleased to meet you, Hildee. You must meet my wife."

Nate was surprised at the effect Hildee had on Mrs. Smith, who was charmed by Hildee's pleasant demeanor. After the introductions, Nate said, "We have a lot to do so, with your permission, we'll get to it."

Mrs. Smith watched Nate and Hildee carry in the heavy equipment and seemed amazed Hildee was able to carry such large items. As usual, Hildee and Nate worked together quickly and efficiently. They had the camera work done by noon after which they walked the septic bed and found the ground was soft and flooded with raw sewage. It was not good.

Nate and Hildee went to talk to the Smiths, who were sitting on the front portion of the large porch.

Mr. Smith asked, "So what is the diagnosis?"

"It's not good and the patient is critical."

Mrs. Smith asked, "How much will it cost?"

When Nate told the Smiths the bad news and the cost of repair he expected the couple would be upset.

Mr. Smith surprised Nate, "That's a lot less than I expected."

Nate replied, "I wouldn't drink the well water until it is tested and the septic problems are resolved."

Mr. Smith looked at his wife, who nodded agreement. They signed a contract for Nate to do the work and for progress payments. Mr. Smith gave Nate keys and a check for the camera inspection work.

As Hildee and Nate were packing up the equipment, the Smiths came out and said goodbye then drove away. Nate said, "Let's get this packed up. I have something to show you."

As he and Hildee got in the truck, Nate handed her a magazine in which there was a bookmark. He said, "Have a look at that and tell me what you think?" She looked at the pictures and said, "This was an old stone barn?"

Nate said, "Yes."

Hildee looked at the pictures and read some of the article. She asked, "Why are you showing me this?"

"You'll see."

He drove down the long lane stopping by the old barn near the county road, "Come have a look."

Hildee got out and followed him to the old barn. She looked at him and said, "Really?"

"Yup. It's under contract and it'll close in sixty days."

"How much land goes with the barn?"

"Five acres."

"The old roof is all caved in."

"So was the roof on the one in the magazine."

Hildee smiled, "It's nothin' we couldn't do."

Nate smiled, "I agree, but it's got to be our secret. It'll be a while."

"I reckon I can keep it zipped."

They got back in the van and headed for the rental company to return the equipment.

"That's a big contract, Nate."

Nate said, "Yes it is."

"How much do you figure we will normally make an hour?"

"Around here, maybe fifty an hour average after expenses if we are working smart and together. It depends on how far we have to travel."

Hildee whistled, "That's good wages for these parts."

"Only if we keep busy. What we make is not for sharing with others, Hildee."

Hildee made a motion of zipping her lips.

"Good. Loose lips ruin businesses."

Hildee stretched her hands and Nate had a moment of panic, "Where's your ring?"

"At home. No way I'm going to wear it on the job."

Nate sighed in relief and Hildee smiled.

They got to the rental company before closing and returned the equipment. Hildee said as they left, "I suppose this meant you didn't have to pay another day's rental?"

"You understand perfectly."

Nate climbed back into the truck and went to an ATM, where he withdrew cash. He counted out a hundred and fifty dollars and handed it to Hildee with, "There's your wages for today."

"What about taxes and such?"

"I expect we'll be filing joint returns soon so I don't see that it matters."

"I suppose not. This is the most I ever made in a day."

"We'll stop and have dinner on the way back to celebrate."

As they were driving, Nate said, "We should hire a helper to work with us."

"Why? We can do the work. I can still do pa's books and the stuff he can't do in the evenin's and on weekends."

"Yeah, but our working out there together is going to be a big temptation for both of us. If we have a helper, there's not apt to be gossip and it will dampen the temptation. It'll also allow you to split your time helping me and your pa without getting burned out."

Hildee stated, "I reckon it won't be hard to get someone. I'll call my ole building trades instructor. He'll know someone good. Maybe we could even keep him on if it works out and he can hep us make money."

"Now you're sounding like a business woman."

Hildee didn't let any grass grow under her feet. She got a lead and they ended up hiring Carson Walden, a recent graduate of the building trades program at the technical and community college. He turned out to be a wise hire. He was only twenty-two but was already married with two children. He was a hard worker and got along well with Nate and Hildee.

The Thursday before the Memorial Day weekend, they were locking up the Smith house after a long day. The three of them had worked at the house all day. The job was going much faster than Nate had expected and they were way ahead of schedule. They were going to take a four-day weekend.

Carson said, "I'll see ya later, boss. Enjoy the weekend, Hildee."

Hildee said, "See ya," and Nate waved.

Usually Nate picked Carson up and the three of them came together and Nate drove him home after dropping Hildee off. Nate had arranged things so that seldom were he and Hildee alone; it was to protect them from the temptation they were for each other. Because they were leaving early for the long weekend, Carson had brought his own vehicle today.

They were on the way down the drive when Hildee said, "People been asking me when and where we are goin' to get hitched. They asking ya?"

"Yeah, your pa and my mom have asked me several times. Mom is phoning me regularly and she always asks."

"Maybe we otta reckon on when and stuff."

"Open-air wedding at the campground with a reception at the VFW?"

"Thet works. Pa will like it."

"How would you like to be a July bride; sometime around the fourth?"

Hildee grinned, "The sooner the better says me. I kinda get hot thinkin' about sharin' a bed with ya. I gotta admit, I'm looking forward to finding out what it's really like."

Nate smiled and said, "I understand, believe me."

Hildee undid her seatbelt and slid over on the bench seat and put the middle belt on. She cuddled up to Nate and he sighed. When they pulled up at the house, there was a crew cab pickup parked out front. Len was already sitting on the porch with a man and woman.

Nate announced, "Well, if that don't beat all. That's my mom and dad." They got out of the van and walked quickly hand-in-hand onto the porch. Nate said, "It's good to see you."

His mother and father got up and he said, "Mom, Dad, this is Hildee. Hildee, this is my mother, Janice, and my father, Mike."

Hildee smiled and said, "I'm happy ta meet ya."

Janice and Mike stood up. Janice stood looking at Hildee, who opened her arms and without hesitation hugged Janice. She had to bend over a little to do it as Janice was considerably shorter. Hildee turned to Mike and, to his surprise, hugged him as well.

Hildee noted that Janice was dressed in jeans, sneakers and a very feminine top. Hildee figured Janice was about five six and pretty. Hildee figured men of any age would find her very attractive. Mike was about six foot and had a small belly but she figured for his age he was in very good shape. If Nate looked that good pushing sixty, Hildee would be happy.

Nate began, "Well, this is certainly a surprise."

Mike smiled, "Well, we admit it was spur of the moment."

Hildee said gleefully, "I am so happy to meet ya'll."

"Len told us you and Nate are working together," Janice told them.

"Yes, we are. Your boy is a proper gentleman. He hired a feller to help us jist to protect me from gossip even though we coulda done the job jist the two of us. You raised him good."

Janice laughed, "That is high praise."

Hildee smiled, "It sure is." She motioned to the chairs and they all sat. She looked at Mike and said with a broad smile, "He's a hard worker, too. He's the only man I know works as hard as me. Pa is a close second."

Len laughed at that, and the way she said it made Nate's dad laugh. Janice looked at Nate, who was smiling broadly. Len added, "It's true, too."

Janice changed the subject said, "I can see why you like it here, Nate. Len showed us the campground and where you are staying."

"Yes, this area suits me."

"Len showed us where you are holding service," Mike said. "We're looking forward to attending."

Janice asked, "So Hildee, when and where are you planning to get married?"

"We thought to get married at an open-air service here and have a reception at the VFW."

Mike interrupted, "Nate, did you join the VFW here?"

Len informed them, "He's the chaplain."

"I couldn't get him to participate back home."

"Well, time heals painful memories," Len said.

Mike looked at Len and said, "I never looked at it like that."

Len shrugged.

Janice asked, "Hildee, what did you do for work before you and Nate started working together?"

"I do chores for pa and keep his books."

Len continued explaining, "She does the electrical, plumbing, carpentry repairs, welding, books, payroll, taxes and hires the summer help. I basically just run the store and take the campers' money. She completed the building trades program at the Pearce Community and Technical College. Also took some bookkeeping courses."

"Pa is understatin' what he does."

Len smiled and added, "She and Nate hep with the big stuff when they ain't workin' on buildin' their own business."

Hildee interjected, "Well if'in ya'll will excuse me, I'll go get cleaned up for dinner." She looked at Nate and smiled, "You should clean up, dear; you are a little ripe."

Nate smiled and said, "Yes, love."

Hildee went into the house and Janice said, "I think I'll freshen up."

Hildee was feeling really gritty. She decided she needed a shower unaware that Janice would be lying in wait when she got out.

Out on the porch, Len said, "I'll go check on the store then come back and we'll grill us some steaks." Len got up and started walking to the store.

Mike looked at his son, "She's a looker, Nate, but nothing like the girls that used to chase you. She's quite young."

"I think she's gorgeous and just the right age for her. More importantly, she's a good Christian woman and I love her."

"She has quite an accent. Her father does, too."

"I suppose the folks around here say that about me."

"I suppose."

"It was quite a surprise, you showing up unannounced."

"Well, it was your mother. It was driving her crazy that she didn't know Hildee and you didn't ask for your mother's approval like your brothers did. The name was enough to make her wonder what you were thinking. I came out of self-preservation."

"It's the price of marrying a strong woman."

"You're right and it seems you are facing the same thing."

"Uh huh."

"It's happened a little quick hasn't it? You sure?"

"Yes and yes."

Mike responded, "Ok."

"I'd better go shower. I won't be gone long."

While Nate was gone to shower and Mike was waiting on the porch, the fun upstairs was just beginning. Hildee had dumped her dirty clothes, all of them, in the hamper in the bathroom and taken a long shower. When she finished, she went to her room with a towel wrapped loosely around her and using another to dry her hair. She went into her room to find Janice sitting on the edge of the bed. Janice stood up.

"I'm not sure I approve of you and Nate getting married."

It was the wrong thing to say. Hildee walked up to Janice and got into Janice's personal space. Hildee was looking down on the shorter woman.

Janice said, "Back off."

Hildee pushed her and in the process dropped the towel covering her. Janice was forced backward onto the bed. It was then that Janice realized just how strong Hildee was. Janice was also faced with a naked and Amazon-like athletic woman towering over her.

Hildee pointed and commanded, "Stay put! You are Nate's mother so I am going to restrain myself and not deck you right off. Let's get it straight. I love Nate and, if you get between us, I will make minced meat of you, little lady, mother or not. I don't want Nate not having a relationship with you but if you force it, that's your problem. If you ever invade my privacy and blindside me like this again, I won't be responsible for what will happen. Now having said it, the Lord says I am to forgive so it's your choice - war or forgiveness."

Janice broke out laughing, which disarmed Hildee. Hildee watched her double over in laughter so picked up one of the towels and went back to drying her hair and waited for the laughter to stop. It had not been lost on Janice that Hildee had lost her folksy speaking style during the stern warning.

Janice had tears in her eyes from laughing so hard as she said, "I'm now sure I do approve, Hildee. May I get up?"

Hildee said, "I reckon."

Janice got up and hugged her naked future daughter-in-law and left without another word. She went downstairs and out onto the porch. Nate had returned and she sat down with him and Mike.

Janice announced, "Well, I've been put in my place."

Mike looked at his wife and asked, "Did you deserve it?"

"Oh, yes, I did and that fireball gave it to me. I think if I'd have pushed her a little further, she'd have decked me."

Nate sighed before saying, "She could have, too."

Janice said, "Oh, there's no doubt. That woman is strong. I approve. The woman has spunk and she'll be an able partner who will have your back, son."

Mike asked, "You tell her you approve?"

"Yes."

The three of them sat swinging and a few minutes later Len came up from the store. He took a seat and said, "Everything's fine. The young uns have it under control. I'll grill some steaks in a while."

Hildee came out onto the porch and sat between Nate and Janice. She had on clean jeans, a nice blouse, her engagement ring, and brown sandals.

Janice said, "Len, your daughter and I have come to an

understanding." Len looked at Janice and didn't say anything. "We agree she is right for Nate and they should get married. I think he's lucky to have her."

"I have me a problem with them gettin' hitched."

Janice looked shocked and Mike asked, "What's that?"

"He won't take no I.O.U. for the horse and two sheep dowry."

Nate interjected, "It is three sheep."

Both Janice and Mike look dumbfounded so Hildee proceeded to let them in on the joke, which they enjoyed.

Janice asked, "Where's the nearest hotel?"

Len told them, "Won't do no good. It's the Memorial Day weekend so you'll have to accept my invitation to hole up here. If not, then you'll be drivin' a hundred miles or sleepin' in ur pickup."

Mike said, "Thank you, Len. We accept your kind invitation."

Hildee agreed, "Janice, you and Mike can stay in my room. The guest room has twin beds and a married couple should be in the same bed."

"Thank you very much, Hildee."

"Uh huh."

Janice looked at Nate, who said, "The local interpretation of 'uh huh' under the circumstances is you're welcome. It can also indicate appreciation or agreement."

Hildee grinned, "I forgot ya'll don't know local talk. You are welcome, Janice."

Janice laughed, "This will be a fun weekend I reckon."

Hildee smiled, "Now ya's gittin' it."

"Women," Mike said.

Len said, "I'm callin' Marilee to join us for dinner."

He went inside and Janice asked, "Who is Marilee?"

Nate replied, "Len's squeeze."

"Pardon?"

Hildee chimed in, "I'll interpret. It's pa's girlfriend."

"Oh. What about your mother?"

"She passed when I was a wee girl."

Mike said, "Sorry."

Hildee added, "No problem. Pa moped around for years and years. Nate finally brought him around and he started dating Marilee. She's good for him. Good Christian woman, too."

106

Janice commented, "I notice you lose the local dialect and accent when you want to."

"Most of the time I don't want to. I'm doin' it outta politeness for ya aliens."

Janice smiled and looked at Hildee, who had a broad smile.

Mike chuckled, "My dear, I think you've finally met your match."

Nate looked at Hildee, "Mom has my brother's wives intimidated."

Hildee looked at Janice, "When we go to visitin', I'll make sure not to ruin that fer ya but don't push it."

Janice laughed before saying, "Uh huh."

Hildee looked at Nate, "Yar ma's a fast learner."

Nate nodded agreement.

Len came out and said, "Marilee's comin' to et with us."

"We'll have a regular little party," Nate said.

Len said, "Uh huh."

Mike put in, "Meaning you agree."

Len looked at Mike, "We're learnin' ya, Mike."

Hildee got up, "I'm goin' to git a beer. Anybody else want one?"

Janice said, "Uh huh."

The men all indicated they'd like one. Janice offered, "I'll help you, Hildee," and the women went to get the beer.

Mike shared, "I could get used to this."

The men sat quietly until the two women came out of the house and handed the bottles of beer to the men and then sat down. There were no glasses and Janice twisted a cap off her bottle and took what could be called a swig. Mike asked about the area so Len proceeded to tell him. They talked for about ten minutes before a vehicle came up the drive. Marilee got out and waved as she walked up to the deck. Marilee said, "Hi, y'all."

Len stood up and kissed Marilee on the cheek, "I'll git ya a beer."

Marilee sat down and Hildee said, "Marilee, this is Janice and Mike, Nate's parents."

"Pleased to meet ya. I didn't know ya were comin'."

Mike said with a broad smile, "That makes two of us."

Janice added, "It was a spur of the moment thing. Curiosity was driving me crazy and I wanted to meet Hildee."

Len came out and handed Marilee a beer and sat down beside her and

107

put his arm around her shoulders. She snuggled up to him.

Marilee accepted it, "Thanks, hun."

Mike asked, "What's the plan for the weekend?"

Len provided, "Well, Friday afternoon and evening is the big check-in time so Hildee and I will have to work. Saturday evening there is a dance at the fairgrounds. Sunday is church and Monday is the laying of the wreath at the memorial followed by the parade. Nate is riding the VFW float while I'm ridin' with Ben in Ole Beauty. Afterwards is the big BBQ at the fairgrounds."

Janice asked, "What's an Ole Beauty and who is Ben?"

Len answered, "Ole Beauty is a classic pickup that pulls the VFW float. Ben owns Ole Beauty and is a good friend. Nate helped Ben put in a rebuilt motor so Ole Beauty would be runnin' in time for the parade. On Monday, it's Hildee's turn to watch the store. Other than that there's no plans. Either Hildee or me needs to be here to keep an eye on things."

Janice looked at Nate, "Hildee tells me you are planning the wedding for July sometime around the fourth."

"It depends if the VFW can handle our reception with all that will be going on around that time."

Mike asked, "Who will do the service?"

Nate sighed, "We haven't discussed that yet."

Janice turned to Hildee, "I'll help you anyway you want."

"Thanks Janice." Hildee turned to her father, "It will be nice to have a ma again."

Len nodded.

Hildee said, "Maybe two."

Marilee choked on her drink and Len just looked at Hildee with a puzzled look on his face.

Janice looked at Hildee, "Men can be so clueless."

Hildee smiled and said, "No doubt."

Len choked out, "I don't git it."

"No kiddin', pa."

Janice declared, "When they get married, I'll be her mother-in-law; that's one."

Len asked, "Who's two?"

Janice looked at Len and said, "Duh," as she looked at Marilee, who broke into a broad smile. Len turned bright red and everyone laughed.

Mike changed the subject, "I suppose you'd better come meet the rest of the family, Hildee."

"Uh huh."

"I'll arrange a family get together," Janice said, "so you can come visit and meet everyone at one time."

Nate remarked, "Oh, that will be like letting a tiger in with the sheep."

Len looked at Mike. Mike said, "Nate's brothers' wives think they are something when Janice isn't around. Janice has them all cowed, but they'll try Hildee on for size and she'll eat them alive."

"I don't git it."

Mike explained, "None of them stood up to Janice, but they'll try to bully Hildee."

Len grinned, "They'll go to regretin' it."

Hildee smiled and looked at Janice, "Could be fun." Janice chuckled which came out like a high pitched snort and it sounded so funny they all started to laugh.

Nate decided, "That could be worth the trip."

Len changed the subject, "I reckon the grill should be fired up." Nate stood, "I'll do it." Len said, "Uh huh," and turned to Mike, "What say ya we go hep him?"

They got up and followed Nate. When they were out of ear shot, Marilee was the first to speak.

"Hildee, did you see the look on your pa's face?"

Hildee smiled, "I ain't never seen pa blush before, so he must a bin thinkin' on it."

Janice agreed, "Well, it's obvious he's bonkers over you, Marilee."

Marilee sighed, "Well, he sure does set my heart to runnin' like a racehorse in the home stretch."

Hildee said, "Well, I know ya are fer shore good fer him."

Janice asked, "How long have you two known each other?"

Hildee jumped in, "They were high school sweethearts. They went to the senior prom together. Then ma's family moved here and the whole thing changed."

Marilee confessed, "He sure loved yar ma, Hildee. I always had a thing for Len, though I was happily married until my Bob passed."

Janice remarked, "Life sure is strange sometimes."

Marilee made a profound statement, "Yup."

Janice looked at Hildee, "When do you think you can come and visit?"

"I'll have to talk to pa and it will have to be a short visit because this is the busy time of year."

"Could you do a weekend?"

"Probably not because of church and all. Maybe a Friday and Saturday trip would work."

Marilee put in, "I'd be willing to help Len out on a weekend."

"Uh huh. That'd work. I'll talk with Nate and pa."

The women talked until Mike came to tell them the steaks were ready. The women followed Mike to the back deck.

Janice exclaimed as they reached the deck, "Well, isn't this something." The men had the picnic table set complete with a table cloth. Len brought the platter with steaks and Nate was carrying a plate covered with baked potatoes and corn on the cob wrapped in aluminum foil.

Marilee noted, "You fellers sure set a nice spread."

Nate bowed, "We aim to please."

They all sat. Len said the blessing and they all started to eat. Len started the conversation with, "Nate tells me, Mike, that you and his brothers are in construction."

Mike affirmed, "Yeah. It's a family business. Nate's two brothers and half a dozen employees. Janice takes care of the office. It's a good living. How did you get started here?"

Len told them, "I inherited the farm from my folks but I'm too lazy to farm, so I sold a few acres to some city folks and built the campground. I've been buildin' it for decades and it ain't finished yet."

Janice asked, "How big is the property?"

"A few hundred acres."

Mike whistled, "That's big. You have a lot of river frontage?"

"Uh huh."

Mike was wise enough not to ask further. The conversation turned to plans for the weekend.

Chapter 6

Friday morning Nate had just finished getting ready for the day and was sitting in a chair drinking his first coffee when Hildee and Janice showed up in the campground pickup.

Nate got up to meet them and called out, "Good morning, ladies."

His mother got to him first and said, "I had to see the inside of your camper."

Nate hugged his mother and kissed her on the cheek. Hildee smiled and hugged him and whispered, "Don't you dare kiss me in front of your mother."

As she started to move away, Nate kissed her on the lips and held her tight. She turned beet red. Nate smiled.

"You'll pay for that, love."

"Yes, dear, but it was worth it."

Hildee smiled.

Janice was already going inside. Nate and Hildee followed her. Janice said, "My, but this is nice. You two did a good job. I've not seen anything like it."

"You should have seen it when we started."

His mother replied, "Hildee told me."

Janice went and looked in the tiny bathroom and then the bedroom. She came out nodding.

"You've done a nice job. It's a little smaller than the efficiency apartment Mike and I had when we first married but not by much."

Hildee observed, "God willing, someday we'll build a home."

Janice asked, "Where did you get those unique kitchen cabinets?"

"Hildee made them from scrap aluminum we bought."

"Very creative," and opened one of the doors and added, "And very functional. I suppose lightweight too."

"Fer sure and strong," Hildee agreed.

Janice looked at Nate, "Your father's up at the store with Len. Hildee offered to take us on a tour of the river. Want to come?"

"Of course."

They went to the store where Len was already working with the summer staff checking in campers. Len waved at them. Mike came over and said, "Len is swamped and I said I'd stay and help him."

Janice smiled and kissed Mike then left with Hildee and Nate. They walked down to the river. As they passed the canoes, Janice asked about them and Hildee explained what they were used for. Some weekenders were already starting the downriver float trip. At the river, the trio got into the smaller of the campground's two boats. The first mile or so the river had a lot of floaters so Hildee went slow but then was able to travel a little faster as she and Janice talked.

Hildee suddenly slowed the boat and motioned with her head and Nate saw it. She nudged the boat toward the branch and Nate took a grappling hook and snagged the log and they pushed it to the shore. Hildee beached the boat and helped Nate pull the log up onto shore. The couple got back into the boat.

Janice asked, "Why did you do that?"

"That one coulda caused trouble. A tube snag on it might hang-up or puncture a tube and panic a newbie."

Janice just nodded. They started out again and came to some young people who had beached their small boat on a sandbar and were swimming. Hildee and Nate waved.

Janice asked, "You know them?"

"No, but here it's just neighborly," Nate said.

Janice smiled, "I see."

Halfway down to the highway bridge crossing the river, Hildee pointed and said, "That is one of the landing sites. We pick up the short trippers there. There's another at the bridge. It's a state park with restroom facilities, if you need 'em. It's a little way to the bridge."

Janice said, "Let's stop."

Hildee took the boat to the shore and beached gently on the sand then said, "You may need this, Janice." She took a roll of toilet paper and two individually wrapped sanitary wipes from a water tight container under her seat and handed them to Janice, "We women folk need to go prepared."

Janice smiled and said, "Uh huh."

Nate got out and helped his mother out. The washrooms could be seen from the landing and Janice headed for them.

Hildee said, "Your ma seems nice. I think we'll git along like bread and butter."

Nate said with a broad smile, "My mother is a good judge of people. My brothers' wives are prissy snobs and my mother never really took to them, though she treats them well for my brothers' sakes. She seems to really like you. Probably because you are so much alike."

"We don't look nothin' alike."

"True. You are alike in other ways."

Hildee thought about it a bit and added, "I reckon'. I suppose that's not a bad thing."

Nate smiled, "I don't think so, love." He stood admiring his fiancée for a few minutes and she just sat there silently, smiling. Finally, he said, "Have I told you today you're gorgeous? Those shorts show off those beautiful long legs and there's your beautiful…" and he cut off his compliments.

Hildee had her finger over her smile indicating he should hush. Janice said behind him, "Son, you have a bad case."

Nate sighed deeply then turned and offered his smiling mother his hand and helped her into the boat, though Hildee doubted she really needed the help. Janice handed Hildee the toilet paper.

"Thanks, but there was still some there but not a lot."

Hildee responded, "You never know," and started the motor. Nate pushed off and Hildee backed the boat out into the channel and headed downstream. At the bridge, Hildee beached the boat and said, "There's a snack trailer usually parks here. I'm going to get a drink."

Nate put the boat anchor on the shore and the three of them got out of the boat and walked a short distance to the vendor. The man and wife were preparing to receive the floaters already on the river and those spending the day at the river shore. The little parking lot was already full and there were cars parked up and down the highway. People were already staking claim to spots along the riverbank and under the bridge.

Nate asked, "I'm hungry and I'm going to get a hot dog. What can I get you?" Nate ended up having a hot dog and bottled water. Janice had a soda as did Hildee. They both had eaten breakfast.

In no time, they were headed back upriver. They got back to the campground a little after eleven. Hildee beached the boat and Nate chained it around a tree then padlocked the chain. Hildee disconnected the fuel tank from the outboard motor and carried it up to the pickup. They all loaded in and went to the shop, where Hildee filled the tank from the large bulk storage tank. They then drove to the store.

Hildee was the first one in and Len, who was sitting behind the counter with Mike, asked, "Did you enjoy the trip, Janice?"

"Oh, yes! I'd like to spend some time on one of the sandbars swimming and have a picnic."

Len nodded, "We can make it happen."

Hildee asked, "How'd it go, pa?"

Len smiled, "About eighty percent of those folks that reserved are already in. We had a morning rush; unusual thet." He turned to Mike, "Folks usually don't start comin' till later in the afternoon."

Mike said, "These camper folks are real nice people." He looked at his wife, "Maybe we should get an RV and spend some time in the summer here."

Janice came behind the counter and sat down and said, "Uh huh."

A woman came in, "Hi, Len. I need some ice." She put three dollars on the counter and added, "I know where it is."

Len said, "Alice, this is my daughter's fiancée, Nate, and his parents, Mike and Janice."

Alice said, "Howdy. Pleased to meet ya."

They all shook hands and Alice said, "I'd better get back 'cause the kids will be driven' my hubby wild by now. They's wired. See ya." She rushed out.

Len rang up the sale and put the money in the till. He said, "Alice and her family are seasonal people. Her family pays to leave their camper here year round but they only come off and on from Memorial Day 'til Thanksgiving. I have two couples who stay here year round like Nate."

Mike looked at the clock and took out his wallet and handed a twenty to Len, "I'm buying two large pizzas for lunch; my treat."

Hildee offered, "I'll put them in. Everybody like all dressed?"

Everyone agreed and Hildee went to prepare the pizza. Len said, "Thanks, Mike," and rang up the sale.

One of the summer workers showed up for her shift which started at noon. As it turned out, Hildee didn't get to eat any of the pizza because there was an unusual lunch rush and she had to help the young worker cook and serve. After lunch, Hildee and Nate said they'd hold down the fort while Len took Janice and Mike on a tour of the area. They returned around four-thirty to find Nate and Hildee sitting on the porch.

Len was first out of the truck and said, "I can see you two are workin' hard." As Len went into the store, Hildee said, "Uh huh," knowing her father couldn't help himself and was going to look to see what the total sales receipts were.

Janice and Mike took seats beside Nate and Hildee.

Hildee asked, "Did you like what ya saw?"

Janice replied, "Uh huh."

Len came out of the store, "Boy, ya sho nuff had a passel of folks."

Hildee said, "Crazy busy. All those folks checkin' in early were comin' all afternoon to buy what they forgot to bring."

Len asked, "What about the dump cans?"

Hildee looked at her pa, "Nate was good enough to go 'round and empty them after the lunch rush. They should be good 'til mornin', but Charlie comes on at eight so he can check again before Susie leaves. Nate also had to bring up another pickup of firewood as we sold out by one-thirty. We'll probably need another load brought down in the mornin', pa."

"Ok," Len said.

Mike asked, "How come you have a worker come so late?"

"With hundreds of people a stayin' here, we have an all-night worker to make sure the toilet and shower houses is in good shape and sort a keep an eye on things. The two young fellas that work twelve hour shifts every other night mainly camp out at the gate house most of the time. They does make regular like trips 'round after midnight in an electric golf cart. They call me if there's a problem. The gate closes at nine and only registered guests can come in then."

Mike replied, "I see."

Hildee said, "We seldom have trouble as this is a family campground and it's known in these parts that pa don't tolerate no nonsense."

Marilee drove up to the store and parked. She got out and waved as she walked toward the store. She came up on the porch and said, "Hey," then bent over and kissed Len on the cheek before taking a seat.

Len informed them, "Marilee is going to hep me hold down the fort tomorrow, but we are going to the dance tomorrow evenin'. I put on an extra worker."

Hildee asked, "Jess?"

Her father replied, "I reckon." Hildee said, "Good choice. Ya put her in charge?"

"Yup."

Hildee added, "Even better." Hildee turned to Marilee, "She's our most mature worker; bin with us for years. Her husband is a seasonal worker also, so this suits her. She could run the place more if pa weren't so pig-headed."

Len looked at Marilee, "Well, now I have reason not to work the fields day 'n night. I reckon Jess will just have to boss the crew fer me so's I can go courtin'."

Marilee agreed, "Good," and smiled.

Len asked, "You goin' to the dance, Nate?"

"I'm waiting for Hildee to tell me."

Janice laughed, "You are learning son."

Hildee smiled while trying to keep from laughing and said, "We wouldn't miss it."

Mike turned to his wife, "They are practicing up for being married," then looked at Janice and asked, "We going?"

"Uh huh."

Len added, "Ben and Betsy are bringin' Billie and his gal and meetin' us there."

Hildee looked at Janice, "It's jeans; western dress."

Len looked at Marilee and asked, "How about we take Mike and Janice out for dinner? It's Hildee and Nate's day to watch the store."

Janice said, "Sure," and Mike just nodded dutifully with a smile.

The foursome left and Nate and Hildee stayed sitting on the porch.

Nate asked, "Think we'll get slammed again at supper?"

"Naw. The campers will be set up and anxious to do their first grillin'. Tomorrow will be busy with folks pickin' up stuff they forgot to bring and we'll be steady at the grill around meal times for the couples who like to come to socialize."

Hildee was right and it was a quiet evening. The summer worker handled the check-ins. They restocked the coolers and shelves, but spent most of the evening on the store porch as the student workers went about the routine work. When the store closed, Nate walked Hildee up to the house. Hildee tried to go in but the knob wouldn't turn.

"I think pa locked the house and he still hasn't give me a key. Let's try the back."

The back door was locked as well. The couple went back out front and sat on the porch. Nate put his arm around Hildee and she put her head

116

on his shoulder.

Nate offered, "This is the life. I suppose as we have tomorrow off, I'll get up early and write a sermon. What about I pick you up around eleven and we go to the diner for lunch and then see if we can make arrangements for the wedding reception and wrangle up a pastor to hitch us?"

"Sounds romantic like."

They sat there quietly and they both drifted into sleep. They were both sitting there asleep when Len came up on the porch with Mike and Janice.

Len woke them asking, "How come you two aren't inside?"

Hildee opened her eyes and shrugged then said, "My pa don't see fit to give me a key to his house so's I expect I'll have to git married so's to have my own key to my own place." She looked at Nate, "I think I kin use my charms as a new bride to wrangle a little key." She smiled.

Len was looking at her with a stunned look. Nate was now awake and said, "The dowry is now two horses and four sheep."

Len was still stunned and without thinking asked, "How come?"

Nate smiled and said with emphasis, "It's because I didn't realize how badly you wanted rid of her so there's got to be a reason and it must be bad because you make her sleep on the porch."

Hildee started laughing and Len said dramatically, "It ain't funny!"

Marilee started by trying not to laugh, but, when Mike and Janice started, she couldn't help herself. Len went to the door and fished for his keys in his pocket and opened the front door and went inside. The rest of them followed Len inside and to the kitchen, where everyone but Len sat down at the table.

Len said, "I'll get coffee a brewin'. It'll be a bit."

Nate teased, "Good. I was getting a little chilly outside."

Len said in a low voice almost pleading, "Enough already." He started the coffee and came to the table.

Janice asked, "When you and Marilee get hitched are you going to give her a key?"

Marilee smiled and Len turned beet red then turned to Hildee and said, "Daughter, I am truly sorry about razzin' ya about marryin' Nate before he asked ya."

Hildee smiled, "All's forgiven, Pa; it worked out. When ya goin' to ask Marilee?"

Len sighed, "So much fer forgiveness."

117

Hildee replied, "Oh, I forgive ya, but I'm not lettin' ya off in the hook. I kinda like the idea of havin' not one ma but two."

Marilee spoke, "Hildee, I think you should give your pa some space."

Hildee looked at Marilee, "Don't worry. He ain't goin' to get scared off. He's obvious got a yearnin' for ya and everybody sees it'd be a good thing for ya both. It's just that pa is a little slow gettin' things done without someone lookin' over his shoulder and he ain't gettin' no younger."

Len sighed deeply, "I resemble that ree-mark." Everyone was exchanging glances and Len got up and went outside onto the back deck. Marilee said, "I think he's upset. I'd better go see," and she followed him out.

Hildee said, "The coffee is done," and got up and got mugs out of the cupboard.

They had no sooner all got their coffee than Len came back holding hands with Marilee. Len took a seat and Marilee went and got coffee for her and Len.

Len said, "I reckon we should all go to dinner together before the dance tomorra. What say y'all?"

Mike remarked, "Sounds good."

Nate jumped in, "It'll be fun."

Len said, "When I finish this coffee, I'd best see Marilee to her ride."

Janice turned to Nate and asked, "What do you and Hildee have planned for tomorrow?"

"I'm taking her out for lunch then we are going to the VFW and see about a reception, then arrange for someone to marry us here; that last is just a phone call."

Your father and I can rest up then so we can keep up to you and Hildee tomorrow evening."

Marilee s finished her coffee, "I think it's time to head home."

Len said, "I'll walk you out," and with that the couple left to walk through the woods down to the store where Marilee's car was still parked. Once they were out of the house, Janice looked at Hildee.

"How long before he pops the question?"

Hildee shrugged, "Pa's been thinkin' on it so it won't be long. Maybe a day or two but no longer than a week."

Mike asked, "Kind of quick isn't it?"

Hildee replied, "Nah. Pa has known Marilee all his life. They probably

118

woulda got hitched if ma hadn't come along. Now Nate and me is quick, but I ain't complainin'." She smiled at Nate, who added with a huge smile, "Me, either."

Janice got up from the table, "Well I'm turning in. You coming dear?" Mike got up, said, "Good night," and followed Janice upstairs.

Hildee noted, "Your ma and pa are cute; like young uns a courtin' and they bin married a long time."

Nate agreed, "Yes. I think it's great."

Hildee asked, "You hangin' 'round so's not to embarrass pa and Marilee before ya go back?"

"Uh huh."

"I never thought about them kissin' on one another."

"I'm a realist. Your pa and Marilee aren't old, just older than us."

Hildee smiled, "Well, ain't you the romantic."

Nate smiled, "You said you wanted two mothers, so I have to do my part. Tonight that means giving the other lovebirds some time, seeing as my dear one tormented her pa greatly."

Hildee sighed, "I like that. The other lovebirds."

Nate shrugged. They sat talking for almost fifteen minutes before Len showed up.

"You were gone a long time, pa," and looked at Nate then added, "I guess Marilee must be a good kisser."

"Alright, Hildee, enough already. I don't want ya talkin' about your future step-ma that a way."

"Congratulations," Nate said.

Hildee was sitting with her mouth open and a shocked look on her face. Len looked at his daughter and said, "It were the only way to git ya to stop tormentin' yar poor ole pa."

Hildee gave her father a big smile and said, "Well, first of all ya ain't that old and, second of all, them that gives it better be able to take it."

She got up and gave her pa a big hug then pulled out her cell phone and called Marilee's number. Len refilled his coffee cup and did the same for Nate and they both sat eavesdropping on Hildee's call.

"Marilee, it's awesome you and pa gettin' hitched. We have so much to talk about. No, I didn't know he'd gotten a ring. Pa usually is pretty good at keepin' secrets." There was a pause and Hildee said, "We'll just have to coordinate the honeymoons. I'm pretty sure I can talk Nate into hepin' me with the campgrounds, 'sides, Jess can do more. Ok then, tomorra. Bye."

Hildee looked at the two men, "You fellers done made two women folk very happy. I have to tell Janice."

Hildee left the room and Len said, "And two women folk made us very happy."

"Uh huh. You decided when?"

"Nope."

They sipped on their coffee silently each lost for a moment in their thoughts. Hildee came back into the room and she was blushing. Nate asked, "What?"

Hildee said as she took a seat next to Nate, "Well, it didn't sound like I should disturb your ma and pa. Sounds like your folks are doin' what only married folks should and your ma ain't bein' none too quiet. I think she's bein' carried away."

Len smiled, "Then I'd better wait before goin' up or it may give me ideas and I don't want to do nothin' to offend Marilee afore we's hitched."

"Well, you know what it's like and I don't. All them sounds upstairs has set me to wonderin' though."

Len and Nate looked at her. Hildee realized what she had said in front of the men and started to blush then put her face in her hands on the table.

She says, "I don't believe I just said that."

Len teased, "Just don't wonder too hard."

Hildee still had her face in her hands and said, "Oh pa, please leave it be. I'm embarrassed enough." Nate put his hand on Hildee's back and said, "No need to be embarrassed. Those feelings are natural. It helps to bond husband and wife together."

Hildee sighed, "I think I'd prefer to be a June bride."

Nate said, "Alright." Hildee took her head out of her hands and looked at Nate.

"Hildee, you are a great temptation for me and I've had to do some powerful praying because of how you affect me. I even told your pa so he could help me." Hildee looked at her father who just nodded.

"Really?"

Len said, "Yup."

Nate added, "I don't think you realize just how sexy you are, love."

Hildee broke out in a broad smile and said, "Well, isn't that just the nicest thing to say." Without thinking, she put her hands on Nate's cheeks and leaned over and kissed him. It was intense.

Len said, "It'd better be June or I'll have to clean my shotgun."

Both Nate and Hildee had to stop the kiss because they started laughing.

"You two are gettin' too bold kissin' on each other and it's got me ta worryin'."

Hildee teased, "And I suppose you don't kiss on Marilee?"

Len started to laugh and it was contagious. They didn't hear Janice come into the room. She had on a housecoat and was barefoot. She went to the counter and got a coffee before coming to sit with them. She seemed to have a certain glow.

Hildee told her, "We are in a joyful mood. Marilee and pa are gettin' hitched."

Janice said, "Congratulations, Len."

He smiled, "Thank you."

Janice continued, "Len, Mike and I would like to get a seasonal site. We are going to get an RV and come here often. Mike realized just how much he needs to get away from the stress of business. It has a good effect on him."

Len smiled and looked at Hildee, who started to blush.

Janice said, "What?"

Hildee shook her head no.

Nate explained, "Hildee started upstairs to tell you, but decided it was not a good time."

Janice smiled and said to Hildee, "Thank you for your good judgment."

Hildee again had a shocked look on her face. Len said, "Hildee close your mouth. It ain't ladylike."

Hildee giggled and Janice started to laugh lightly. Nate did not resist the temptation, "Hildee is very curious and so we are moving the wedding up to June."

Janice now started laughing hard and through the laughter said, "Oh, Hildee!"

Hildee blurted out, "Well, I don't want to miss the good stuff."

Now Janice was doubled over in laughter and her pa and Nate weren't far behind. Hildee said, "What?" That little remark just prolonged the laughter. It was contagious so Hildee found she was laughing, too.

When they calmed down, Len announced, "Well, I'm tired and I'm turnin' in." He went upstairs.

Janice asked, "You really going to move the wedding up?"

"Yes, mother. We are too much of a temptation for each other."

Hildee agreed, "Ain't that the truth."

Nate got up and leaned over and kissed Hildee, who sighed.

Janice said, "Good night, son."

"Good night, mother."

Nate touched Hildee's shoulder and she was looking into his eyes as he said, "Good night, love." He left going out the back door. Hildee got up and locked it after him.

Janice asked Hildee, "How bad?"

"So bad he torments me in my dreams. Most times, I have trouble sleepin'. I have these hot feelings I ain't never had before."

"Been there. It'll turn to joy once you are in the marriage bed."

"Will it hurt at first?"

Hildee and Janice sat up talking for a long time.

Nate was happy as he returned to his camper. He found he could not sleep because of thoughts of Hildee. He stayed up until well after two in the morning writing a sermon before he could go to sleep. He woke to the sounds of children and smiled.

Nate rolled out of bed and looked at the clock. It was after nine so he made the bed and got ready to face the day. He was just getting out of the shower when the knocking on his door started. Wrapping a large towel around his lower body, he went to the door, "Who is it?"

His mother answered, "It's me." Without thinking he opened the door to find Janice was there, with Hildee and Marilee.

"Sorry, mom. I thought you were alone."

Hildee said, "You are lookin' good, Nate." Nate shook his head, "Come on in. Coffee's on. I'll go get dressed."

Nate went back to his bedroom and closed the door and put his clothes on. He found the women sitting in the small living area drinking coffee. He went to where Hildee was sitting and leaned over and kissed her, "Good morning, love."

Nate then went and hugged his mother and said, "Good morning, mother."

122

She smiled.

Nate then went and kissed Marilee on the cheek, "Good morning, mother-in-law to be."

The three women were smiling.

Janice said, "There's been a small change in plans. We decided but Hildee wanted to talk to you about it."

Nate went to the cupboard and took a mug then poured coffee as he asked, "So what's up."

Janice started off, "There's only one date open in June for a reception at the VFW and that only because they had a cold feet cancellation."

Marilee was smiling broadly, "Len and I reserved it. We plan on getting' hitched then. I always wanted to be a June bride."

"I see."

Janice said, "They want you to marry them."

Nate said as he took a seat with his coffee, "No problem. They just need to get a license."

Hildee said with a broad smile, "But I reckoned to be a June bride and you promised, Nate."

"Let me guess. Double wedding, shared reception. I do the ceremony for Len and Marilee, but who marries Hildee and me?"

Marilee looked at Janice, "Your boy is quick."

Hildee told him, "Reverend Rick from Chesterville will come down and hitch us on the Saturday. He was booked but it was for the same cold feet wedding."

Nate said with a smile, "When's Len going to bring me the dowry because I'm not taking an I.O.U."

Hildee jumped up, rushed over and sat in Nate's lap and gave him a big kiss. Nate almost spilled his coffee.

Nate whispered in Hildee's ear, "You'd better get up because you're having an effect on me."

Hildee smiled and whispered, "You owe me," then got up and went back to her chair.

"Well, that's all settled," Nate said. "So what's the plan?"

Marilee answered, "Well today, we are going to steal Hildee away and we're goin' shoppin' for wedding clothes. Don't worry, we'll be back in time for dinner and dancing."

"Good. I'm looking forward to a night on the town. I even stayed up half the night preparing the sermon for Sunday."

Janice chuckled, "Well, we finished his coffee so we'd better get moving because we have a lot to do."

The women all got up and Nate walked out with them to their vehicle. He hugged them all and watched them as they drove away. Nate thought how lucky he was to have these women in his life.

Nate locked his trailer and walked up to the store where he found Len and Mike sitting in chairs on the store porch.

Len said, "Mornin'," and Mike nodded.

"I just had a tornado blow through my place."

"They are sho nuff wound up," Len noted.

Mike told his son, "Your mother and I are taking a place here. Len has agreed to let us turn one of the campsites into another year round site but we'll need to do the electrical meter work. Will you help me with that?"

Nate took a seat, "Sure, dad. It won't take long with the two of us working on it."

"It seems, Nate, our lives aren't our own anymore," Len conceded.

"Great, isn't it?"

"Uh huh."

Mike continued, "Your mother and I are going shopping for an RV when we get back. We also want one of those carport structures like you have."

Nate asked, "Where you going to be?"

Mike answered, "Two sites up from you. That too close?"

"No problem. Mom and Hildee get along real well."

"Hildee's already like the daughter we never had."

Len asked, "What about them other daughters-in-law?"

Mike said, "At best, they tolerate Janice, though I don't understand why they don't take to her. She's pretty much an open book. I think those women are afraid of her because she sees through their pretention."

Len said, "Ain't none of that with Hildee."

"There you have the difference."

Len said, "I see. What ya say I have Susie make us some sandwiches?"

The men spent a pleasant afternoon on the store porch talking. Every once in a while Len would go inside to help out when it got busy. Around four, the men left to get ready for the night on the town and Len left to go to town on an errand.

Sometime later, Nate was sitting in a lawn chair waiting when Janice and Mike pulled up in their crew cab pickup with Hildee. Nate climbed in next to Hildee, "Hi." He leaned over and kissed Hildee and she smiled.

Janice said, "We decided to go to the steakhouse over in Chesterville so Betsy can be away from the diner."

Nate asked, "How was your shopping trip?"

Hildee told him, "I found an outfit right off, but Marilee's took some lookin."

Janice agreed, "We found outfits for the wedding, too. It was a very successful trip." The women told the men about their shopping trip and the plans for the wedding. The men listened dutifully and smiled at their women's enthusiasm.

Ben, Betsy, Len, and Marilee were already there and seated when Nate and his group showed up. After exchanging greetings, they gave the waiter their drink orders. It was a pleasant meal and they left around six-thirty.

Nate, Hildee, Len, and Marilee arrived at the fairgrounds just before the dance was to start. Ben came a few minutes late with Betsy as they had to pick up Billie and his date. Ben introduced Billie and his date, Jessica, to Nate's parents and their party found a place to sit. The group left their jackets and sweaters on the chairs and went out to the dance floor.

The music started and so did the dancing. It was a fun time and they were all happy but good things sometimes get interrupted. The band took their mid-dance break and the little party went back to their seats to find Cal Cartwell and two of his friends and two women at their table.

Len demanded, "What did you do with our jackets, Cal?"

Cal smiled, "What jackets, old man?"

Nate could tell that Len was about to lose it and stepped in front of Len and looked him in the eye, "Take a deep breath, Len, then go get a couple of deputies. Our clothes have been stolen." Len nodded and motioned to Marilee and they left to find deputies.

Nate heard a gasp and turned to find one of Cal's friends had grabbed Hildee's left wrist and was trying to twist it. The man had made a tactical mistake. Hildee punched him in the nose and he screamed as blood went everywhere. He let go of Hildee.

Hildee quizzed him, "Didn't yer ma teach ya not to lay hands on a woman?"

Cal was getting up and Nate moved quickly to cover Hildee's back.

125

Cal stopped in his tracks. Two deputies came to the table.

One asked, "What happened here?"

Nate explained, "Someone stole our jackets, this group took our table, and the fellow with the bloody nose was stupid enough to grab Hildee."

Hildee advised them, "He won't be grabbin' at me no more."

One deputy looked at Cal, "Where are their things?"

Cal smiled, "What things?"

A man at the next table said, "The feller with the bloodied nose put them under a table a few down."

Cal glared at the man who stood up. He was a giant of a man and said, "Anytime, anywhere Cal. You name it."

The deputy said, "You'd better leave, Cal, or I'm gonna take ya in. As it is, your friend is bein' arrested for assault on Hildee."

Cal choked out, "It ain't fair. He's the one bleedin' all over."

The deputy replied, "And it's his own fault. Now git or I'll arrest ya, too."

Cal and his friend and the two women left. Nate went and retrieved their jackets and brought them back to the table.

Len remarked, "There's peckerwoods wherever you go."

Hildee scolded, "Pa!"

Len spoke, "I'm sorry ladies but they is, well you know." Janice broke the tension when she smiled, her hands on her hips and said half laughing, "Yes, I know, so you don't have to say it again."

Len broke into a smile and they all sat down.

Nate suggested, "Hildee and I will go get beverages. Who wants what?"

The rest of the dance was enjoyable and the group had fun. The dance ended at midnight and Nate, Hildee, Mike and Janice were walking to the truck when Cal and another man came out from behind a truck and stood between them and Mike's truck.

Nate murmered, "Dad, take the ladies inside."

Hildee disagreed, "I'm hepin."

Mike warned, "Son, try not to hurt them too much."

"I'm going to try and not hurt them at all."

Mike turned to Hildee, "Please, Hildee, Nate's coverin' our retreat and we need to call 911." Hildee nodded and the three of them headed back to the building. Hildee asked, "Ya sure he can handle 'em?"

Mike assured her, "There's only two of them."

Hildee looked over her shoulder to see Nate following them at a distance keeping an eye on Cal and his friend, who seemed to be closing the distance to Nate.

Mike and the two women met two deputies at the door and Mike said, "Same fellows that were causing trouble before seem to be looking for more trouble," and pointed.

They watched as Cal and his friend suddenly charged Nate. The deputies set out on the run and Mike took the ladies inside. A moment later, Nate came inside.

Hildee asked, "What happened?"

"I escaped and the deputies set out after Cal and his friend." Hildee looked at Nate and cocked her head.

Mike contended, "I'm afraid that sooner or later that one is going to catch up to you and then he'll wish he hadn't."

Nate shrugged, "I'll deal with it, if it comes to that."

Mike announced, "Well, let's head back." The four of them walked back to the truck and drove off. Hildee looked at Nate, "You really try to avoid trouble, don't ya?"

"Yes. I'm afraid, though, that Cal is the typical bully and he's going to interpret my not wanting to fight with fear or inability."

Mike jumped in, "That's what's going to get him hurt."

Nate sighed, "I'm afraid so. I'd rather it wasn't me that did the hurting."

Hildee questioned him, "I don't get it. You disarm a guy with a gun stuck in your face during a robbery but you run from an unarmed man?"

"I can't outrun a bullet, but I can avoid Cal. Your father was also at risk because of the weapon."

Hildee paused a moment then said, "Now I think I understand."

"There are always two extreme possibilities in a fight; you get killed or you kill. Neither are desirable, so avoidance is the best policy."

Janice changed the subject, "I had a good time tonight. We'll have to do it whenever we are staying over."

Mike added, "I'd like that."

It didn't take long to get back to Len's place. Len was gone but this time Hildee pulled out a key and smiled. She opened the door and they went in.

Hildee asked, "Anybody want coffee?"

Janice said, "No, thanks. I'm for bed," and grabbed Mike's hand and he smiled. They went upstairs.

Hildee looked at Nate, "You goin' to stay for a spell?"

"Sorry, love. I need to sack out. I have to preach in the morning."

Hildee put her arms around Nate's neck and kissed him passionately then said, "Now git, preacher man."

Nate turned to leave and Hildee slapped him on the butt and he jumped just a bit then chuckled.

He was walking through the trees when he sensed it. It was a small sound but out of place. Nate recognized the sound of a charging handle being worked. Suddenly he was back in combat mode. Nate slipped behind a tree just as the first shot rang out. The slug hit the tree and he slipped low and, following the shadows, moved to better cover. Nate knew the shooter was probably using a twenty-two caliber from the sound. The shooter fired a few more rounds wildly in Nate's direction. He could tell the shooter was undisciplined. Nate listened to the sound of the shooter leaving through the woods.

Nate decided there was no reason to risk closely pursuing an armed opponent who was withdrawing. Nate kept his distance following the shooter. He was too far to make out anything but that the shooter left in a pickup. Nate heard sirens and walked to the lane where the deputies were getting out of their cars.

Nate walked over to them and one asked, "What's goin' on?"

"I think someone tried to kill me. The shooter was undisciplined and using a twenty-two rifle."

Hildee came running out of the house and jumped into Nate's arms, "Oh, thank God yar ok." Janice, Mike and Len were not far behind.

Nate said, "I suggest we go inside," and looked at the deputy who nodded. Inside Janice said, "I'll put some coffee on."

Janice hurried back to hear Nate give a statement to the deputy about what had happened.

The deputy asked, "Do you have any idea who might do this?"

Nate sighed, "Well, there's Terry if he's out of jail and that Cal fellow that caused trouble at the dance."

Len added, "Cal Cartwell," paused for a moment then added, "And them fellers who tried to rob me, too."

Nate nodded, "If they made bail or have friends, maybe."

The deputy said, "I reckon they are all three possibilities. We'll look into it. Another deputy is going to stay to secure the crime scene until daybreak."

Len stated, "I need to go to the store. Campers will be wonderin' what's a goin' on." The deputy looked at Len, who said, "I'll drive around."

The deputy said, "Good."

Len added, "Our night security might have seen somethin' so's I reckon someone should talk to him."

The deputy nodded, "Somebody will go talk to him."

Len looked at Nate, "You otta stay here tonight." Nate nodded agreement.

Len left and Nate, Mike, Janice, and Hildee went into the kitchen.

Hildee declared, "Well, one thing fer sure, life isn't boring with Nate around."

Nate reasoned, "God wants me here, but apparently Satan has other ideas about my presence."

Hildee looked at Janice, "If'in I wasn't so much in love with 'im, I might have second thoughts."

Janice smiled, looked at Mike and said, "I understand." Mike smiled back at his wife.

It was after two o'clock when Len got back and they all sacked out. Nate slept on the downstairs sofa. Before drifting off, Nate decided he'd better keep his concealed carry weapon with him all the time.

Chapter 7

Nate woke early but a little groggy. He got up and tidied up. He quietly slipped out of the house and walked the long way around back to the campground. He was almost back at his camper when his cell went off.

Nate opened the phone to, "Where are you?"

Nate smiled to himself then said, "Good morning, love. I'm almost at my camper. I have to get cleaned up for church."

Hildee chuckled, "Well, make it hurry up quick and come on back fer breakfast. I'm goin' ta cook."

Nate replied, "I'll be there shortly."

Twenty-five minutes later, Nate was pulling up in his van at Len's house. Marilee's car was already there. Nate went inside and found the group in the kitchen.

Marilee saw him first, "Good mornin', Nate."

Nate said, "Hi everybody," then went and kissed Hildee's neck from behind as she was standing watching the stove. He said, "Good morning, love."

Hildee turned beet red but said nothing; she just sighed. Nate then went and kissed his mother on the cheek and Marilee as well.

Marilee seemed surprised so Nate explained, "You are about to be my mother-in-law."

Marilee smiled and said, "Uh huh. This is goin' to take some gettin' used to, but I will." She looked at Len, who sat back and smiled broadly.

Marilee asked, "You preaching in sandals and shorts, Nate?"

"Yes. We have three baptisms this morning and I can go in the river in this."

Hildee still had her back to the group and Nate was looking at her and said without thinking, "She looks as good from the back as from the front." Everyone stopped and looked at Nate with shocked looks. Nate shrugged and said sheepishly, "I didn't mean for that to be a spoken thought."

Hildee said, "Nate, you are embarrassin' me somethin' fearful," and didn't turn around but continued to tend the stove. Nate could tell she was blushing again.

"Sorry, love," then looked at Len and said, "I'm thinkin' I'll take the I.O.U. for the dowry."

Len smiled, "I knew you'd cave."

Janice couldn't help it but started laughing. That set everyone off.

Nate said, "I just hate to see Hildee blushing all the time."

Hildee blurted, "It's your ma's fault and all them sounds she and your pa makes comin' from my bedroom."

Janice had been in the middle of a sip and choked on it. Mike looked at Len and shrugged, "We're on vacation and we are just enjoying ourselves." Janice turned a deep shade of red.

Len looked at Marilee, "I hope to be doin' the same soon." For the first time, Marilee went red and Len's smile broadened.

Marilee declared, "You men had best start behavin' and stop embarrassin' your good Christian women folk so."

Len demurred, "Yes, dear," and that started laughter again because of the way he'd said it.

Hildee announced, "Foods ready," and started bringing the food on platters to the table. She hurried back, opened the oven, took out hot biscuits and quickly brought them in a basket to the table. It was a feast of sausage, bacon, scrambled eggs, biscuits and gravy, along with home fries.

Len said the blessing and the eating started. "One thing Hildee got from her ma is cookin'."

Mike finished a bite and said, "The girl sure can cook."

Nate looked at Hildee longingly and said, "Yup."

Hildee correctly thought he didn't mean food and blushed again. She sighed deeply and dug in.

The breakfast conversation turned to the events of last night.

Marilee asked, "What did ya tell the campers 'bout the shooting Len?"

"The truth. Some nitwit was shooting in the woods and the sheriff's department was investigatin' who was the idiot."

Mike asked, "Do you think it will affect the church attendance?"

Nate shrugged, "Only God knows."

When they finished, Janice and Marilee helped Hildee clean up so they would all get to church on time. They arrived at the pavilion almost an hour early and went to setting up. The summer staff had arranged the tables and brought extra seating. Since it was a nice day, they decided to use the flatbed truck for a stage and ran the necessary extension cords.

Shocky and Jean showed up a half hour before service and were

131

introduced to Nate's parents. The ladies took seats to talk while Shocky set up his bass amp. Five minutes after Shocky arrived, Tiny showed up. The worship group did a sound test and satisfied with it went to socialize.

The place was swamped because the campground was full and more folks from the surrounding area showed up. All the picnic tables were occupied and there were people on truck tailgates, blankets, and folding lawn chairs.

At the appointed time, Len got up and welcomed everybody and announced there would be baptisms at the river. He also announced the upcoming weddings then said the introductory prayer. The worship group then started the playing and singing. Many joined in and the service became a joyful praise event that had most people going with the music.

The group did a couple of more songs than usual and then Nate started preaching. It was a good but short message about people's need for salvation. There was an altar call and several came forward for prayer. Two responded to the call to salvation. Hildee and Janice helped record the people's names to arrange appointments for them to meet with Nate.

Nate made a call for volunteers to help establish a Sunday school and asked anyone interested to stay after service.

There were two more praise songs then they moved to the beach for the baptisms. Most everyone went to the river. It was a touching time and many had tears in their eyes. After the baptisms, everyone went back and they sang two more songs before the service ended. It had all taken just a little over an hour and a quarter.

Few left and people started to socialize. Out came the picnic lunches and Len left with Marilee to check the store and see that the summer staff had started work. Many of the campers drifted away to their campsites but some stayed.

It turned out they had five volunteers who were willing to teach Sunday school and several who volunteered to help with the smaller children. Hildee and Janice took their names. Nate was talking to people who wanted pastoring of some sort or another. He took their names and numbers and promised to contact them. In the meantime, Tiny and Shocky had broken down the equipment and stored it away.

Finally, Nate had a chance to breathe and Sheriff Pilcher came to him, "Good message, preacher."

Nate offered his hand, "Hello, Sheriff."

Cory said, "Nate, this is my wife, Myra."

Nate asked, "Are you a hugger, Myra?"

She smiled and opened her arms and Nate gave her a hug saying, "I'm so happy you came."

Myra said, "I'm hearin' good things about yar services here and jist had to come see for meself. We've been goin' to Chesterville and it's such a long drive."

Cory asked, "What are you goin' to do when there's bad weather?"

Nate shrugged, "We haven't figured that out yet, but I expect God will lead us to a solution. We can only get about a hundred in the pavilion and I think we had considerably more than that this morning. I guess we'll go to planning and praying."

Cory said, "Well, we made our minds to come back next Sunday."

Nate smiled and said, "Good. I'll look forward to seeing you."

Myra put in, "The weddin' announcement about you and Hildee I 'spected based on the local grapevine, but Len and Marilee was a surprise. I've been wonderin' for years if them two would get back together."

Nate smiled and said, "Well, now you know."

Myra nodded, "See ya, preacher," and led her husband away.

Nate couldn't find his guitar and then realized one of his friends must have put it away; at least, he hoped they had. Nate walked to the store carryin' his Bible. He arrived to find the family sitting at a table eating sandwiches. Hildee was sitting behind the counter and Nate went and joined her.

"You know who packed up my guitar?"

"Pa's got it. You should be more careful like with it. Pa said it was a really expensive classic."

Nate nodded, "I had other things on my mind."

Hildee smiled, "I know."

Len came over, "You two otta come join the talkin'."

They got up and went to join the others and pulled up two chairs from another table.

Ben announced, "We got nuff folks comin' we needs to be thinkin' 'bout a place for when the weather's bad."

Nate remarked, "We could just rent the room at the fairgrounds where they hold the dances."

Len agreed, "Great idea. We could easy cover the hundred dollar daily rental."

Ben shared, "We could book it startin' after Labor Day. We could start a regular like church membership roll. I'll take care of makin' arrangements Tuesday, if it's agreeable."

Nate offered, "I think we should invite the church to the weddings and have a bring your own picnic lunch afterwards. Then we could have the reception for the wedding party at the VFW."

Mike asked, "Why not have it all here and invite your VFW friends. We could rent a big tent and serve BBQ."

"That's not a bad idea 'cept a lot of campers will come," Len said.

Mike continued, "You can serve a lot of people BBQ and baked beans for not a lot of money. Janice and I will chip in."

Ben added, "I'll talk to the fellers at the VFW and tell them we have too many people comin' to have it there but we'll make a good donation if'in they hep us with the BBQ. The fellas at the VFW got a big portable smoker."

Janice spoke up, "Doesn't Hildee get to have a say in her own wedding plans?"

"Janice is right," Len declared, then looked at his daughter and added, "Sorry, Hildee."

Hildee smiled, "I don't care where it happens as long as me and Nate gits hitched."

Ben said, "I can ask Shocky if his band will play at the reception. We can have dancin' in the pavilion."

The little party spent an hour planning and then everyone started drifting away. Nate's parents got ready to leave.

Mike came to Nate, "We're real proud of you son. You are a good preacher and that was the best service we've been to, ever."

"You belong here," Janice concluded.

Hildee smiled, "I'm glad to hear ya say thet."

Janice smiled back and nodded. They all shared hugs and then Janice and Mike went back to the house.

Nate and Hildee went to sit on the porch. Hildee sat in the swinging love seat and Nate sat beside her. She lifted his arm around her shoulders.

She sighed, "Life will be simple and we'll face it together. With God's help, we'll be all right. How many little ones you expectin' we'll have?"

Nate said, "I suppose that's in God's hands."

"I reckon that's the right answer. I always thought I'd have a passel of kids when the time came."

Nate just nodded.

Hildee asked, "How old are ya, Nate?"

"I'm twenty-eight."

"I just turned twenty-one."

"That's about what I figured. Dad asked if you were too young for me and I told him you were just the right age."

"That's only about half the difference in age between Betsy and Ben."

Nate just nodded.

Hildee asked, "How long were you in the military and what did you do?"

Nate sighed, "I was in for six years. They trained me to kill people and that's all I want to say about that, please. In my spare time, I studied for my bachelor's degree."

Hildee asked, "How did you get into building trades?"

"I graduated high school at seventeen and apprenticed with my father and brothers and went to school at night. I was the only unmarried one so after the 9-11 attack I started to get the patriotic itch and finally signed up, with my father's blessing. I got out after two tours in the Mideast. By then, I'd almost finished my degree on the internet. I went to school full-time for six months when I got out. I just graduated before I came here."

Hildee sat thinking and said nothing more.

Shocky pulled up in his car with Jean. They got out and approached Nate and Hildee. Shocky greeted them, "Hi, Nate, Hildee." Hildee got up and hugged Jean.

Shocky said, "Jean and I wanted to talk to ya 'bout a day ta git hitched. We've been goin' over to Chesterville to church until ya came 'round. We talked to Pastor Rick over there and I told him I was on the praise team here and we would be joining here. He said he'd vouch for us. He also said a church was needed here and he blessed our work."

Shocky handed Pastor Rick's business card to Nate then said, "We'd like to talk to you about a personal matter."

Hildee offered, "I'll skedaddle," and started to get up.

Jean pleaded, "You can stay, Hildee. Please!" The pleading look caused Hildee to sit down and she looked at her friend and smiled.

"We want to get married and very soon," Shocky began.

Jean agreed, "We almost lost control the other night and came close to doin' what we hadn't ought to until we're married."

Shocky continued, "It's time we got hitched. The temptation is getting too strong."

Jean was starting to tear up.

Hildee looked at Jean and took her hand, "I understand. We are movin' up our weddin' for the same reason. We take 'cautions to make sure we ain't together alone much."

"Really?" Shocky asked.

"Yup," Nate said. "The temptation is real."

Jean started crying lightly, "We was afraid you wouldn't understand, preacher."

Nate empathized with them, "What God uses to bind husband and wife, Satan uses to try to cause us to sin and to corrupt the body before marriage. You did the right thing in resisting though."

Shocky concluded, "We talked to Jean's parents. We aren't going to be together at night until after we are married unless we are chaperoned. They are supportive and we'd like to do it next Saturday. Just a small wedding, a few friends and family. We were hoping to do it here at the pavilion. It's now our church."

Nate nodded and Hildee stood up, "I'll go clear it with pa," then went inside.

Shocky told him, "We expect maybe a couple of dozen at the wedding."

"Well, having it here may result in a lot more."

"Well, I guess the more witnesses the better," Jean agreed.

Shocky added, "We are not having a reception. We'll be leaving directly on our honeymoon. That ok?"

"There's no requirement for a reception."

Jean sighed, "You don't know how settlin' it is talkin' ta ya and Hildee."

Hildee came out, "Pa said it's ok. Nothin's booked for next Saturday."

"What's the rental fee?" Shocky asked Hildee.

Hildee answered, "You's church members so there ain't no fee."

Jean reported, "We'll be back in time for your new weddin' date the followin' Saturday."

"Good. Then it's all settled," Hildee smiled.

Shocky smiled and said, "Thanks, Nate."

"You're welcome."

The couple rose and so did Nate and Hildee. After hugs, the couple left.

Nate and Hildee sat down and Hildee noted, "Don't that beat all?"

Nate said, "Uh huh."

Hildee cuddled up to Nate, "Bein' a preacher's wife will have its rewards."

"True."

Nate thought and it will have its trials, too, but he knew Hildee realized that so didn't ruin the moment by giving the thought voice.

Hildee allowed, "I suppose it will also have its trials, too, but we'll have each other and God to see us through."

Nate said, "True," while thinking Hildee was already reading his mind.

Marilee came out and sat on the porch, "So Shocky and Jean are tyin' the knot next Saturday."

"Yup. Then we're up the next Saturday."

Marilee said, "I should be frettin' 'cause this is all happenin' so fast but I ain't.'

Hildee smiled and looked at Nate, "Me neither."

Len came outside and took a seat, "It must be somethin' in the water that's got folks in the marryin' mood."

Nate chuckled, "It isn't the water."

"I reckon' not," Len said, then turned to Hildee, "What's this I hear about you callin' Jess to cover for ya tomorrow?"

"Well, the preacher's future wife has to be there when he does official stuff, like give the message at the wreath layin' ceremony. Specially seein' he's the VFW chaplain."

"Good excuse for not workin'."

Hildee smiled at her father. "I reckoned so. Jess needs to get in practice to hep ya when me or Marilee ain't around. We got other work, too. Besides, ya need to spend time with Marilee and someday you'll have grandpa duty and ya all will need extra time off."

Len conceded, "I reckon you're right."

Hildee said tongue-in-cheek, "Nate and I won't abandon ya altogether, pa. We'll hep with the big stuff that requires skilled trades people and young strong bodies. Where's Mike and Janice?"

Len laughed, "Up at the house probably having some more enjoyment of the vacation type."

Hildee started to blush and Marilee laughed, "Girl, you sho nuff do blush easy."

Hildee answered, "I'm glad Nate and I are gettin' hitched, so I don't have to hear ya'll makin' them noises."

Marilee started to blush and Nate said, "Hildee, behave yourself."

Hildee smiled and said, "Yes, love."

Nate added, "Even if she did deserve it."

Len started laughing and that set Nate and Hildee to laughing.

Marilee insisted, "It ain't that funny," which set them to belly laughing. Hildee was laughing so hard she jumped up and said, "I'm goin' to pee my pants," and ran into the store to use the employee restroom.

Now Marilee was laughing and blurted, "That girl is fer sure somethin' else."

The student worker popped her head out of the store and looked strangely at the trio and for some reason that set them to laughing again. The young woman went back inside shakin' her head. She'd never seen Mr. Cole carry on like that before and didn't know what to make of it. If getting married did that to a person, she supposed marriage couldn't be a bad thing.

Hildee came back outside and sat next to Nate. They were all sitting quietly when Janice and Mike came walking hand-in-hand.

Mike asked, "We heard you laughing half way to the house. What's goin' on?"

Len smiled, "You just had to be here."

Mike handed Len a check, "That's for the seasonal rental. We'll be coming back next Thursday; hopefully with a camper. I'll put the meter pole in as soon as Nate can help me. That ok?"

"Uh huh."

They all sat there listening to the sounds of the campers and the laughter of children at the playground. They could hear the squeaking of the swings.

"I'll git one of the young uns to grease those," Len said.

Mike shared, "This is a nice change of pace. I can see why so many people come here."

"Yeah, it's a real good spot for workin' folks to git away."

Hildee changed the subject, "Nate never said. Do you have grandchildren, Janice?"

"Unfortunately not."

Mike added, "It seems our daughters-in-law want to put off having kids. They are all in their thirties now and they are going to find it harder if they have children now."

Hildee asked, "So, Nate's the baby of the family?"

Janice smiled, "Yes. You planning on making us grandparents anytime soon?"

Hildee said, "Nate and I talked 'bout it. We's leavin' it up to God."

Janice's smile was even wider, "I'm liking you more and more all the time, Hildee."

Nate looked at his mother, "You really want grandchildren and I didn't realize it. Is that part of the tension between you and your daughters-in-law?"

"I never consciously thought about it, but I suppose it might be part of it."

Len agreed, "Grandchildren would be nice."

"Yes, they would." Marilee said. "They'd round out the family."

Janice asked, "You not have children, Marilee?"

"No, not that I didn't want them. My husband, God rest his soul, couldn't father children. It was just one of them things. Now I'm too old so I'll have to settle for grandchildren and that will be a blessing."

Marilee smiled at Hildee.

Len injected, "I didn't know Marilee."

The group sat quietly enjoyin' the warm day and the noises of the campground for several minutes. A camper came by and said, "Hi, Len."

Len nodded, "Good to see ya again, Ted."

The man went into the store.

Mike said, "What say we go for a walk around the campground?"

They did just that, the couples walking hand-in-hand. They greeted people and stopped to have short chats, thoroughly enjoying the walk. It took them almost three hours to complete the circuit of the campground on foot. When they arrived back at the store, Len found things were running smoothly. The sales at the store had been steady but not hectic.

The group went inside and sat at one of the chrome tables. Len inspected the grill area, reviewed the register sales, and walked around the store.

He told Susie, "This is good and clean and restocked. Good job, Susie."

Susie smiled, "Thanks boss. Lynn hep'd."

Len looked at the high school student behind the register, "Good work, Lynn."

Lynn smiled and said, "Uh huh."

Len looked at the group, "Would y'all like subs?" Everyone indicated they would and Susie said, "I'll make 'em." Len smiled and nodded and went back to the table and pulled up a chair.

Hildee noted, "I told ya, pa. We have a good crew and ya could trust 'em more."

"Uh huh. Ya know, I think it's getting' to the point we should add some more campsites."

"Yup. I guess we should start plannin' out the sites. Ya thinkin' serviced sites, pa?"

"Ya. It seems more and more of the folks need services for these new campers."

Nate offered, "Hildee and I could help, especially with the plumbing and electrical."

"Ok. Thanks."

Hildee told them, "It's the clearing that's most work and we have a small tractor with a backhoe attachment we use to trench."

Mike asked, "How do you handle wastewater, Len?"

"Septic for the store and house. We got big holding tanks for the dump stations and a few trailers are hooked directly inta 'em. We pump 'em three times a week during season and take it ta the county treatment plant."

Marilee chided, "This ain't proper meal time talk."

"Sorry, hun. You're right."

Janice looked at Marilee, who smiled. She asked, "Don't it bother ya, Janice?"

Janice chuckled, "We do electric and plumbing, Marilee. This talk doesn't bother me because it's part of how we've made a living for decades."

Marilee said, "I see."

Susie brought the subs and asked, "What do y'all want to drink?" They all gave their orders and Susie brought the drinks. After eating, they all headed for the house and sat on the porch talking. It was a pleasant evening. About ten, Nate headed back to his camper to turn in.

Nate was up early, did his devotional, and decided to go for a run. He had gotten out of some of his habits since he came here and he decided he needed to get back into his old routine. During the run, he found the layoff had affected his level of fitness. It took him longer than usual to complete his run and he was more winded than he'd expected when he got back to the camper.

Nate turned the coffee maker on while he showered. He was sitting outside drinking coffee when Hildee pulled up. Nate got up and went to greet her. They embraced and kissed lightly. It was enough to make them both smile.

"You got more coffee?"

"Have a seat and I'll get you a cup."

Hildee smiled and sat down. Nate went into the camper, came back with a mug of coffee, and handed it to Hildee, who smiled.

"Looks like it will be a nice day."

"Forecast says so. You hungry?"

Nate shook his head, "No. I don't usually eat much breakfast. You hungry?"

"Nah. I had some oatmeal before I left the house."

Nate didn't know why he said it, but it just came out, "Are mom and dad behaving?"

Hildee giggled, "Yeah, like rabbits."

Nate started laughing lightly and Hildee smiled, "For older folks, they sure are frisky and they don't seem to care who knows it. Their room's right next to mine and it's kinda uncomfortable. Even when they's trying to be quiet, it don't end up that a way."

"Well, dear, let's hope it runs in the family."

Hildee started blushing and said, "Stop, Nate. We got two weeks so don't go drivin' us both crazy."

"Fair enough."

Janice and Mike pulled up in their pickup and got out to come to sit with Nate and Hildee. Nate said, "Coffee's hot. Help yourselves."

Mike sat down and Janice went to get coffee.

Nate said, "How are you this morning, dad?"

"Great. This place is good for us. I haven't been this relaxed in years. We are going to spend a lot of weekends here."

Hildee said, "Good."

Janice heard the remark as she came to sit down and handed Mike a mug. Mike said, "Thanks, lover."

Hildee couldn't help it and snickered. Janice looked at Hildee and said, "Get over it."

Hildee laughed, "I will, in a couple of weeks."

Mike looked at Janice with a look of obvious confusion. Janice looked at Hildee and said, "Men can be so dense."

"Uh huh."

Nate was wise enough not to say anything.

Janice looked at Nate, "Don't you have anything to add?"

"Nope."

Hildee looked at Janice, "He ain't no dope."

Janice smiled, "I like you more and more, Hildee."

"Good 'cause we's kinda stuck with each other seein's we both love Nate."

"Well put, daughter-to-be."

Mike asked, "What time we need to be at the VFW, Nate?"

"Ten. The ceremony is at eleven."

"We've got a while then," then asked, "Not to be insensitive, but how are you two fixed for money?"

"Ok, thanks. We have good paying work and I still have some laid back."

"Good then."

Hildee laughed then added, "Then there's my dowry."

Janice asked, "How much can you get for a horse and three sheep?"

Hildee laughed, "No, it ain't that. Pa hasn't been payin' me but puttin' my wages back for when I got hitched. He's told me how much it is and it's considerable. Several years of wages adds up."

Mike agreed, "It does. It appears you will be starting out ahead of where we did."

Nate pointed out, "And our housing costs are minimal."

Janice told her husband, "We don't have to worry about them, Mike. They'll make their own way."

It was then that Hildee figured that just maybe Nate's brothers were somehow being helped financially by Mike and Janice and that was why the strain between Janice and her daughters-in-law. Could be the sons' wives knew it and probably resented the dependence the sons had on their parents. It fit.

Mike announced, "I'm hungry so I'm taking Janice into town for breakfast. You want to come?"

Hildee shared, "I ate already and I have to get more presentable for the goings on."

Janice said, "Well, we'll see you later then," and she and Mike got up and left.

Hildee asked, "Your parents hepin' ur brothers out moneywise?"

Nate looked at Hildee, "You are very perceptive."

"It just fits. The wives know and resent the ties your brothers have to your parents."

"You have it. It's part of the reason I left the family business. It would be too easy to fall back on my folks. I figured that wasn't healthy."

"And, as a result, you're closer to you parents than yar older brothers."

Nate nodded, "Seems so."

"Some people just don't appreciate what they got. Well, I'd better go get gussied up so's I don't embarrass ya."

Nate laughed, "Yeah, like that could happen."

"You're too sweet, love," and leaned over and kissed him. Nate realized his motor was racing. It felt like his heart was going to burst out of his chest.

Hildee straightened up, "You can come fetch me about a quarter of ten. We'll take the pickup."

Nate nodded. He watched Hildee as she walked back to her truck and drove off. He thought to himself how lucky he was. He came to the house about nine-thirty to find Len sitting on the porch. Nate got out of his van, picked up his Bible and his head cover, and went to join him.

Len said as Nate got to the porch, "Hildee ain't ready yet."

Nate nodded and took a seat asking, "Where's Marilee?"

"I'm pickin' her up at her home."

"I haven't heard anything about the shooting."

"I reckon it means they don't have nothin' much yet. You worried about it?"

"Actually concerned because Hildee is around me a lot."

Len added, "Well, if'in it's them robber fellers they could be after me, too."

Nate nodded, "That's why I'd like it resolved. There's too many unknowns."

Hildee came out and Nate's reaction was to say, "Wow, you look gorgeous, love."

Len added, "You do clean up nice."

"Ya fellers look handsome in them sports coats. The last time I saw ya in one pa was at last year's wreath layin' ceremony."

Nate didn't pay as much attention to what Hildee was saying as what she was wearing. She was wearing a dress for the first time since Nate had met her and he thought she was a 'knock out'. She was also wearing high heel shoes which accentuated the fact she had long shapely legs and the dress length was modest just above the knee. The neckline did not reveal any cleavage but it was obvious Hildee was all woman.

Hildee twirled around, "You like?"

Nate exclaimed, "Oh yes, I do!"

"Your ma helped me pick it out. She said I was just a little too 'servative and needed to show off my feminine side."

Len said, "Well, let's git this dog and pony show on the road."

They all went to Len's truck and Nate helped Hildee in. She showed just a little leg above the knee and Nate had to concentrate not to ogle his fiancée. He did help her buckle up and, when he was buckled in, put his arm around her shoulder.

Hildee smiled, "I feel different. I liked what I saw in the mirror."

"You probably now know what I see every time I look at you."

"Nate, remember her pa's in the truck," Len said.

Hildee laughed, "Pa, you ain't that much a prude."

Len smiled and stifled a little laugh.

They arrived at Marilee's and Nate and Hildee got in the back. Len went and opened the door for Marilee who said, "Mornin'."

Hildee said, "Mornin', ma."

Len said, "Hildee!"

Hildee looked at her father, "Just practicin', pa."

Marilee laughed lightly, "Loosen up, Len."

Len just nodded. Marilee's house was not far from the VFW and it took them no time to get there. They got out in the parking lot where the vets were assembling before marching to the memorial across from the courthouse to lay the wreath.

Nate got out, helped Hildee out, then fetched his Bible and hat. He put the cover on just as Len was doing. They each walked with their fiancée to the marshalling area. Cory and his wife, Myra, met them before they could get to the area.

Cory called, "Good mornin'."

Len replied, "Good morning, sir." In addition to being the elected sheriff, Cory was the commander of the branch.

Hildee said, "Hello, Myra."

Myra smiled, "I don't remember seeing ya in a dress before, Hildee."

Hildee smiled, "My work doesn't lend itself to this type of dress."

Myra had a stunned look and Hildee realized she had not spoken local. Suddenly Myra smiled and said, "There is more to ya, Hildee, than most folks know."

Hildee winked and said, "Yes'm."

Apparently Myra and Nate were the only ones who had noticed the lapse because the others weren't paying attention. Nate wore a broad smile.

Cory stated, "Nate, ya was right about the rifle used. We found slugs in them trees and they was twenty-twos. We questioned the most likely suspects and none of 'em had alibis. The young feller at the gate saw a dark blue pickup go past just after the shots."

Len asked, "So what's next?"

Cory replied, "We're still workin' on it."

Nate turned to Len, "It means they'll be checking records and asking around about who owns a twenty-two and a blue pickup."

Cory just nodded, "That needs to stay with us uns here."

Len nodded agreement as did the others.

Cory said, "Let's git organized."

The memorial service went off without a hitch. Nate noticed a lot of the young and not so young men were paying attention to his fiancée. He didn't blame them for Hildee looked gorgeous. When the service ended, the members went to gather for the parade. The women went to the reserved seating to watch.

Nate thought it was a typical small town parade with floats, emergency vehicles, the high school marching band, the community marching band, the color guard, local marching groups, the local reserve unit, and finally the VFW float and marching members. Nate found he enjoyed it.

After the parade finished its route, Nate climbed down from the float and went with Len to the truck to meet the ladies. There they found Cal harassing Hildee. Nate could tell Hildee was trying to control her temper and succeeding.

Nate walked up behind Cal, "Cal, please leave my fiancée alone."

Cal turned around and smiled, "Well, if it ain't the yeller feller."

Nate got in Cal's face, "You keep looking for trouble and you're going to find it and be in a world of hurt. Now skedaddle out of here before I lose my temper."

Cal backed up a step and took a swing at Nate. His fist caught nothing but air and he found himself on his knees, his shoulder just about popping out of the joint and he screamed in pain. It was loud enough that people were now watching.

Nate bent over and whispered in Cal's ear, "Turn from your evil ways, Cal. You don't want the angel of death throwing you kicking and screaming into the fires of hell. " Nate let go of him and said in a quiet voice, "Go and sin no more."

Cal stood up and left not looking back.

Hildee came to Nate and put her arm through his, "What did you say to him? He went as white as snow."

Nate sighed, "It was spiritual advice."

Cory came over, "Ya want to press charges?"

Nate shook his head, "No need. If he's smart, he'll stay away from Hildee and me and change his ways."

"I don't think he's so stupid as to mess with ya again."

"I hope you're right, Sheriff. I don't want to hurt him."

Cory just nodded, "I'll go talk to his folks and tell them he's playing with fire and likely to get himself burned."

"Thanks. He is certainly playing with fire, the eternal kind."

Cory nodded and walked away.

Len announced, "Well, now I've seen it all. Let's go eat BBQ."

Nate agreed, "Yes, lets."

"Here come your folks, Nate," Hildee said.

Mike, Janice, Ben, and Betsy showed up.

Mike told them all, "This was fun and the place was crowded."

Len informed him, "You ain't seen nothin'. The BBQ is huge around here. We'd better claim a table unless ya wanna eat standin' up."

They all left for the BBQ. When they got to where the tents were, they staked out a table and the men stood guard while the women went to fix plates.

"I heard that you had a little set-to," Mike prodded.

Nate sighed, "Word sure does travel fast around here."

Ben put in, "Well, it ain't every day the town bully gets his comeuppance from the local preacher, who is also a war hero."

Nate looked at Ben.

Len smiled, "It was certain ta git out. This is a small town and somebody on the committee was bound to say somethin' outta school."

Nate paused then spoke, "It's why I didn't want to join in the first place."

His father exclaimed, "Now I understand." Nate looked at his father and shrugged.

Mike asked, "They sell beer here?"

Ben nodded and said, "Let's go."

He and Mike went to buy beer.

Len muttered, "Don't look now but here comes trouble."

Carl Johnson came over and stood glaring at Nate, "So ya's the trouble maker."

"Good afternoon to you too, Mayor."

"Don't smart mouth me."

Nate noticed what the mayor didn't. A lot of people were listening to the exchange of words.

"That was not my intention, Mayor."

Carl cautioned, "I don't want you marryin' my son to that nasty sharecropper's daughter."

Nate observed, "Your son and his fiancée are good Christians and both are adults. I think they are well suited and both of good character. I know for certain one of them is even from a Christian family of good character."

Carl snarled, "What's thet s'posed to mean?"

Nate smiled, "Exactly what I said; no more no less."

"I won't have ya badmouthin' me and my wife."

"I don't think I did that, Mayor."

"Ya think you're somethin' better, don't ya?"

"No. We are all God's creations and we are all sinners."

"Stay out of my way, preacher. Hear me?"

"I hear you and I will keep you in my prayers."

Carl retorted, "I don't need yar stinkin' prayers!"

Nate watched the mayor stomp away. Len looked at Nate and shrugged, "Weren't that interestin'?"

Nate agreed, "Sure was."

Mike and Ben returned with carriers, on which were eight cups of draft beer. The women came back each with two plates at about the same time. Hildee put one in front of Nate and smiled.

"Thanks, love."

"Uh huh," and she sat down, then said, "We saw from the line that the mayor stopped to talk at ya."

Nate nodded, "That's an accurate description of what happened."

Hildee asked, "What'd he want?"

Len explained, "For Nate not to hitch Shocky and Jean."

"He's sure got his nerve," Marilee exclaimed.

Len said, "Yup."

"I hope he don't cause trouble at the weddin'," Hildee said.

Nate offered, "Maybe we should hire an extra duty deputy to be there just in case."

Ben agreed, "Couldn't hurt. We won't even tell Shocky and Jean 'cause there's no reason to upset 'em. We could all chip in as sort of a weddin' present."

Hildee put in, "Good reckonin', Ben."

Nate said, "Let's say the blessing."

They did and started eating.

Mike commented, "This is good BBQ. Who pays for all this?"

Ben answered, "The chamber of commerce, the VFW, and some local businesses sponsor it. They all chip in."

"There's a list of sponsors in the food tent," Hildee added.

A voice from behind them said, "Hi." The group turned to see Billie and Jessica.

Len said, "Come join us. We'll make space." They all slid closer together and Hildee looked at Nate when their sides were touching and smiled. Nate smiled back.

Jessica led Billie to his seat and he said, "Thanks, Jessica."

There were now ten people at the eight person table.

"I sho nuff enjoyed the music and preachin' on Sunday," Billie said.

"I didn't know you were there."

"No wonder. Ya was swamped. We are coming back," Jessica said.

Billie announced, "Now that we have a church here, I plan to come regular like."

Jessica smiled, "He thinks I'm his personal chauffer."

"Yeah, but I don't backseat drive."

"There is that. Besides he can't tell if I'm not wearin' makeup."

Billie shook his head and everyone smiled. Jessica was actually a reasonably attractive woman and good natured. She hardly ever wore makeup because she had a very good complexion.

The group shared about what was happening in their lives and ate. Hildee lost no time telling Billie and Jessica how she was going from having no ma to having two. The couple seemed to enjoy Hildee's enthusiasm.

When the meal was finished, Mike stated, "Well, I hate to eat and run but Janice and I have a long way to drive." He and Janice got up and hugged everyone.

Janice said, "See you next weekend."

When they left no one moved to take up the extra space. The couples were comfortable with the contact.

Len told Nate, "Your ma and pa are really nice, Nate. I reckon' they'll make good kin folk."

Nate smiled, "I'm kinda partial to them."

Billie said, "It seems a lot has happened since ya got here, Nate."

Nate smiled, "Yes, everything is moving at the speed of God. Sometimes that's fast and sometimes it's slow, but it's always the right speed."

Billie allowed, "I s'pose."

Hildee said, "It goes without sayin' ya'll are invited to our weddin'. I know ya'll want to come, Billie, 'cause there'll be dancin' in the pavilion."

Billie turned to Jessica, "Will ya be my date?"

Jessica smiled and teased, "Well, ya do need a driver."

Billie shook his head, "I don't get no respect."

Marilee said, "You don't look so hard done by. Seems to me you cleaned up your act since Jessica came along."

Billie smiled, "Sho nuff."

Len broke in, "What say we go a walkin' here in the park and let some other folks use this table?"

Billie said, "I'm for it."

They all got up and Billie picked up his guide cane. After putting their paper plates and cups in the trash, the couples went walking arm-in-arm. Hildee and Nate were trailing Billie and Jessica as Billie told her what he heard and Jessica told Billie what she saw.

Hildee whispered to Nate, "Ain't they a cute couple. How long you figure?"

Nate said in a quiet voice, "Maybe a month or two. Billie's a little slow on the uptake."

Billie said, "Yeah, but I got super hearing."

Hildee laughed. Jessica asked, "What did they say?"

Billie told her and she looked over her shoulder at Nate and Hildee and they exchanged smiles.

Billie sensed Jessica's movement and said, "Don't encourage 'em, Jessica."

Jessica teased, "It's not them that needs encouragin', Billie."

The walkway through the small park was a winding one that went around a large pond and there were ducks swimming in the pond. Some children were feeding them. The walk was only a quarter of a mile so they finished up fairly quickly.

"Let's walk some more through the downtown," Marilee said.

Billie said, "Lead on."

The group had been walking and talking for about an hour when they got back to where their vehicles were parked. They all exchanged waves and goodbyes as they parted.

After Len, Marilee, Hildee and Nate had gotten in the truck Len asked, "What now?"

Marilee chuckled, "How about my place for coffee? We can set on the porch and give the neighbors somethin' ta gossip 'bout."

They drove to Marilee's home where she gave them a tour of her home after starting the coffee.

When the tour was finished, Hildee said, "Nice place ya got here, Marilee. Real nice."

Marilee poured coffee into mugs and they all went and sat on the porch. She said, "I'm goin' to miss the place just a little."

Hildee looked at Marilee and it dawned on her. Marilee would be movin' in with her pa. She asked, "Ya gonna keep workin' at the county?"

Marilee nodded, "Of course. It's not far from the campground to the courthouse." Marilee smiled and looked at Len then added, "I'm lookin' forward to movin' to the country."

Len advised Nate and Hildee, "We been thinkin' on what furniture we're takin' from here and what we got at the other house that will go. We decided you and Nate can have first dibs on any and all we decide not ta use. Ya'll can store it in the old shed. It should stay good if'in ya cover it with plastic."

Hildee smiled, "Thanks."

Nate said, "That's very generous. Between you there's a lot of nice furniture among the items you won't be using."

Marilee added, "The realtor's comin' Tuesday evenin' to list the place."

Len turned to his daughter, "Hildee, you can have the bedroom suite ur ma and me used. Marilee and me decided it weren't right fer us to be a usin' beds we shared with our passed loved ones; outta respect, don't you see. We're goin' to use the one in the spare bedroom here. It's most like new."

Hildee nodded.

After they finished their coffee, Len kissed Marilee and they said good bye. Hildee and Len dropped Nate off at his camper.

Chapter 8

Nate had just poured himself a cool glass of water when there was a knock on his door. Nate went to answer it and was surprised when he opened the door. Cal was standing there in the dark looking rather sheepish, "Can we talk?"

Cal was in Nate's camper for over an hour before he left carrying a gift from Nate.

Nate was up early Tuesday morning and picked Carson up early before swinging back around to get Hildee. It was a productive day at the worksite and they stayed a little later than usual. Nate drove Hildee home first, as was his practice, then dropped Carson off and circled back. The extra driving would not be necessary once Nate and Hildee were married.

Nate had finished cleaning up and was sitting outside drinking a cup of coffee when he had a visitor come to talk with him. Hildee was surprised when she pulled up at Nate's site to see him and Cal sitting talking. She wondered what that was all about. She got out and walked toward the two men. Cal got up as Hildee walked up.

"Good evenin', Hildee," Cal began.

Hildee smiled, "Hello, Cal." She walked over and kissed Nate on the cheek then took a chair.

Cal sat down, "Hildee, I'm sorry I gived ya such a hard time. I've seen I acted badly and I'm workin' to straighten up and fly right. Forgive me?"

"Ok."

Cal had a puzzled look on his face.

"That's how it works, Cal," Nate told him.

Cal looked at Nate and asked, "God's like that?"

"He's the one that told Hildee to forgive. It's just like I told you. He forgives you once you accept Jesus and work to fly straight."

"It's hard to believe it's that easy."

Hildee sighed, "True, but that's how it works."

Cal sat shaking his head, "Seems too easy."

Nate just nodded.

Hildee asked, "Nate is taking me to the diner to eat, wanna tag along?"

Cal was surprised, "After the way I done ya?"

Hildee said, "That's water under the bridge and flowed into the lake."

Nate reminded him, "We get to start out new."

Cal said, "I'd like that. I don't have any real friends."
Hildee's stomach growled, "I'm hungry so let's go."
"I'll meet ya there," Cal promised.
Nate locked his camper and he and Hildee got in her pickup. They had no sooner pulled away then Hildee asked, "What happened."
Nate shrugged, "It seems God used the little bit of counseling I did in the parking lot to convict Cal. He came by last night and we had a long talk. He apparently talked to his parents for a long time before coming to see me and they worked on him, too."
"God sure do work in the most mysterious ways most times."
"He sure does."
When the three of them walked into the diner, everyone stopped talking and looked at the trio.
Nate said in a loud voice, "Hello everyone. Good to see y'all."
Everyone went back to eating and the little party went to a booth and sat down.
Cal said, "Seems everybody was speechless to see me with ya."
Hildee said, "I reckon' so."
Sue came to wait on them, "Hi. I guess y'all made up."
"They done forgived me. How about you, Sue? You forgive me for bein' a horse's…," and Cal trailed off. "Sorry, for bein' a jerk."
Sue looked at Cal, then Nate, then asked, "Is he for real?"
"Seems so."
Sue looked back at Cal, "Ok, Cal. So what can I get y'all?" She took their orders and went to put them in.
Cal sighed, "I almost still can't believe it's that easy."
Nate shrugged.
Hildee asked, "Ya comin' to church on Sunday?"
"Nate said it's ordered, if I'm to be a real Christian."
"Good."
Sue brought their drinks and looked at Cal, "You seen the light?"
Cal just nodded. Sue left and Cal asked some questions. Hildee and Nate discussed with him what being a Christian meant. They were still talking when Sue brought the food.
Nate asked her, "Sue, we are about to pray. You have anything you want us to include?"
"Yeah, let's pray for Cal. He will need wisdom and strength on his

153

new journey."

They prayed together and when they finished the short prayer and said amen, several surrounding people joined in. The three of them enjoyed their meal and conversation. After eating, they lingered over coffee before leaving.

Wednesday evening after work, the praise team met to practice at the pavilion and, as usual, they drew a crowd. It was a fun evening.

Thursday afternoon, the Smiths dropped by to see the progress being made on the house. Nate and Carson were working inside and Hildee was outside using her pa's tractor and backhoe attachment to dig for the new septic system. She saw the Smiths first and waved but continued working.

Dorcas and Bethany went inside and found Nate and Carson putting in the new laundry room wiring.

Dorcas said, "Hi, Nate."

Nate looked up, "Good morning."

Bethany said, "You are making good progress, Nate."

"Yes, we've been working hard and long and I'm pleased with our progress. This is the last of the electrical to tie into the new service."

Dorcas said, "I saw your fiancée digging outside."

"Yes, she's digging for the septic tile bed. We already pulled the old septic tank and we'll dispose of it. It was in bad shape. It's on the truck out back. The new one is out back waiting to be put in the ground. For the time being, we have a porta-potty out back."

Dorcas nodded, "We'll take a look around." Fifteen minutes later, the couple left after saying goodbye.

At six fifteen that evening, Nate, Hildee, and Carson were still working outside to lower the new septic tank in place. They were lowering the tank with a chain suspended from the bucket of the tractor's front end loader when the Smiths came back followed by another man, who was in a pickup. Nate, Carson, and Hildee were at a point where they could not leave.

The Smiths and their guest went inside for a while and came back out as Hildee was backfilling around the tank. The guest drove away.

Dorcas came toward Nate, who went to meet him. Dorcas smiled, "I had an associate come and look at your work. He said it's top notch."

"Thank you."

"You aren't offended?"

"Why would I be?"

Dorcas smiled, "After we finish the drywall and flooring, would you come back and do the installation of the light fixtures and bathroom fixtures for us? We'll pay your going rate."

Nate nodded, "Certainly. I appreciate your business."

Dorcas said, "Good," shook hands with Nate before he and his wife left.

Nate's little crew locked up and headed home about seven fifteen that evening. It had been a long but productive day. Nate got out of his shower about eight thirty. He was making a sandwich when there was a knock on his door and he opened it. Hildee, Len, and Marilee were there.

Nate said, "Come on in. I was just making a sandwich. Do you want one?" The women started laughing and Hildee was looking away. Nate realized he was in his boxers. He said, "Excuse me," and headed for the bedroom. He came back out barefoot in jeans and a T-shirt to find his company sitting waiting.

"Sorry. What about a sandwich?"

Len smiled, "Marilee and I ate already."

Hildee said, "I'd like one."

"Who wants a drink?"

Len said, "I do," and Marilee indicated she did.

Hildee added, "I'll get them," and went to the fridge and announced what was available. She brought out the drinks and Nate finished the sandwiches and brought one for Hildee.

When Nate got seated Marilee asked, "You always answer the door in your skivvies?"

Nate sighed but did not answer. He changed the subject, "Let's say the blessing. I'm hungry." They did and Nate and Hildee started eating.

Marilee was in a teasing mood, "You didn't answer my question."

Nate said with a smile, "I am ignoring it. Let's just chalk it up as one of life's most embarrassing moments."

Hildee turned to Marilee, "I told ya he looked good without a shirt on."

Marilee smiled.

Nate groaned, "Women!"

Len added, "Yup."

Nate asked, "So what brings you to my humble abode?"

"Don't he talk fancy like," Marilee said.

Hildee added, "Yeah but he's cute, so's I'll put up with it."

Nate sighed, "I'm not going to win."

Len said, "Nope."

Nate shook his head and took another bite of his sandwich.

Len said, "Marilee already has an offer on her house. We are definitely going to add forty full service lots for RVs. There's no reason we can't start right away if you work short hours say ten to four or you can wait 'til the fall. Work as it suits. We want you and Hildee to put in the services. We'll pay ya your goin' rate and the cost of materials. What's the rate?"

"You know we are going to do it for free."

Marilee told them, "We know you offered, but we can well afford to pay and it wouldn't be right with y'all startin' out not ta pay ya."

Hildee smiled, "Thank you, Marilee," and it was settled.

Nate told Len their rate.

Dismayed, Len said, "Is it what you're makin' now?"

"Less. I gave you a family discount."

Marilee added, "I reckon' we don't have to worry about them gettin' by." She looked at Hildee who just smiled.

Nate conceded, "We can work between other jobs."

"Well, your rates is less than what I paid fer the last lots. Suppose that's 'cause of the family price."

Len, Marilee, and Hildee had been there for a half hour when there was a knock at the door. Nate started to get up but Hildee beat him to it. She opened the door and said, "Look who's here. Come on in."

Janice and Mike came in. There were hugs and greetings all round. There weren't enough seats in the camper so Hildee sat on the floor leaning against Nate's legs.

Nate said, "You weren't kidding about coming back Thursday."

Janice smiled, "We realized just how much we enjoy it here."

Hildee jumped up, "I'm a poor hostess. What do you want to drink?" Once they were served, Hildee sat back down on the floor.

Mike looked at Nate, "I'll need some help setting up the new RV."

Nate said, "Sure thing, dad."

Len added, "And I'll supervise. Let's get to it."

The men left and the women sat talking.

Janice announced, "We'll be staying all next week. We decided to take our first real vacation in decades."

Hildee smiled, "Great."

When the men finished setting up the new RV, they came back and everyone went to see it. They talked and Hildee made sandwiches for Mike and Janice. The little gathering broke up about ten.

By Friday afternoon, Nate's little crew had finished the Smith job except for some cleanup. They knocked off early at four o'clock, having already worked over nine hours.

As they drove, Hildee asked Nate, "When ya reckon we'll finish the clean up?"

"Probably early Monday afternoon. With Carson helpin' and you working full-time with me, combined with long workdays, we made really good progress. We are a very good crew."

Carson asked, "What about the next project?"

Hildee told him, "We have work for my pa. That will take quite a bit of time and we can do it when we don't have other work."

Nate added, "We'll have to go back to the Smith's to finish up fixture installation after the drywall is done but that won't be until after we get married. I think Hildee and I will take a few days off next week and we'll get you started on the new lot work, Carson"

Carson said, "Thanks. That will be good. I need the work."

Nate added, "I suppose I should put an ad in the paper."

Hildee agreed, "It'd be smart."

Carson said, "I like workin' fer y'all."

Nate said, "We do get along and work well together. I'm not concerned about having enough work."

The men dropped Hildee off and Nate took Carson home. Nate had showered and was sitting outside in a chair when Hildee pulled up. She came and sat beside him.

"Hi, love."

Nate smiled and looked at Hildee, "I love you."

Hildee smiled, "Are you gittin' nervous? Our weddin's only a week away."

"No, I'm not nervous at all, at all. I'm looking forward to waking up next to you for the rest of my life."

"That's a sweet thing to say to yar future wife. I'd better git along. Sue's pickin' me up as we got to go to Jean's place. Your ma's goin' with.

It's a girl's thing; it's a weddin' shower. I forgot to tell ya."

Nate nodded, "Have a good time."

Hildee got up, leaned over and kissed Nate. It set his motor to racing and, as she stood up, she said, "I can get used to this kissin' stuff."

"I'm sure glad we'll soon be married."

"Me, too." She walked to her truck and, as she got there, she looked over her shoulder to see Nate watching her. She waved then drove off and Nate sighed. He reflected that it was just another week until their wedding, thank God. She was such a temptation and, at the same time, such a blessing.

Saturday turned out to be the nice day that had been forecast. Nate had finished his run and, when he returned to the campsite, Shocky was waiting for him, sitting in a lawn chair. Nate took a seat.

"Good morning, Shocky."

"Mornin', Nate."

'What's up?"

Shocky seemed fidgety, "I ran into my dad at the diner last evenin'. He threatened me. I'm worryin' he might come to the weddin' and cause a commotion. My bride don't deserve that."

"Don't worry, your friends have your back. There will be a deputy at the wedding. It's already arranged."

Shocky sighed, "That's a load off."

He had no sooner said it than a pickup pulled up and a man got out and approached.

Shocky said, "That's my father and he's lookin' fer trouble."

Nate said, "Stay here," and went to intercept Carl.

Carl announced, "I need to talk to my son."

"Carl, I'm asking you to leave. This is my private lot."

Carl almost spat it, "There ain't nothin' private here. Yar jist more trailer trash."

Nate stepped in front of the man, "You leave now or I'll have you arrested for trespassing as I've given you fair warning. You're not welcome here."

Carl tried to step around Nate but Nate moved in front of him. Carl got red but turned on his heel and went back to his truck and got in. He started it and gunned the engine, his tires throwing up gravel.

Nate walked back and sat down beside Shocky, who said, "Thanks."

Nate smiled, "You're welcome, but I don't think he's done."

"I'm afraid not. Mind if I hang out here 'til the wedding? I got my duds in my truck."

Nate nodded agreement, "Ok. Let me shower then we'll go up to the store and I'll buy breakfast."

Shocky nodded. Fifteen minutes later they were headed to the store in Shocky's pickup. The summer girls working the store made them breakfast and they were almost finished when Nate saw Hildee come in.

"Good morning, love."

"Morning. You too, Shocky." She turned to the girls and said, "Hey." Hildee went to Nate and kissed him and Nate smiled broadly. Hildee took a seat beside Nate.

"Yur spendin' a laid-back mornin', Shocky."

"Yup. There is advantages to a small weddin' don't ya see."

Hildee looked at Nate, "I reckon' one of 'em is it's quicker."

Nate smiled, "There's that."

"Well, I done my chores so I'm fixin' to go get gussied up for the weddin'. See ya later."

Nate watched Hildee leave.

Shocky said, "We are lucky men, Nate."

"Yes, we are indeed blessed, Shocky."

Shocky smiled.

Nate asked, "You got the license and rings?"

"In the truck."

Nate didn't know why he said it but it just came to mind, "You sure?"

Shocky said, "Put it in the glove compartment myself." He thought for a moment and said, "I'm goin' ta check," and left and went outside.

Nate watched him furiously looking and, after a few moments, got up. Nate said to the girls, "Put breakfast on my tab," and went to help Shocky. Shocky got out of the cab, "They're gone."

"When was the truck unlocked?"

"Just since I got here," then paused, "And last night at the diner. Ya don't think?"

Nate just shrugged.

Shocky was suddenly in a panic and asked, "What do I do? Jean will be heartbroken and the family will be rightly put out. This ain't good."

"Let's not panic. Let me make a couple of phone calls."

Nate called Ben who answered, "Mornin'."

"Hi Ben. Shocky has a problem, so we have a problem. It seems someone stole his marriage license and rings out of his pickup. We can manage without the rings if we have to, but the license is another matter."

"I heard about the hoopla at the diner and I bet I know who has the license."

"Let's not jump to conclusions. Can you make a call and see about getting it replaced? I'll see about helping Shocky with the rings."

"I'll call in some favors and call ya back," then he hung up.

Nate turned to Shocky, "Where did you get the rings?"

"In town."

"Let's go get replacements and, on the way, you can make a theft report by telephone to the sheriff's department."

Shocky nodded and they got in the pickup and headed for town. They arrived at the jewelry store just after it opened and Shocky was able to get replacement rings. They had just left when Nate's phone rang. It was Ben.

"I'm at the courthouse now. County Clerk Beatrice Lynn is openin' up fer me. We goes way back. She's a cousin by marriage don't ya see. Where's ya at?"

"We are downtown. We'll meet you there."

"We'll be awaitin' fer ya."

Nate noticed that Ben's accent got thicker when he was stressed. At the courthouse, they were met by Ben, who led them to a side door and they went up to Beatrice Lynn's office.

Nate remembered seeing Beatrice Lynn at the Sunday services and offered his hand, "Good to see you again."

She smiled, "I'm glad I could hep the young uns, preacher. It seems there's a plot to keep 'em from getting' hitched." Beatrice Lynn looked at Ben.

Shocky told her, "Thank ya so much for hepin' me out, ma'am."

Beatrice Lynn said, "Everyone jist calls me Bea."

Shocky nodded and said, "Thank ya, Bea."

Bea said with a broad smile, "Just remember this to yar friends and family come election time."

Shocky laughed, "Count on it, Bea."

Nate said, "Thank you, Bea. It's a good thing you're doing."

They all left the courthouse ten minutes later.

As they walked to the truck Ben couldn't resist needling Shocky, "Now hold on to this one, ok?"

Shocky smiled, "Once burned, twice very careful is I."

Ben told them, "I'd better go git cleaned up so's not to shame y'all at the weddin'. Besides, I wanna make a 'pression on Betsy."

So it was that the preacher and the groom arrived early to the pavilion. They pulled up to find Len and Ben setting up Hildee's keyboard and the public announcement system. A sheriff's car pulled up and a deputy got out. It was Cob.

"Afternoon, Cob."

Cob smiled, "Hey, preacher."

The men all shook hands and Cob asked, "Ya got nerves, Shocky?"

Shocky shook his head no, "Nah, I reckon' I'm lucky Jean agreed to have me."

"A good looker like thet and a homely feller like ya, I reckon you should kiss her feet."

"I aim to kiss more than her feet." Both Cob and Shocky looked at Nate, realizing what had just been said.

Nate shrugged, "They'll be hitched so it will be all moral and legal for them to do all the kissing they want."

Cob smiled, "You ain't like no preacher I ever met 'fore."

Nate returned the smile, "That's not the first time I've heard that."

Shocky added, "I reckon' it's so."

They were at the pavilion well before the appointed time waiting for the bridal party. The bride's family were all there as were many of the church folks and a few campers.

Hildee arrived in her pickup and got out. Nate watched her intently as she strode to where he was standing. He knew he was not the only man watching her. She came and kissed Nate on the cheek and whispered in his ear, "You shouldn't had ought to be seen so obvious lustin' after me like that. It ain't proper for a preacher."

Nate said quietly, "I can't help it. You, my dear, are stunning."

Hildee smiled, "Good," before going and taking her place at the keyboard.

Jean arrived and her father helped her out of the car and the wedding party, less Hildee, started walking to the pavilion. Hildee started playing the wedding march. When Jean's father left her with Shocky at the altar, Hildee

161

came and took her place next to Jean.

The ceremony was going on without a hitch and Nate was just about to declare the couple married when a loud voice boomed from behind the pavilion, "I object! They don't have a marriage license."

Carl Johnson came rushing out from behind the storage locker of the pavilion.

He repeated shouting, "I object. They're not legal. They don't have a marriage license."

Cob stepped into Carl's path and Carl, who had been a high school football player, instinctively lowered his shoulder and knocked Cob over. His momentum carried him toward the bride and groom. Hildee was closest to him and stepped into his path.

Nate watched in horror as Carl was apparently going to knock Hildee over. Instead Hildee threw a haymaker that caught Carl full in the face. Carl not only stopped cold but after a moment swaying, dropped like a hay bale thrown from the loft of a barn; hard and with a slight bounce. Hildee had laid him out cold. Cob got to his feet looking at the unconscious Carl.

Nate looked at Hildee who shrugged and stepped back into place beside Jean. Jean and Shocky were trying not to laugh. Nate knew they weren't going to be able to hold it in for long as he was himself fighting laughter. It was too comical. He spoke like a machine gun spewing out the words, "I pronounce you man and wife. You may kiss the bride. Quickly."

Shocky did but the bride and groom couldn't hold the kiss and broke into laughter and the audience that was already snickering and chuckling followed them.

Nate had never heard dozens of people laughing like that - belly laughing. He looked at Carl, who was just starting to come to as Cob put handcuffs on him. Carl starting muttering softly and half crying, "It's not legal. They don't have a license. They don't."

Nate said to the bride and groom, "I will need you and the witnesses to sign the papers." They went to a picnic table and signed the documents as did the witnesses. Nate added his information and signature then gave them a copy.

Shocky shook Nate's hand. Jean had her arm through Shocky's but let go long enough to kiss Nate on the cheek and hug Hildee.

Shocky hugged Hildee and said, "Nice right ya got there, Hildee."

The young couple smiled and left as Cob led Carl away.

Ben came to see Nate, "Cob's takin' Carl off to the clinic for a 'samination afore takin' him to the station. He's a still mutterin' it weren't legal."

Jean's father and mother came to see Nate. Mr. Morris said, "That were some weddin', preacher. Is it always thet interstin' here?"

Ben jumped in, "Not always, but mostly there's somethin' interestin' a happenin' a lot."

Mrs. Morris said, "We gotta come see fer ourselves tomorra. Shocky said we had otta come."

Nate smiled, "You will be most welcome."

Hildee came and took Nate's arm.

Mr. Morris looked at Hildee, "You hit like a mule kicks, Hildee," then turned to Nate, "Preacher, you'd better behave when ya two's hitched."

Nate smiled, "Yes, sir. On the other hand, I have someone to watch my back."

Mrs. Morris said, "Yes, siree," and led her husband away.

Mike and Janice came forward and Mike stated, "Interesting ceremony, son."

Nate nodded.

"I can promise, Hildee, that you won't have that kind of problem from us," Janice said.

Hildee giggled, "Shucks, I won't get to practice my haymaker."

Mike laughed and Janice shook her head in disbelief, "You two sure are something."

Folks started drifting away and Mike asked, "Why don't you kids come over to our campsite for a beverage. Invite Len and Ben and their ladies."

Hildee answered, "I'll ask 'em."

Mike and Janice left. Nate took off his jacket and helped Len and Ben pack up and lock up while the ladies sat and talked. When Nate had finished, Hildee walked over to him.

"Love, I think you'd better take me to the clinic."

Nate asked, "What's wrong?"

Hildee smiled, "I think Carl broke my hand with his face."

Hildee showed Nate her badly swollen hand and he said, "Let's go."

They jumped in the pickup and went to the clinic. The clinic was not busy and when they went to the counter the receptionist said, "Hi, Hildee.

What's up? Another fainting spell?"

Hildee shook her head, "Naw, I'm over swoonin' over my Nate since he's promised to me. My hands busted up, Phyllis."

Phyllis smiled and tried to keep from laughing and it sort of came out stifled. "It'll happen when someone hits yar fist hard enough with their face."

Hildee responded, "News travels faster 'an a racehorse in the home stretch 'round here."

"It's been a slow gossip week. Sides, a preacher's future wife deckin' the mayor would be news anytime. Then there's that Carl was marched in here in handcuffs to see doc. His face is broken worse than your hand."

"Really?"

"Yup. They had to take him to the city to see one of them specialized docs."

It turned out Hildee's hand was not broken just abused and swollen. When they arrived back to the house, the cold compress Hildee had been given had reduced the swelling considerably. Hildee said as she exited the truck, "I'll go change and meet ya at yar parent's camper."

Nate walked back to his camper and, as he passed, he waved to his parents and friends who were sitting in camp chairs talking. He yelled, "I'll be back soon as I change."

When Nate came back, Hildee was already there sitting and sipping a cold drink, an ice pack around her hand.

Len joked, "We bin tryin' to talk Hildee into joinin' the women's pro fight circuit."

Nate said, "She wouldn't last long."

Hildee asked, "Why not?"

Nate smiled, "They'd run out of fighters too quickly."

Janice said, "True."

Hildee smiled, "I reckon' I'll stick to bein' church bouncer."

Everyone smiled at the remark and Mike said, "Good one, Hildee."

Marilee commented, "I suppose what happened today will be all over the county by now."

Nate sighed, "Already is."

Ben said, "Figures. It will sure be interestin' to see how the gossip affects church attendance in the mornin'."

Len put in, "I reckon it'll be up. People is curious and they'll come to

164

see the preacher's pretty fiancée that done decked Mayor Carl."

Hildee chuckled, "I reckon then I'd better gussy up so's not to disappoint."

Nate laughed lightly; half a snicker.

Hildee smiled, "Watch it, love."

"Yes, dear."

Mike suggested, "Let's go to the diner to eat and hear the gossip."

Ben said, "Good idea."

Janice looked at Hildee, "Men are such gossips."

Hildee smiled, "Sho nuff."

The four couples arrived after five and the diner was packed. They were fortunate to enter just as others were leaving. Sue came over and said to her mom, "Right this way, ma'am. Your party's reserved table is ready."

As Hildee passed a table, one of the people said, "Way to go, Hildee," and started humming the theme from a well-known fight movie.

Others picked it up and started humming. Hildee played along. She raised her fists over her head and turned around in a well-known victory stance from the movie. Everyone started clapping and cheering.

Someone started the chant, "Hildee, Hildee, Hildee," and it went on until Hildee's group, who were all laughing, got seated.

Mike said, "That was surreal."

Janice added, "I love it."

Sue came to the table and looked at Hildee, "What can I git ya, champ?" Hildee smiled and Sue took their drink orders.

A couple Hildee did not know came to the table and the man said, "Hey mom, what's that all about? Hi, Nate."

Janice spoke up, "Everyone this is my son, Paul, and his wife, Belle." She proceeded to introduce everyone at the table. Hildee was last and Janice said, "And last but not least, this is Nate's fiancée, Hildee, church bouncer extraordinaire."

Belle looked puzzled but Janice didn't offer an explanation and instead asked, "Have you eaten?"

Paul stated, "We just finished."

Nate told them, "Pull up a chair and watch us chow down."

Belle replied, "The owner may not like that. They are so busy."

Betsy noted, "It's no problem."

Paul looked around, "Why not. Hildee seems to be some sort of celebrity."

Belle elbowed Paul. He ignored it then fetched two chairs which he placed at the end of the table. The rest of the party moved closer together. Hildee was snuggled up against Nate and, much to her amusement, it was causing Nate not a little discomfort.

Hildee shouldn't have done it but she did. She put her hand on Nate's thigh and he turned a deep red.

Janice had noticed and started laughing. It drew attention to the fact Hildee was smiling broadly and Nate was blushing.

Len grinned, "Well, I'll be."

Nate said, "Probably."

Belle said, "I don't understand."

Janice laughed, "I know."

Belle pursed her lips and Hildee couldn't help it, "Belle loosen up. You pucker up any more and ya's goin' to explode."

Belle's mouth dropped open and Paul tried to stifle his laughter, but it came out and that set everyone off. When Belle elbowed him none too gently, the laughter increased.

Belle said dramatically, "Well, I never."

Paul agreed, "I know."

Belle now turned red.

Nate said, "Welcome to the club, Belle."

Belle sighed, "You are all crazy people."

Len said, "I do believe she understands the sit-you-ation."

Hildee added, "If ya ain't crazy when you come, Belle, you'll be when ya leaves."

Sue came over, "So what do y'all want?" The group placed their orders. Sue looked at Belle and said, "And I suppose it will be an order of loosen up for ya, dear?"

Belle's mouth dropped open again.

Sue said, "Gotcha." Everyone laughed and Belle exclaimed, "I give up!"

Paul looked at his wife and said, "Finally," then turned to Sue, "Please just bring us coffee."

Sue nodded and put her hand on Paul's shoulder, "Sure thing, handsome."

Belle's mouth dropped open again and Sue again said, "Gotcha," and turned to the group, "She's kinda a slow learner, huh?"

Belle had a shocked look on her face. She paused a moment then shook her head in disbelief. She looked around the table and said, "You are all really around the bend."

Len said, "There's many bends in the Drift River and we bin 'round most of 'em."

Janice started the laughter and it caught on.

Belle looked at Paul, "And we have to put up with this all weekend?"

Paul agreed, "Seems so."

"Well, when in Rome."

"That's the spirit," Janice said.

Suddenly Paul turned beet red and Belle said, "I guess it's a common trait among the Christian males. I learned something new."

Hildee started the laughing and this time Belle joined in.

Sue came over with the beverages and said to Belle, "Behave yourselves or I'll have to ask you to leave."

Belle retorted, "No and you can ask, but it doesn't mean I will."

Sue replied, "She's a learnin'," and put out the beverages.

"Thank you, Sue," Janice said.

As Sue walked away, Paul watched her leave. Belle reached over and grabbed her husband's chin, turned his face toward hers and said with a broad smile, "If you know what's good for you, husband dear, you'll only have eyes for me."

Paul smiled, "Yes, dear."

Janice said, "The order of loosen up seems to have worked."

Marilee added, "Seems so."

Belle ignored them and kissed her husband passionately. Paul turned beet red.

Hildee said, "She sho nuff knows how to corral him."

Janice agreed, "It works on all the Christian men."

Marilee blurted, "It works on 'em all."

Len looked at Marilee, who realized what she had said and just shrugged and said innocently, "Well, it's so." They all started laughing.

Sue brought the food. When she had laid it all out, Belle spoke.

"Man, that looks good. Sue, would you bring me one of those cheese burgers with fries please?"

"Uh huh."

167

Everyone was looking at Belle, who said, "Well, I just had a salad before. I'm in Rome so I'm going to eat like you all."

Hildee corrected her, "It's y'all."

Belle repeated it, "Y'all."

Betsy remarked, "Now ya got it, girl."

Nate interrupted, "Let's say the blessing."

They did and started eating. Cory came to the table with his wife and said, "Evenin'."

Ben said, "Evenin', Sheriff. Myra."

Ben introduced everyone and Cory shook their hands. When the introductions were finished, Cory looked at Hildee.

"Hildee, I hear ya helped Cob this afternoon."

Hildee said, "Yes, Sheriff."

The sheriff looked at Nate, "The young folks ain't goin' to press charges. Carl is pretty beat up and Cob thinks it's a hoot. Hildee did quite a number on Carl and he's sorta the laughing stock of the county. Do ya reckon you can let bygones be bygones?"

Nate looked at Hildee, who nodded, and Nate said, "Certainly, Sheriff."

Cory said, "Good. That's Christian of ya. I think Carl has learned his lesson."

Nate smiled, "I hope to see you in the morning."

Cory smiled, "We'll be there, God willing."

"Would you like to join us?"

Myra said, "Thanks for the invite but we just finished and we are goin' to visit some friends."

Hildee told them, "Have a nice evening."

Belle told them, "Y'all are going to have to let me in on the story."

Janice recounted the goings on at the wedding to much laughter in the telling of the story. After dinner, they all got in their vehicles and headed to the campground where they all went to the store and drank coffee and talked until after dark when the party broke up.

Paul and Belle left with Mike and Janice. Nate walked Hildee to the house while Len drove Marilee home. They walked holding hands and didn't say anything until they got to the porch. Hildee suddenly turned and kissed Nate passionately. It just sort of happened and Nate pulled her close his hands slipping too low on her back; actually way too low.

It took only a minute and he let go and said, "My love, you are a blessing and my greatest temptation. Forgive me."

Nate moved apart from Hildee but was still looking into her eyes.

"I'm as guilty. I didn't want ya ta stop."

Nate realized his love was breathing hard and said, "You go sit there and I'll sit here on the step until your pa gets back. You are altogether too dangerous, my love."

Hildee sighed and nodded and went to sit in the chair. Nate sat down on the steps and leaned against the banister.

"I reckon we'll be happy together."

"Yes, happy and content. God is good."

"Yup! All the time."

They sat quietly and Nate didn't realize he'd drifted off until Len pulled up and closed the truck door. Hildee was asleep in the chair.

Len asked quietly, "How come ya's sittin' on the step?"

Nate said in almost a whisper, "Avoiding great temptation."

Len just nodded and said, "It was also good I reckoned ya'll was waitin' on me."

Nate just nodded. It seemed the temptation was rising for Len and Marilee as well. He left and walked back to his camper. He slept in fits and starts that night then woke to the alarm and quickly got ready. He realized he had not prepared a sermon. Going through his notes from sermons he had practiced at bible college, he found one he thought would be appropriate.

He grabbed his Bible and guitar and headed for the pavilion. The praise team was setting up when he arrived. Hildee was already there and had on a new dress Nate had not seen her in before. His hormones started to rage and he went and sat at a picnic table and prayed.

Hildee came over, "Somethin' wrong, love?"

Nate sighed, "Just prayin' for strength to overcome the temptation that is a part of my blessing."

Hildee was looking puzzled. Nate said in a low voice, "One look at you and my hormones started raging. You, my dear, are driving me crazy."

Hildee agreed, "My dreams was tormented last night with lustful thoughts of ya. I thought I'd never sleep."

"Well, we'd better keep family around us this week."

Hildee smiled, "By the time we's hitched, we'll be exhausted from lack

169

of sleep."

Nate smiled, "I doubt that will stop us."

Hildee blushed slightly and said, "I reckon."

Len came over holding hands with Marilee.

Marilee said, "We's thinkin' we'd better stay in groups 'til Saturday."

Hildee grinned, "Ya got that right!"

Marilee laughed lightly, "I'm glad we ain't the only ones bein' tormented."

Nate affirmed, "You aren't."

Janice and Mike arrived with Paul and Belle and set up lawn chairs. There was quite a crowd around already.

Len said the opening prayer then announced after Labor Day the church would be meeting at the county fairgrounds center. He also told those present that they would have Sunday school once they were holding services inside.

The music started and it was another foot stompin', soul singing, loud praising of God. Nate noticed Belle had tears coming from her eyes. After five hymns, Nate started preaching.

Nate preached about marriage, first from the Song of Solomon. It was a touching message that had the adults listening intently to his explanation of the passages. Nate also explained how God had ordained the marriage bed to be a sacred thing between only a husband and wife to become one flesh. When he finished, there was dead silence. Nate looked around and saw husbands and wives with their arms around each other and some young people looking at the ground.

The silence lasted until the praise team started singing. Ben and his helpers took up a collection. The service ended with an alter call but no one came forward. Len said the closing prayer and the service was officially over.

People came to talk to Nate and he noticed Hildee was being approached by several young women. He knew God was at work. Forty minutes after the service had ended, Nate finally got to speak to Hildee. She came and put her arm through Nate's.

Nate asked, "I take it the sermon got some of the young women to thinking."

"Oh, yes. I'm goin' to meet with some of 'em to talk about chastity before marriage."

Nate just nodded.

"I think even some of them what gave it up already are now thinkin' they made a mistake. I told 'em God will forgive 'em and that they get to start over if'in they's really repentin' of their sin."

Nate smiled, "You are starting to talk like a preacher's wife."

Hildee smiled back, "I figured I should start practicing as the time is getting close."

"You sure can lose the accent when you decide to."

Hildee smiled, "Ya, but I loses some of my charm in the doin' of it."

Nate smiled.

Chapter 9

Monday was an easy day for Nate, Hildee and Carson. They had the Smith job site cleaned up and the trailer loaded for the dump by lunchtime.

As they were getting into the van, Nate said, "Why don't we drop this load at the dump and then I'll buy lunch at the diner?"

They arrived at the diner a little after one o'clock. As they were going in, they met Cal.

Nate said, "Hey, Cal," and offered his hand and the two men shook.

Cal smiled, "Hello, Hildee."

Hildee smiled and surprised Cal by hugging him, "Hey, Cal."

Nate said, "Carson, this is Cal," and the two men shook hands.

Hildee said, "We's jus goin' fer lunch. Ya want to come with?"

Cal said, "Sure thing."

The four of them went inside and sat down. A waitress came and took their orders. She had no sooner left than Sue showed up. She didn't have an apron on.

Sue said, "Hi, y'all."

Hildee said, "Hey, Sue," and noticed she wasn't wearing an apron, "Ya not workin', girl?"

"Nah, just gettin' off."

Nate asked, "Why don't ya pull up a chair and join us?"

She said, "Thanks," and she did. She looked at Cal, "I hadn't expected seein' ya at church, Cal."

Cal smiled, "That makes two of us. I reckon my folks is almost happier 'bout it than me."

Sue looked at Carson, "How's the wife and kids?"

Carson smiled broadly, "My sweetie is as great as ever and still puttin' up with me. The kids is growin' like weeds. Seems like they needs new clothes 'bout every other week."

Sue asked, "Y'all hear what happened at court?"

Hildee said, "What?"

"Terry Bradson pled guilty to a lesser charge and was sentenced to ninety days in the county lockup and five years of probation with a condition he stay at least a hundred yards from Nate and the deacons or officers of Drift River Church or its services."

Hildee replied, "Really?"

Sue answered, "Ya. Don't that beat all?"

Out of nowhere Cal said, "Sue, would you let me take you ta eat and to the dance comin' up?"

Sue looked at Cal, "Let me think on it. It would have ta be a double with a couple I approve of."

Cal nodded, "I git it. I have to earn your trust. I bin such a jerk in the past."

Sue looked at Hildee, who just smiled.

Sue asked, "Where ya wantin' to go?"

Cal said, "The steak place and then the dance. There's one a week Friday. I maybe can find a couple ya approve of to double with by then."

Sue said, "Well, ya know where to find me."

Cal smiled, "Thanks."

He looked at Nate and Hildee, who looked at each other. Hildee nodded.

Cal said, "Will ya double with us?"

Hildee looked at Sue ,who smiled, so Hildee said, "Sure. It'll be fun."

Cal looked at Sue who said, "All right then, it's a date."

Cal smiled, "Bein' a Christian has its vantages; I mean 'sides bein' right with God. Sue would never go out with me afore. Course I can't says as I kin blame her."

The waitress brought the food and Sue had a sandwich brought for her. After they finished eating, Nate took Hildee to the house and then took Carson home. Nate returned to his camper, cleaned up, and then went to his parents' campsite. His father and brother's trucks were there but they weren't so Nate walked up to the store.

Len was sitting on the store's porch and said as Nate took a seat, "Y'all got back early."

Nate nodded, "Job took less time than I figured on."

Len announced, "Your family's on a float trip. Left this mornin'. Should be returnin' shortly."

Nate just nodded.

Len asked, "Ya gittin' nervous? Weddin's only four days away."

"No. You?"

Len shook his head no, "Nah. I reckon' Marilee and me is suited."

Nate just nodded agreement. The men sat quietly for a couple of minutes until Hildee showed up.

She said, "Hi, pa," but went to Nate, leaned over and kissed him. He sighed when she stood up.

Len looked at Nate and said, "As her pa, I'm glad y'all's gettin' hitched Saturday or I'd be a sweatin' it for my baby girl."

Nate chuckled and added, "In case you haven't noticed, she isn't a baby anymore."

Len looked at Hildee as she sat in a chair next to Nate, "She'll always be my baby girl."

Hildee smiled, "Sho nuff, pa."

Len asked, "Have you decided what to do about a honeymoon?"

It was Hildee who answered, "Nate's got responsibilities. The church is too new for us to go gallavantin' on a Sunday. Just bein' with Nate will suit me."

Len said, "I think y'all should go away for a few days. Ya can leave after church Sunday."

Hildee looked at Nate, "That'd be nice."

Nate nodded, "I'll take care of it."

They all looked up as a sheriff's unit drove up. It was the sheriff who got out and came up onto the porch.

Nate was the first to speak, "Hi, Cory."

Cory replied, "Hey. How y'all doin' on this fine day?"

Len said, "Enjoyin' it. Take a load off."

Cory sat down and took his hat off, "I suppose y'all heard about Terry Bradson."

Len said, "Yup."

Cory admitted, "The judge gave him a light sentence seein' as it were his first offense and he has roots in the county."

Len said,

"Uh huh."

"Well, we found out who did the shootin' here."

Nate said, "Who was it?"

Cory looked at Nate, "Young Tommy Crenshaw. He still had the rifle in his room. He fessed up. At first he was all worked up and blamin' y'all for Tye's death. His folks have put him right 'bout it. The county prosecutin' attorney's is wantin' to let him plead out seein' he's a minor. I think the boy's true all broke up 'bout it now. He ain't been in trouble before. The prosecutor don't want ya'll raisin' a ruckus seein' as ya's all celebrities of a sort, so wants to know if ya got objections. Tommy will do a short time in a juvie lockup if he pleads. His record will be sealed and won't affect his getting' a job when he comes ah age. Ya want him tried as an adult?"

Nate shook his head no. "You all know him better than me and if you say that's best, it's ok by me."

"The young fellers who tried to rob ya, Len, is goin' to be tried in a few weeks. They all couldn't make bail so's they's stayed locked up. Y'all will need to testify here. After, they's goin' to be sent for trial for a holdup over in Hebstville."

Len looked at Cory, "Too bad they jist didn't plead guilty."

"May still happen. Well, I guess I'll be gettin' on home. Myra will be 'spectin me home early tonight."

They said goodbye and Cory left.

Len said, "He's a good ole boy."

Cory had no sooner left then the bus bringing back floaters arrived. Mike, Janice, Paul and Belle got off. They saw Nate, Len, and Hildee sitting on the porch and waved. The men were wearing shorts and tee shirts while the women had beach dresses on over their swimsuits. They unloaded their cooler and put it on the grass then walked over to the porch. Mike had his arm around Janice while Paul and Belle were walking hand-in-hand.

When they got to the porch, Paul said, "Hey everybody. Boy, was that fun. I feel like a teenager on summer vacation."

The four new arrivals took chairs. Janice plopped down saying, "That really was fun."

Belle added, "There's this tree overhanging the river and we all got to swing on a rope from a branch over a cliff and drop into the water, about a ten foot drop. It was a blast."

Paul agreed, "Being outdoors does work up an appetite, though. We thought we brought more than enough food but we gobbled it all."

Nate looked at Hildee and they both smiled.

Belle said, "We are going to have to get our own RV. It doesn't have to be as fancy as you all have. Something more basic will do."

Nate noticed his mother and his father exchange a look. Nate knew that, in fact, Belle's willingness to settle for something "basic" was a little out of character for her.

Len reported, "There's ah older one that's in real good shape up fer sale. It's on lot 212. I can vouch everythin' in it works. The couple what owns it give me a key. You might wanna have a look see. There's a list of what comes with it on the kitchen counter."

Paul said, "We'll go look at it."

Marilee pulled up and got out of her vehicle and came to the porch, "Hey, everyone." Len got up and brought another chair over beside his. Marilee kissed him lightly then sat down in the chair, saying, "Thanks, dear."

Paul announced, "Belle and I will be leaving shortly. We'll be back by Friday though."

Nate said, "I pray you have a safe journey."

"Thanks, Nate," Belle said.

Paul announced, "We'd better get going. I want to swing around lot 212 before the long drive back home."

Len told them, "I'll git the key," went into the store then came back and handed it to Paul.

Paul and Belle got up, "We'll be back shortly."

Mike looked at Hildee, "Nate's oldest brother, Ted, and his wife, Kathleen, will be coming down Thursday."

Hildee said, "I look forwards to meetin' 'em."

Mike got up, "It's been a long day and I'll think I'll go back to the campsite and relax."

Len shouldn't have said it but he did, "I'm lookin' to have some of that vacation relaxin' soon."

Hildee said, "Behave, Pa."

Len said, "I ain't sayin' nothin' ain't true."

Janice took Mike's arm and said with a broad smile, "It's time to relax, husband dear."

The couple left and, on the way, Mike picked up the empty cooler with one hand and the couple walked hand-in-hand back toward their campsite.

Marilee said, "You should otta behave, Len."

"Ain't no fun in behavin', sweet cheeks."

Marilee blushed slightly and Hildee giggled.

Len turned to Hildee, "What?" Hildee just smiled and looked at Marilee, who was smiling broadly.

Nate added, "Hope we are as frisky when we get to be as old as you are, Len."

Len half rose from his seat shaking his fist, "I object to the ole part." Nate started laughing and the women followed.

Len asked, "What?"

Hildee smiled, "Pa, ya sure are comical when ya tries to be intimidatin' like."

Len was now fully sitting, "Don't git no respect no how."

Marilee replied, "You bring it on yarself."

Hildee added, "Sho nuff."

Len looked at Marilee, "Don't encourage Nate as he's goin' to be kin folk and then we's goin' to have to put up with him."

Hildee said smiling broadly, "Nate, ya should ought ta preach on them what gives it otta be able to take it."

Len retorted, "That's not fightin' fair."

"Pa, who said the teasin's ever fair?"

Marilee said, "Uh huh."

Len turned to Marilee, "Whose side you takin' anyway?"

Marilee put her chin up and looked sideways at Len, "The right side uh course."

"I might jist as well surrender seein's y'all gangin' up on a poor ole man."

"That's pitiful, Pa. Ya must be runnin' out of witty sayin's and comebacks."

Len threatened, "Ya's still my young un until Saturday and I can still take ya over my knee."

Nate countered, "You'd best think on that, Len. Remember the way she laid Carl out cold."

"Oh yeah. I forgot."

Nate chuckled, "I won't."

Hildee said playfully and smiling broadly, "Good. That will make things go easier fer ya."

Nate changed the subject and announced, "I'm gittin' hungry."

"Hey lookie, it's rubbin' off. Hear him speakin' local."

Nate's phone rang and he answered it, "Hello. This is Nate."

Hildee and the others listened to his side of the call, "Yeah, it's all taken care of. Oh no. I forgot. Yeah, first thing in the morning. I don't know. Because it was family, I never thought to ask. Yes, it would be embarrassing. We'll take care of it. Thanks, Rick."

Nate hung up and asked Len, "Have you got your marriage license yet?"

Len looked at Marilee and then at Nate, "Nope. I reckon love's got me all conflabberated don't ya see."

"That makes two of us. We'd better see about it first thing in the morning."

Hildee noted, "That's somethin' men folk is supposed to take care of."

Marilee agreed, "Well, the part 'bout love havin' 'im all confused gits him some leeway."

"I reckon," Hildee giggled.

Len looked at Marilee, "Well, you'll be at the courthouse anyway."

Marilee teased, "If'in we're busy, I might not be able to leave."

Len looked shocked.

Hildee chuckled, "Pa, I reckon she's teasin' ya."

Marilee smiled, "For this, I can git time."

Len appeared relieved, "That's good. I sure do fer certain want to get hitched to ya on Saturday."

Hildee pointed out, "Licenses is one of them first things Nate usually asks couples."

Nate sighed, "True."

Hildee sighed dramatically, "I guess he's havin' doubts."

Nate looked at Hildee and smiled, "Don't even go there. I'm not letting you push those buttons. I'm too happy you are going to marry me."

Hildee smiled, "Good answer."

Len piped up, "I ain't the only one wants vacation relaxin' time."

"Pa! Behave yarself."

Len looked at his daughter, "I s'pose ya's lookin' forward to some as well."

Hildee blushed and Marilee said, "Len! You are embarrassin' her."

Len looked at Nate, "Serves 'em right, harassin' an ole feller like me."

Nate sighed, "I guess I'll have to preach on them what gives it otta be able to take it."

The women started laughing and Len insisted, "It ain't funny!"

Hildee said through the laughter, "Ya, it is, pa."

Nate was now laughing as well and Len was shaking his head

muttering, "What is I gittin' into?"

Hildee declared, "I'm goin' to order us some food," and went into the store. They ate grilled cheese sandwiches and soup for supper. About six, Marilee left with Hildee to go to Hildee's bridal shower. It was dark when the women returned and Nate was sitting on the house porch talking with Len when they pulled up.

Marilee was first out and called out, "Come hep us bring Hildee's loot inside."

The men went to help. Hildee got out of the truck and greeted Nate with a kiss. They took the bags inside then Nate and Hildee went to sit on the porch. They sat in the loveseat swing chair and Nate put his arm around Hildee's shoulder.

"Did you have fun?"

"Oh yeah, even though it was embarrassin' at times. Some of my friends have a pure wicked streak 'bout shower gifts."

Nate smiled.

"You will be gentle with me on our weddin' night."

"You're nervous about it?"

Hildee sighed, "Sorta." She paused and added, "Yes. I know what I been told but 'cause it's new and the tellin's not the same as doin', if ya understand."

Nate could tell she was concerned about it. He said, "We'll work through it together and go at a pace you are comfortable with. I'll be just as gentle as you need me to be."

"Good. I'm tired so I think I'll turn in."

Nate got up and held out his hand and helped Hildee up. When they reached the door, they exchanged a long lingering kiss and Nate said, "Good night, love." He watched as Hildee went inside then walked back to his campsite.

Nate was up early on Tuesday morning and met Carson at the store. He got Carson started on the cutting brush for the new RV sites using Len's tools. He then went to the store where he met Len and Hildee and they all headed for the county offices where they joined up with Marilee to get the marriage licenses.

They walked into the office and a man came to the counter, "May I help you?"

Nate was closest so said, "We would like to get a marriage license, please."

The man asked, "May I see your documents?"

Hildee and Nate were issued their license fairly quickly because they had never been married. They just filled out the forms, showed their paperwork and Nate paid the fee.

After Nate and Hildee were processed, Len said, "We'd like a marriage license please."

The man asked for their application and documents. He looked at them and said, "I see you have both been married before."

Len answered, "Yes."

The man said, "May I see your divorce decrees, please."

"We's both lost our spouses."

"Their being missing does not provide a grounds for remarriage."

"Ya don' understand. They's passed on."

"That's not what your application says."

Len said, "Then change it."

"I can't because you signed it and I accepted it."

Len said, "But my wife passed."

The man smiled, "I can accept a death certificate."

Marilee fished in her purse and took her copy of her deceased husband's certificate out of her purse.

Len said, "I gave mine to the insurance company."

"I'll have to have one."

Len stood open mouthed.

Marilee said, "I'd like to talk to George, please."

The man said, "Just a minute, please," and left.

An elderly man came to the counter and Marilee said, "Hi, George."

He smiled, "Hey, Marilee. What's happenin'?"

Marilee said, "Len and I are fixin' to get hitched on Saturday and the new feller says 'cause Len filled out the form wrong," and with that Marilee gave Len "the look" and then continued, "He has to provide a death certificate for his wife."

George looked at Len, "How's it goin', Len?"

"It was a goin' good until I messed up the paperwork."

George turned to his man, "I known Len since he was a knee high to a grasshopper. He's never bin good with paperwork. I did, though, attend his wife's funeral, God bless her soul." George looked at Hildee, "Yar ma was a fine woman, Hildee."

Hildee said, "Thank you, sir."

George looked at Len, "Too bad Hildee's mother didn't learn ya good like she did Hildee."

Hildee agreed, "Pa's a little hardheaded."

George said, "Don't I know it," and picked up the application and said, "Change this here and initial it and I'll see ya's issued a license."

Len said, "Thanks, George."

As they changed the application, George commented, "Ya know y'all's marriages is the talk of the county."

Len stammered, "No kiddin'?"

"Yup. Folks is a wonderin' how it is an ole fart like you got the pretty widow Marilee and how this young homely feller got a knockout like Hildee."

Nate interjected, "We are just blessed, I guess."

"Preacher, ain't ya bin taught not to interrupt?"

"The way I was taught, a fellow could defend himself."

George chuckled, "I reckon," then asked Len for the fee.

Len stated, "Thet's highway robbery."

"Ya sayin' Marilee's not worth it?" George smiled.

Len looked at George, "Ya's a slippery ole politician is what ya are."

"It's why I bin reelected all these decades, don't ya know."

"Well, it ain't because ya's Mr. Personality."

George advised, "Careful Len, I ain't prepared the license yet."

Len bowed down from the waist with a broad hand flourish, "Yar most high potentate honor, may I has a marriage license, pretty please?"

George laughed, "Good un, Len. Jist give me a minute."

Len looked at Marilee, who was smiling broadly.

Nate reckoned, "The entertainment here is worth the price of admission."

George called out, "I heard that."

"We already got our license."

George called out, "Ya can learn from 'im, Len."

Len gave Nate a dirty look but Marilee elbowed Len lightly. He said, "What?"

George brought the license and Len said, "Thanks, George. Would ya and yar wife like to come to the weddin' on Saturday at the campground?

We's havin' BBQ after the ceremony and there'll be dancin' in the pavilion."

George remarked, "Ya coulda saved us both aggravation by jist invitin' me up front."

Len smiled, "It wouldn' a bin as much fun, though," and offered his hand, which George shook.

George asked, "What time?"

Len told him and the little group left George's office.

In the hall, Marilee said, "I'd better git back to my office," and kissed Len and hurried away. Len watched her hurry down the hall.

Hildee said, "Whatcha lookin' at, pa?"

"None y'uns."

Nate looked at Hildee, who said, "It means none of you uns business."

Nate just nodded understanding.

The rest of the morning and that afternoon, Nate and Hildee helped Carson with brush clearing. They called it a day at four and went and got cleaned up. After showering, Nate was sitting on a chair reading when his mother showed up. Nate rose and hugged her.

Janice took a seat and Nate asked, "Would you like something to drink?"

"No thanks, son."

Nate noted, "It seems you and dad are having a good time here."

Janice nodded, "The place suits us. Kathleen, though, probably won't take to it."

Nate agreed, "Kathleen and Ted seem to get along together, but she's a hard core snob."

Again Janice nodded, "I've been praying about that. Belle seems to be coming around though."

Nate nodded as he said, "Uh huh."

Janice looked at her son, "You've got a good one in Hildee."

"I know."

Janice said, "Paul told Belle she wouldn't have to work if she had lower expectations and that made her think. They've got the big house sold and they're going to move to a nice but modest three bedroom bungalow."

"Wise move. There's just the two of them."

"It's supposed to be a secret but I think Belle's pregnant."

182

Nate looked at his mother, "How did you find out?"

"It's hard to keep that a secret when you have morning sickness and you're staying with somebody else in an RV. It also explains the move to the bungalow."

"Uh huh."

Janice sighed, "I suppose she's planning to be a stay at home mom."

"Good for her."

"Want to hear a shocker?"

Nate asked, "What?"

"I'm pregnant, too."

Nate was stunned and blurted out, "How did that happen?"

Janice smiled, "The usual way."

"Congratulations, mom," and Nate got up, leaned over and hugged her. He then returned to his chair.

"Thank you, son."

"You're forty-eight, mom."

"I know how old I am son. I haven't been through menopause and it's happened so it's God's will. Believe me it was unexpected. We purposely started young so our children would be grown while we were still young enough to enjoy each other."

Nate paused, "You really have been enjoying yourselves. No wonder dad's acting like a teenager."

"He ain't the only one. My hormones have me wired for fun."

"Too much information, mom."

Janice smiled.

Nate smiled back, "What did the doctor say?"

"You know, I've always been active and I'm in really good shape. It's not all that common for this to happen, but there are lots more women my age than you would think who successfully deliver. Still there's risks for me, but we are going to keep a close eye on my health. I'm going to the doctor regularly."

Nate asked, "May I tell Hildee?"

"No reason why not. Just don't tell your brothers yet. They don't know."

"How come?"

Janice sighed, "I didn't think they'd be as understanding as you."

Nate asked, "How far along are you?"

"About six weeks."

"I'm going to have a new brother."

"Or a sister."

"Yes, there is that possibility, isn't there?"

"You are taking this well."

Nate laughed, "It's you and dad that will be changing diapers again. Dad will be what, about sixty-eight, when the new addition is graduating high school."

"I'm aware of that, son. We know what we're facing. We may need some help down the road."

"I'll be there for you."

"Thank you. Imagine how we felt. I thought I was sick at first. You know with my age and all. I have sons from twenty-eight to thirty; almost thirty-one. Imagine if I hadn't married your father at seventeen and gotten pregnant right off. After all those years, we didn't think it would happen again. We thought we were past all that then boom."

"This has surely been an unusual year."

"That's an understatement."

Nate looked up and saw Hildee coming. Hildee greeted them when she got close, "Hey."

Janice said, "Take a load off. I have news."

"Ok."

"I think Belle is pregnant," and told Hildee about her observations.

"I reckon you're right. That's great news but I suppose we'll have to wait for Belle to tell us afore we throw a party."

"You want to hear a shocker?"

"Shoot."

"I'm pregnant."

Hildee jumped up and hugged Janice, saying, "Oh, that's great, another family member."

"Not the reaction I anticipated."

"Why not?"

"My age."

Hildee shrugged, "Might as well rejoice. God's done decided the matter."

Janice laughed, "You'll make a good preacher's wife."

Hildee sat down and asked, "Have you told the brothers yet?"

184

Janice shook her head no.

"You gonna wait until after the weddin' to tell 'em?"

"Mike and I thought that might be the thing to do. I'm not sure, though."

Hildee nodded, "Ya don't think they'll take it well?"

"Probably not, but they might surprise us."

"I pray they do."

Nate added, "When my sibling gets older, my mom and dad might need some help."

"We can hep. He or she can come here for the summers and play with our kids."

Janice smiled, "So you're certainly planning to have a family?"

Hildee looked up at the sky and said, "I reckon it's part of the big boss's plan."

Janice laughed, "Oh, you are such a delight Hildee."

Hildee looked at Nate, "Dependin' on how your brothers and their wives take it, you may have to send me to your ma for a bit. When the new baby comes, I can hep her out for a while. The birth could be hard on her seein's she's a little older." Hildee looked at Janice, "I mean no offense."

"None taken. Your offer is appreciated and accepted."

Nate just nodded agreement.

Janice got up, "Well, I'd better go tell Mike we have at least some of the family being supportive."

Hildee got up and hugged Janice again before Janice walked away. Hildee sat down.

Nate said, "Who'd have thought?"

"It sure do beat all. You ate yet?"

"Not yet."

"Well I'll go in and make us somethin' if'in you promise to stay out here."

"I understand and promise."

They ate outside and talked. Nate walked Hildee home before dark.

Chapter 10

Wednesday started out like any regular work day. In the morning, Hildee and Nate worked with Carson chipping the previous day's cutting and started some new work. Nate and Hildee stopped at lunch time but Carson would work alone in the afternoon cutting brush. For safety, they had agreed not to run the chipper unless two of them were working.

After lunch, Hildee fetched her swim suit then she and Nate went to see Mike and Janice. They were sitting out reading.

Nate mentioned, "We thought we'd take the boat down to the sandbar and go swimming. Want to come?"

Mike looked at Janice, who smiled, and he said, "Give us a minute to get our swim suits on."

The four of them spent about two hours on the river but a gentle rain started to move in so they cut their outing short. They spent the rest of the afternoon under cover at Mike and Janice's, sitting in lawn chairs talking. About four-thirty, Nate's oldest brother, Ted, and his wife, Kathleen, showed up.

Ted got out first, "Hi." The four got up and went to greet Ted and Kathleen. Janice did the introductions, "Ted, Kathleen, this is Nate's fiancée, Hildee. Hildee, this is Ted and his wife, Kate."

Kathleen said coldly, "I prefer Kathleen."

As Hildee went to embrace Kathleen, Kathleen held out her hand to shake indicating she didn't want to hug Hildee. Hildee shrugged and shook Kathleen's hand. Hildee was surprised when Janice shook Kathleen's hand as well.

Janice went to Ted and hugged him so Hildee followed her lead. Ted broke into a broad smile.

Mike asked, "Can I help with your luggage?"

Ted sighed and Nate could tell he was uncomfortable, "Kathleen thought it would be too much of an imposition to stay here. We have a room at a bed and breakfast."

Janice broke the tension by saying, "Come and have a seat. How about a beverage?"

Kathleen said haughtily, "No, thank you."

Ted replied, "I'd like a cold beer if you have one."

Kathleen gave Ted a dirty look as Mike got up saying, "I'll get you one."

Kathleen asked, "Did Belle tell you she's pregnant?"

Janice answered, "No, but I figured she was because it looked like she was having morning sickness."

Kathleen sneered, "Can you imagine being pregnant at her age?"

Hildee had just taken a sip of ice tea and choked on it. She looked at Janice, who was trying to stifle laughter.

Mike had come out of the RV and, as he handed Ted the bottle, commented, "Belle is still a young woman."

Kathleen retorted, "She's too old to be starting a family. I can't imagine at her age. It's a disgrace to the family."

Mike choked back a retort and looked at Janice. Nate looked at Hildee, who had turned her head away and was struggling not to laugh. Nate could almost guess the reaction when his mom told Kathleen the other news.

Janice smiled and said innocently, "It think it's wonderful. In fact, we'll be having another baby in the family"

Kathleen looked at Hildee, "I guess I know now why the hurry up marriage for Nate."

Hildee couldn't help it any longer and broke out in laughter and that set Janice off. Mike and Nate were not far behind. They were bent over in laughter.

Kathleen continued, "I don't see what's funny about Nate marrying a slut."

The result was not what Kathleen expected. The laughter increased and Hildee and Janice were doubled over, tears running down their faces.

Kathleen looked at Nate, "As a man of the cloth, I wouldn't have thought you'd find humor in your situation."

The laughter was now louder. Nate could tell by the look on Kathleen's face she was frustrated at the response to her comments. Nate thought the look on Ted's face was priceless.

Nate saw Kathleen look at Ted, "We had best go."

Ted sat back, "I don't think so."

Kathleen looked shocked and the laughter that had begun to die down started up again.

Kathleen looked at Ted, "I think they are drunk."

Janice got out between the laughs, "Drunk on love."

The laughter grew again and Kathleen was sitting with what Nate thought was a pouting look on her face.

Kathleen looked at Ted, "I'm leaving."

Ted cautioned, "Suit yourself but it's a long walk back to the bed and breakfast."

Kathleen's mouth pursed and she folded her arms across her chest.

When the laughter died down, Ted asked, "Will someone let me in on the joke?"

Mike got it out, "It's your mother who is pregnant."

Ted's mouth dropped open and he blurted out, "How?"

Mike looked at Janice, "No wonder Kathleen's never been knocked up."

Kathleen turned a deep red and that set off laughter again. Kathleen was now sitting looking at the ground with what Nate thought was an angry look on her face.

Hildee looked at her, "Oh, loosen up, Kate. Life is too short ta be goin' round like you have a corn cob up your rear end."

Kathleen jumped out of her chair and charged Hildee, who stood up and, when Kathleen was close, stepped sideways and put her in a bear hug. Hildee lifted her off the ground with hardly any effort and carried her to Ted and dropped Kathleen into Ted's lap.

Hildee announced, "She's your problem, Ted. You handle her," and then Hildee calmly walked back to her chair.

Kathleen moved to get up and Ted put his arms around her and said sternly, "Stay put, love. You've pushed it past the limit."

Kathleen broke down and started sobbing. Hildee acted instinctively and went to her. Ted let go and Hildee picked her up effortlessly talking in soothing tones. Janice went and opened the RV door and Hildee carried Kathleen inside.

Ted looked at the other two men, "Well, that was certainly unexpected. I wonder what it's all about."

Mike declared, "It's never boring around here."

Nate injected, "There's more here than meets the eyes."

Inside the RV, Kathleen had lost it entirely. Hildee was sitting on the sofa rocking her as she sobbed, the tears wetting Hildee's blouse. Janice was kneeling on the floor stroking Kathleen's head. Hildee looked at Janice, who had tears in her eyes. Suddenly the three women were crying together. Almost twenty-minutes had passed and Kathleen was still lying with her head in Hildee's lap.

Kathleen's eyes were red and she didn't seem to have any energy left. It was then she said, "I've never used birth control and yet no pregnancy," then started crying gently. She cried herself to sleep.

Hildee looked at Janice, "I'll stay with her. You should maybe go talk to Ted."

Janice nodded and went outside and looked at Ted, "She's sleeping. Hildee is staying with her. Son, we need to take a walk and talk." Janice motioned and Ted got up and started walking with his mother. They were silent until they had walked about a hundred yards.

Ted asked, "Is she going to be ok?"

Janice looked at her oldest son, "It's a woman thing. Did you know she's never used birth control?"

Ted suddenly got sad, "We didn't talk about it. She seemed embarrassed about it."

"She thinks she can't have children."

"I didn't think she wanted any. It seemed to be the only thing we couldn't talk about because it always set her off and she'd get all angry and emotional."

"I'll bet she doesn't have any close women friends."

"No, she doesn't."

"You might want to comfort her and reassure her when you are alone. You might also want to consider it might not be her and there may be something a good doctor could help you with. Thank God we have good insurance. Use it, son."

Ted nodded, "I will."

"We should get back."

"Thanks, mom."

The mother and son went back to the campsite. Nate and his father were talking about buying boats.

When they sat down, Mike asked, "Everything alright?"

"I think it will be."

Nate said, "We should pray. Janice, you know what's going on so why don't you lead." They all prayed together then started talking. Hildee and Kathleen came out of the RV about a half hour later.

Ted went and embraced his wife and said, "Let's go for a walk."

Ted took Kathleen's hand and they walked away. They were gone for almost an hour and returned smiling to find Mike grilling burgers and corn on the cob. Hildee and Janice were just finishing setting the picnic table. Nate was not there.

Ted asked, "Where's Nate?"

Hildee replied, "He had ta go 'cause one of the church folks was rushed ta the hospital. Got a phone call. Don't know when he'll be comin' back."

Ted just nodded.

Mike said, "I hope everyone's hungry."

Kathleen announced, "I'm very hungry."

The family enjoyed the meal and it was as though the events of the afternoon had never happened. Nate returned after a two hour absence to find everyone sitting around Mike's fire pit watching the logs burn and talking.

Hildee got up and greeted Nate with a hug, "How'd it go?"

"It was a stroke. They got to him in time and he's going to be all right."

"Good. Have ya eaten?"

Nate shook his head no.

Janice said, "I'll make you a sandwich," and hurried off.

Nate sat down and looked at the fire, "This is nice."

Hildee said, "We should get one."

Nate nodded agreement.

Out of nowhere Kathleen, who had been sitting quietly next to Ted holding his hand, said, "I can see why you like it here."

Hildee said, "Uh huh."

Mike looked at Kathleen and said, "That's local talk for I agree or you're welcome depending on the circumstances."

Kathleen just nodded.

Janice came out with a sandwich and a bottle of water and handed them to Nate, who said, "Thanks, mom."

Ted declared, "We'd better head out to the bed and breakfast. It's getting late."

Kathleen sighed, "I suppose so," and got up and hugged everyone goodbye including Hildee.

As they drove away, Nate started eating.

Janice said, "It was an interesting day."

Hildee nodded, "It were thet."

Mike asked, "What was all that with Kathleen about?"

Janice looked at Mike and smiled, "It's woman stuff, dear, and not for a man's ears, no matter how wonderful and understanding the man is."

Mike smiled, "Understood," and looked at Nate.

Nate shrugged and said between bites, "Some things are best left to the women."

Hildee agreed, "We need other woman folk we can talk ta, knowin' it'll stay between."

Nate finished his sandwich, "It's dark so I'd best walk Hildee home."

Chapter 11

The next morning Nate got up late, about seven-thirty. He had just had his first cup of coffee when there was a knock on the door. Nate opened it to find Hildee standing there.

Hildee was holding a clipboard, "Hi, love. Ya best come outside."

Nate stepped outside still in his bare feet. Hildee handed him the clipboard to which was attached a check, "Ya best sign Carson's paycheck fer last week. He's got a family to feed."

Nate nodded, "Thanks, Hildee. Next week we'll have to get you signing authority on our accounts."

Hildee smiled, "I like the 'our'. Ya sure are bein' a lay-about this mornin'. Carson's already hard at work."

Nate smiled, "Nag, nag, nag."

Hildee shook her head and smiled, "I'm in too good a mood ta be harassed this mornin', even by a man practiced at it like ya is."

"Can I buy you breakfast in town? I'm takin' the day off."

Hildee said smiling, "Only if'in you put on shoes and a shirt. Betsy ain't goin' to serve ya like that."

Nate nodded, "I'll get right to it. Meet you at the store."

It took a little longer than Nate had thought to get to the store. Len was just coming outside when Nate arrived.

"Mornin', Len."

"It are thet. Bee-u-tee-full is what it is. Warm an' sunny with just the wind as gentle as a lover's hand on yar cheek."

"Love sure does have you talking funny."

Len smiled and sat down in porch rocker, "Fer sure. Hildee had to go up to the house. Said she'd be back directly."

Nate took a seat, "I am sure lookin' forward to being married."

"Bein' with Marilee is sho nuff pleasurable. Can't wait for the weddin' bed."

Nate laughed, "I guess you've still got some life in you."

Len looked at Nate with a smile, "I reckon."

The men talked for a while and Nate started to get worried about Hildee and called her. She picked up the phone and Nate could tell she was crying.

"What's wrong, Hildee?"

192

Hildee said as she cried, "It's ruined is what it is."

"What's ruined?"

"The weddin's wrecked I tell ya," and started sobbing.

"I'm coming up there."

Nate could tell Hildee was in tears as she said, "Don't ya dare." Hildee hung up on him. Nate sat staring at the phone.

Len asked, "What's wrong?"

"I don't know but she said not to go up to the house."

Nate would later think it was providence that his mother had been coming to the store and overheard the last part of the phone call, "What's the problem, son?"

"Hildee's crying and I don't know why. I said I'd go to the house and she said not to dare. She said the wedding is ruined."

Janice said, "I'll go see what's up. You bring your father some milk for his coffee."

Nate nodded and his mother set off. Nate hurried into the store and bought a carton of milk, which he delivered double-time to his father.

As Nate arrived his father said, "What's got you all in a rush and where's your mother?"

"Hildee's upset and I don't know why. Mom went to talk with her."

Mike teased Nate, "Probably having second thoughts."

"That's not funny, dad."

Without saying anything else, Nate headed back to the store. His father called out, "Thanks for the milk."

Nate was now very worried. Was Hildee suddenly having second thoughts? Nate could not imagine that. He prayed it wasn't that as he rushed back to the store.

Len was still sitting on the porch when Nate got back. Nate said, "Mom not back?"

"Does it look like she's back?"

Nate sighed, "I don't understand women."

"Ya might as well reckon ya never will. Ya won't never."

Nate was pacing the porch. Len ordered, "Boy, chill! Ya's restless as a 'coon in a trap."

"Easy for you to say. Marilee isn't all emotional."

Len shared his country wisdom, "Women folk is always 'motional 'round times like this. Weddin's, funeral's, and babies bein' born makes 'em all mushy like." Len paused then added with a smile, "The rest of the time they's sure good to have 'round."

"I wonder what's wrong?"

"Ain't no tellin' what's in Hildee's mind 'til she says."

Nate sat fidgety for about ten minutes until his mother came around the corner of the building and said, "Hildee's waiting for you on the house porch."

Nate nodded, got up, and then rushed up the path to the house. He went quickly hoping it wasn't as bad as he imagined. Nate rushed up onto the porch and found Hildee sitting in a chair waiting for him. Her eyes were red from crying. Nate took a seat next to her.

"We can't git hitched tomorrow."

Nate felt like a knife had gone through his heart. It took all the strength he could muster to keep from breaking down. As it was tears started to flow. Nate got up and walked off the porch. He didn't want Hildee seeing him break down.

Hildee was taken aback and saw him with his head hung low and slouched over. It occurred to her how she had said it and what he was probably thinking.

She screamed, "Nate, it's not that!"

Nate looked over his shoulder to see Hildee running to him. He turned and she jumped into his arms and kissed him. Then she clung to him saying, "It' ain't what ya's thinkin', Nate. Truly it ain't."

"What is it?"

Hildee backed away and looked at the ground, "My time came."

"What?"

Hildee looked up but not directly into his eyes repeated it, "My time came?"

"Huh."

"My woman time came early."

Nate blurted, "All this because your period came early?" Hildee looked down and Nate interpreted it as a guilty look. "For the love of God woman, I thought you were throwing me over."

"Oh no!" She grabbed on and clung to Nate, "Oh, no! Never that! Never that."

Nate said gently, "Woman, you sure can be a trial."

Hildee let go of him and said looking at the ground again, "But the

194

weddin's ruined, Nate. It's my fault 'cause I didn't reckon on it and I'm usual jist as regular as a clock."

"This doesn't have anything to do with the wedding."

"But what about, well, you know."

Nate asked, "Do you know how many times this will happen over our married life? Do you? Do you think I'm so stupid I don't know how this all works."

Hildee looked surprised, "I never thought on it." Nate threw his arms in the air dramatically, "I'm going to marry an idjit that's what I'm doing!"

Hildee smiled, "You said you was goin' to."

Nate said forcefully, "Well of course I'm going to. I love you."

"In spite of the fact I can be as dense as fog in the river valley durin' a weather change."

Nate smiled, "Yes."

Hildee said with a smile, "Ya didn' have to agree," and hit Nate playfully.

Nate sighed, "Let's go eat."

"Not 'til we kiss and make up."

They did right there on the front lawn. It was a passionate kiss that Nate broke off breathing hard and said, "Saturday seems to be forever away."

"Ya got thet right, preacher man."

Nate looked at Hildee, who was flushed. He put out his hand and she took it. They got in the pickup truck and drove to the diner. The early breakfast rush was over so they went to a booth as soon as they went in.

Betsy came to their table, "Good mornin'. Ya'll getting' nervous yet."

Nate murmured, "Hildee has me a basket case."

Betsy looked at Hildee, who said, "He's maybe exaggeratin' a little."

"It's not me that's dense as fog in the river valley during a weather change."

"Like I said, he's exaggeratin', like makin' the Grand Canyon out of a molehole."

Hildee gave Nate the look. He was looking at the menu and looked up with his eyes. They both broke into smiles.

Betsy said, "Ya two can't even fight right."

Nate asked, "You and Ben going to teach us."

Betsy smiled, "We's lovers not fighters."

Hildee looked shocked and Betsy said, "Not that kind of lovers. Girl. Ya need to git hitched quick; your mind's in the gutter. What can I git y'all?"

Betsy took their orders and hurried off. She'd no sooner left than two old fellows walked by their table. Nate recognized one of them.

"Hello, Mr. Washington."

The men stopped and one said, "Well, hello there, young feller. Ya look familiar. Where do I know ya from?"

Nate said, "I met you on a bench across from the Bryce River Community Church. I'm Nate Christian."

Willie Washington brightened up, "Ya, I remember now. This is my friend, James Butterman."

Nate held out his hand, "Pleased to meet you Mr. Butterman. Gentlemen, this is my fiancée, Hildee Cole."

Hildee said, "Pleased," and shook hands with the men, "Would y'all like to join us?"

Willie said, "Thanks for ta offer but James's kids is come to visit and they's parkin' the car."

Nate said, "Maybe another time then."

James asked, "Ya the feller preachin' down at the camp?"

Nate smiled, "That's me."

Willie remarked, "I'd be comin' to service if I had a ride."

Nate advised, "I can arrange a ride but you might have to come early and stay a little late."

Willie smiled, "Ain't got nothin' else ta do."

"Well then, that's what I'll do." They arranged the time and the two men went to find a table.

Betsy came with the food, "Here it is. Y'all enjoy. I'm busy so I can't talk. Anything else?"

Hildee looked at Nate, who said, "We're good."

They had just started eating when Ben came in with Billie. They came over, "Mind some company?"

Hildee said as she finished chewing, "Ya'll is welcome."

Nate swallowed and added, "Good to see you."

The men sat down and Ben said, "Ya'll seem ready."

Nate looked at Hildee ,who smiled and said, "I was earlier wound tighter than a wire coil in a 'lectric motor."

Ben sat back, "Ya seem over it."

Hildee nodded, "Nate done comforted me."

Billie put in, "He didn' wan ya backin' out."

Hildee smiled, "No chance ah thet."

Ben asked, "Ya hear the latest on First Community Church of Bryce River?"

Nate shook his head no.

"Seems the bank is foreclosin' an' the one's that run it don't want to pay outta their own pockets. They's no longer playin' at church. Interestin' how's when push comes to shove, some folks show their true colors. Rumor has it they jist signed it over ta the bank. There's a fer sale sign on the lawn."

Nate just nodded in acknowledgement, "Somebody may end up buyin' it to turn into a house."

Ben agreed, "Not likely it'll remain a church seein' it has a bad rep."

Billie jumped in, "Mos' likely we'll be havin' more folks come to our services. Words gittin' out."

Hildee added, "Goes to show church is about folks seekin' God, not a buildin' to gather in."

Ben answered, "Amen to that, sister."

The little group had a pleasant breakfast and a leisurely coffee afterward. When Nate asked, Ben said he'd arrange a ride for Willie.

Nate and Hildee were back at the campground by eleven. Hildee got out at the store and went to make the rounds for her pa to make sure everything was going well. Nate drove past his parent's and noticed all the Christians were there. Nate parked his van and walked back to his parent's site.

"Good morning."

Nate's father said, "Pull up a chair and join us."

Nate took a chair, "Thanks, dad."

Paul advised Nate, "We are going to spend a lot of time here."

Belle added, "We bought the RV on two twelve."

Nate said, "Good for you."

Belle grinned, "We just did it so we could torment you and Hildee."

Nate was in too good a mood to take the bait, "It'll be good having family come to visit." Nate looked at Belle, "Even those with tormenting on their minds."

Belle smiled.

Paul asked, "You getting nervous, Nate?"

"Not a bit."

Janice asked, "Where's Hildee?"

Nate made a sweeping motion with his right arm, "She's checking on things for her father."

Belle said, "You are invited over to see the RV we bought. We are going to add on to the deck during vacation and ask Len about putting up an aluminum carport and a prefabricated portable shed."

Nate smiled, "I can help with the deck when I'm not working."

"Thanks, little brother."

Nate smiled even wider, "You may be a great electrician and plumber, but you are more or less useless with hammer and saw."

Paul laughed, "That's why I gave you the hint."

Mike looked at Paul and added, "You are smarter than you look, son."

Belle told them, "I wish I'd kept my mouth shut about the harassing."

Nate smiled, "Too late, Belle."

Paul got up, "Well then, come on and see our vacation retreat."

The family started walking to lot two twelve and they met Hildee coming in the pickup. She stopped and Nate went to the driver's window.

Hildee asked, "You headed to Belle and Paul's."

"Yes. They are going to show us their new place."

"I've got to tell pa somethin' then I'll meet ya there."

Nate nodded and Hildee drove away.

The RV Paul and Belle had purchased was a ten-year-old model but it had been recently renovated and was in excellent condition. It was parked tight to a small deck with a roof. When Paul told them what he had paid, Nate said, "You got yourself a good deal."

Paul agreed, "I thought so. It will be a comfortable and affordable vacation get away spot for us."

They had no sooner gone out to sit on the deck than Hildee pulled up and got out. She walked up on the deck. There were not enough chairs so she sat on the step, "Hi, ya'll." Everyone returned the greeting.

Janice asked, "You getting nervous, Hildee?"

"More like 'cited. I've got a nice outfit, a wedding license, a preacher to hitch us lined up, and a great fiancé, so I'm ready."

Belle asked, "What's your dress like?"

"Can't tell with Nate here. Needs to be a surprise. If'in you want to come up to the house, I'll show it."

Janice said, "Let's," and the women went to Hildee's pickup and left.

Paul looked at the sky, "It's good to get out of the city and away from the hustle and bustle."

Nate's phone rang and he looked at it, "I should take this."

His father and brother nodded. They listened to Nate's side of the call.

"Good morning, this is Nate." There was a pause and Nate added, "Sure, Carson. Be there directly."

Mike asked, "Something wrong?"

"Carson has a problem with some equipment. I have to leave. I'll talk to you later." Nate left.

He'd been gone for about fifteen minutes when the women returned. Hildee walked to the deck and asked, "Where's Nate at?"

Paul responded, "Carson called and needed help."

Hildee looked at the women, "I'd best go see if I kin hep. See y'all later."

When Hildee arrived Nate and Carson had the chain saw partially dismantled. Nate was shaking his head.

Hildee got out of her pickup and walked to the men, "What's up?"

Nate answered, "Chain saw died. I think it needs a decent burial."

Carson smiled.

Hildee sighed, "Well, it ain't nothin' to be surprised 'bout. Thing's older than Methuselah. It's the only one we got. Its sister died last year."

"I suppose we'd better go buy a new one. Carson, why don't you gather up the cut brush then take an early lunch and we'll go buy a new one."

Carson said, "Will do."

Nate looked at Hildee, "You up for a road trip?"

"Sure, but I need to stop at the house first."

They drove to the house and Nate waited in the truck. Hildee was inside for a few minutes and came out carrying a small brown leather purse with a long strap over her shoulder. It occurred to Nate why Hildee would carry a purse once a month. Nate watched Hildee walk to the truck. He thought he sure liked looking at her.

Carson was eating a sandwich on the tailgate of his truck when Nate and Hildee returned. Nate got the new chainsaw out of the truck's bed and put it in the bed of Carson's truck.

Carson finished chewing and said, "Ya got a nice un."

Hildee said, "Nate says buyin' cheap don't pay when it comes ta tools."

Carson nodded agreement.

Nate looked at the pile of brush Carson had gathered, "You've been busy, Carson. We'd best get the chipper and grind up that lot."

Hildee agreed, "Let's do it."

The three spent the afternoon on the site. The three worked hard, teased, smiled, and laughed with each other. About five they were finishing work for the day when Len arrived.

"Y'all sure bin busy. Ya'll works faster than any of them others I had doin' this in the past."

Nate smiled, "I want to make sure you have enough money to pay the dowry."

Hildee snickered.

Len looked at his daughter smiling, "I see ya's pickin' up Nate's bad habits."

Hildee put her hands on her hips and stuck her tongue out at Len.

It was so unexpected the men laughed. Len seemed at a loss for words and shook his head in disbelief. He went and looked at the new chainsaw, "Thet uns a beauty."

Nate said, "Cuts like a hot knife through butter."

Carson said, "If it's ok, boss, I'm headin' home fer dinner."

Nate nodded, "See you."

Carson sais, "Back at ya," and got in his truck and headed home.

Len said, "Yar family and some friends are comin' to the house fer a grillin' party. Y'all need to come."

"I'll shower then come over."

When Nate arrived at the Cole home, the party had already started on the back deck. He was the last to arrive and was pleasantly surprised to find Ted and Kathleen were there. Kathleen was sitting talking to Hildee.

Marilee was closest when Nate came onto the deck and she gave him a big hug, "Hey."

Nate smiled, "Hey back at you."

Marilee said, "The kin folk is all here."

Nate went to Hildee and gave her a light kiss. She smiled.

Kathleen asked, "So what's the schedule for the next few days?"

Hildee replied, "Well early in the mornin' Nate and me have to unload the big truck so's it's free if'in its needed. We should probably work 'til least noon with Carson then we're free 'til the weddin'."

Nate added, "I haven't got my message prepared for Sunday. I need to do that tomorrow."

Belle asked, "Well then, what say all us girls have an afternoon outing tomorrow after lunch? The men can fend for themselves."

Janice jumped in, "Let's."

Marilee offered, "I can go. I'm on vacation now."

Janice smiled, "Good."

Belle asked Kathleen, "Where are you staying?"

Kathleen answered, "With mom and dad."

Janice smiled. Nate knew it was the first time Kathleen had referred to his mother and father that way. She had always used their given names in the past. The family was coming together.

The family gathering broke up about nine after everyone had helped clean up. Nate's family started walking back to their campsites but Nate stayed behind. He and Hildee sat on the front porch. Nate put his arm around Hildee's shoulder and she nestled her head against his neck.

Hildee sighed, "We sho nuff blessed."

"Yes, we are."

"Will it always be like this ya think?"

Nate thought for a moment, "The feelings can be if we rely on God and nurture each other. There will most likely be challenges though."

"I reckon as long as ya's beside me I'll be all right."

Marilee and Len came to the front porch and sat down.

Marilee spoke first, "It's good to be part of a big family."

Len looked at Hildee, "And likely to git bigger."

Hildee didn't blush but instead said, "I's countin' on it. Maybe y'all will add to it. I ain't got no objection to havin' a baby brother or sister."

Marilee said, "I'm too long in the tooth."

Hildee said, "Nate's mom reckoned so, but she's in the family way. Ya ain't old enough to bin through the change."

Marilee looked shocked. She then looked at Len.

Len smiled and said, "There's no tellin'. It's up to the Big Feller

201

above."

Marilee blurted, "I never thought 'bout it."

"You ain't backin' out, are ya?" Hildee asked.

Marilee smiled, "Too late now. I sold my house and I don't mean to be homeless."

Len said with a broad smile, "Thet's a relief is what it is."

Friday morning was overcast but warm. The day went pretty much as planned, though after lunch it started to rain lightly and Carson went home early. Nate spent the last part of the afternoon under his aluminum carport writing a sermon for Sunday. He had almost finished when the sound of the gentle rain on the aluminum roof put him to sleep.

Nate woke to the slamming of Len's pickup door. Nate stretched and looked up as Len came and sat down beside him.

"It's goin' ta seem strange without Hildee in the house."

Nate smiled, "Now you'll have to get used to Marilee being there instead."

Len smiled, "I reckon thet won't be no problem."

"I suppose not."

"Seein' the women folk are still missin' in action, what say we go eat at the diner?"

Nate nodded agreement, "Let me put my stuff away and lock up."

Nate's cell phone signaled an incoming call as he and Len were returning from dinner. Nate looked at the caller identification.

"Hi, love."

"We're headin' home. I guess I won't be seein' ya until the wedding tomorrow."

"It is tradition, but I'll miss not seeing you. I guess I'll survive."

"Try to be brave."

Nate said, "See you tomorrow. Love you."

"Back at ya."

Hildee disconnected and Nate put the phone in his pocket.

"Ya nervous?"

Nate smiled at his future father-in-law, "Not a bit."

"I'm 'bout ready to crawl outta my skin."

"How come?"

"It's bin a long time and there was only Hildee's ma."

"And?"

"Well, it has bin a while."

"It will all work out. Just go with the flow. God made it so it comes naturally. Besides you have the rest of your life to practice."

Len smiled, "Ya done cheered me up. I guess there ain't no harm in practicin', Nate. Eventually I'll git it right."

"There is that."

Len punched Nate playfully on the shoulder, "What makes ya reckon I won't git it right the first time?"

Nate smiled broadly, "Age. You aren't exactly a spring chicken."

Len punched Nate's shoulder again and this time a little harder, "Well, I ain't dead yet."

Nate looked at Len and grinning from ear to ear said, "Just pointing out the obvious."

"I ain't over the hill yet."

Nate chuckled, "Yeah, but you're sure enough getting close to the crest."

"I should pull over and whup your butt. Ya young uns don't have no respect no how. And you bein' a preacher should know better."

Nate, not to be outdone, said, "Yes, but you'd just keep picking on me if I turned the other cheek."

Len kept his left hand on the wheel and slapped his knee with the other, "That's a good one, Nate."

"I haven't forgotten you still haven't given me the dowry."

"You said in front of witnesses that ya didn' care 'bout no dowry."

"I didn't say I'd forgive you the debt just that I'd take the I.O.U.."

"I ain't got them animals so I guess we'll just have to postpone the hitchin' of my sweet daughter and the uppity preacher."

Nate smiled, "If it's postponed, you'll just have another wedding to pay for. You may want to reconsider your position. Besides, I said I'd take an I.O.U. so all you have to do is make your mark."

Len muttered, "For a preacher, ya is slipperier than bald tires on black ice."

"Give it up. You are just going to be stuck with me as your son-in-law."

"Ya and I'll need divine guidance to deal with thet."

"Yeah. I can see you'll need lots of prayers."

They pulled up in front of Nate's place and Len said, "See ya in the mornin'. Get a good night's sleep. I don't want ya messin' up Marilee and me gettin' hitched."

"I'll do my best. Night, Len."

"See ya in the mornin', Nate."

Nate got out and went into his camper. He got a drink and set about finishing his sermon for Sunday. He then pulled out his pastor's handbook and went to reviewing about performing the wedding ceremony.

Saturday morning, Nate woke to the sounds of children playing. He looked at his alarm clock. It was seven and he'd slept in. Nate prepared for the day, made his bed and laid out his clothes for the weddings. He was sipping coffee and just finishing his morning devotional when there was a knock on the door.

Nate opened the door and his mother was there with Marilee.

Nate greeted them, "Good morning. Coffee's on. Please come in and join me."

As the women entered Janice hugged him first and then Marilee did.

Janice said, "Coffee sounds good. You, Marilee?"

"Yes, please."

Janice went to the counter and got two cups and poured them while Marilee and Nate took seats.

Marilee asked, "Are ya nervous, Nate?"

Nate smiled, "No, but people keep asking me that."

Janice stated, "Most people are nervous before getting married."

Nate shrugged, "I'm not afraid to commit to spending my life with Hildee. I'm secure in our decision to marry. I feel certain it's the way God wants it to be."

Janice nodded, "I suppose so."

Marilee looked at Janice who nodded then said, "Len was as nervous as a hound just before the hunt. What did you say to him last night that settled him down?"

Nate shrugged, "Can't say. It's between a man and his preacher. Suffice to say he's head-over-heels for you, Marilee."

"That's good enough for me. I was just worried he was havin' second thoughts."

Nate smiled broadly, "Oh, you don't have to worry about that."

Janice looked at Marilee, "Told you."

"It's just that it's been a while for both of us."

Nate smiled, "You both have the rest of your lives to figure it out but I think you'll get it right." Nate paused and added, "And quickly, with God's help."

Marilee smiled, "I reckon so."

Janice asked, "How did you get so wise so young, son?"

Nate smiled, "It's not me; it's the Holy Spirit leading. I'm just along for the ride."

They finished the coffee and talked. The women left and Nate washed the coffee cups and put them away. He put a fresh pot of coffee on and it had just finished brewing when there was another knock at the door. Nate opened it to his father and brothers.

"Mornin', son. You have any coffee left?"

"Yes, come on in."

Nate poured cups and the men all sat down.

It was Ted who asked, "What are we supposed to wear to the wedding?"

Nate smiled, "Well, I'm wearing slacks and a summer sports jacket but then I'm marrying Len and Marilee. It's an informal place and I expect most guests will be dressed very causally like on Sundays."

Paul asked, "So casual pants, a sport shirt and jacket would be ok?"

"You'd probably be over dressed. It'll be hot so I'd forget the jackets."

Mike put in, "I'm glad we asked. I was thinking we'd be wearing suits and that's what we all brought."

Nate smiled, "Your wives kind of left you out on a limb on this, did they?"

Mike continued, "I guess it was their way of showing us how much we depend on them for the social stuff. We'd have been in suits if Ted hadn't overheard his wife talking to your mother about what they were wearing. It was Paul who suggested we ask you."

Ted smiled, "I like this campground marriage. Kathleen was so wired from the stress of our wedding preparations, I thought she was going to have a stroke."

Paul agreed, "Oh, I can relate."

Ted added, "The bridesmaids have it easy here. They are all wearing khaki Dockers and fancy blouses. Imagine how it would've looked if we'd showed up in suits."

Nate chuckled, "You know, we can have some fun with them. What say you we take a trip into town?"

Mike asked, "What do you have in mind?"

Nate told them and they all agreed to turn the tables on the women. Nate made some phone calls to make arrangements and then they headed to town together. By the time they got back to Nate's campsite at eleven-thirty, the males of the wedding party had everything they needed. They agreed the family men would all meet at Nate's camper to "get ready" for Nate's wedding.

At three, Nate's father and brothers headed for Nate's camper carrying their suits. It was not lost on the men that their wives were smiling or snickering when they left. They said nothing.

Nate arrived at the pavilion at a quarter of four. The place was swarming with people who came for the wedding and reception. The VFW smokers had put the wonderful fragrance of BBQ in the air. Nate greeted Pastor Rick from Chesterville who would marry him and Hildee and quickly filled him in on what would happen. Len and his grooms were already there fidgeting and waiting for the wedding to start. Nate got them in place.

Marilee and her wedding party showed up at five after four and the wedding march started. The wedding ceremony for Marilee and Len went without a hitch. The audience burst into applause when Len kissed Marilee. No one noticed that Nate slipped away after the necessary documents were signed.

Marilee took up her position as mother of the bride and Len left to meet his daughter so he could give her away.

Hildee and her party showed up at the appointed time but had to wait in the cars as the males of the wedding party had not showed up. The arrival of the bride's party triggered the entrance of the men in Nate's party.

Two jeeps and a pickup, all with high lift kits, roll cages, and lots of lights came up the road revving their engines and pulled up beside the pavilion and revved their engines a couple of more times. The sound was very loud.

Nate was standing in the bed of the pickup holding on to the roll bar. The Christian family men jumped down waving to the crowd with their camo-colored caps and dressed in camo pants and T-shirts. The crowd started laughing and clapping then whooping as several men lifted Nate onto their shoulders and carried him to the place where the preacher was standing. He was dressed the same as the rest of the men in the wedding party.

The crowd was enjoying the spectacle.

The men took their positions. The ladies got out of their cars and the wedding march started. Nate watched the women coming down the aisle between the folding chairs and all of them were struggling to keep a straight face. Hildee came on her father's arm and Len was shaking his head and trying not to laugh. Hildee started laughing just a little and that started a laughter chain reaction. The procession stopped because Hildee was now laughing too hard to keep walking. It seemed everyone was joining in the fun.

Hildee got control of herself and looked at her father and they started walking again. Hildee came to the front and Len left her beside Nate. She was wearing a summer weight white pant suit that modestly accentuated her womanly endowments.

"You look beautiful, Hildee."

She smiled, "You look ridiculous."

Nate said with a broad smile, "Thank you."

Hildee was smiling broadly, "I love ya but y'all is goin' to pay for this."

"I'm counting on it."

Rick asked, "Can we start now?"

Hildee said, "Please, before I start laughing again."

The rest of the wedding went without a hitch. When it came time to kiss the bride, Nate and Hildee made a spectacle of themselves. Their kiss was a quite passionate public display of affection with which the crowd seemed pleased by the applause and whooping. They were both flushed after the kiss. The two wedding parties gathered for pictures.

After the pictures, the single women gathered and Hildee threw her bouquet over her shoulder and Sue caught it. She had a stunned look on her face. Hildee smiled and Sue blushed.

The Christian family gathered around and Janice said, "Well, you men certainly made a spectacle of yourselves."

Mike grinned, "Didn't we, though."

Kathleen said, "I never."

Ted laughed, "It serves you right, dear, and we're the ones who get to say gotcha."

Janice smiled, "We'd better surrender ladies and admit our ambush backfired."

Hildee had a hold of Nate's arm, "I already done surrendered."

Nate looked into her eyes and smiled, "And I'm blessed as a result."

Len looked at Marilee, "And to think we's now related to this lot."

Marilee smiled, "Ain't it grand?"

Len replied, "Yes, dear."

Hildee said, "Ya's learnin', Pa."

Len added, "With them as kin it'll never be dull; lots of ups and downs."

Hildee laughed, "And what a glorious roller coaster ride it'll be."

www.ingramcontent.com/pod-product-compliance
Lightning Source LLC
Chambersburg PA
CBHW070833120626
46556CB00002B/749